THE

wrath

OF

wolves

Dark is the Night Book 3

KELLEY YORK
ROWAN ALTWOOD

ALSO IN THE DARK IS THE NIGHT SERIES
A Light Amongst Shadows
A Hymn in the Silence
A Calm Before the Storm
A Shimmer in the Night

ALSO BY KELLEY YORK and ROWAN ALTWOOD
Other Breakable Things

ALSO BY KELLEY YORK
Hushed
Hollowed
Suicide Watch
Made of Stars
Dirty London
Modern Monsters
Howl

BY KELLEY YORK WRITING AS AINSLEY GRAY
Unchained

www.kelley-york.com

Editing by Natalie Andrews
Cover design by Sleepy Fox Studio
Interior Design by Sleepy Fox Studio

First Edition January 2020
THE WRATH OF WOLVES

And as the world comes to an end
I'll be here to hold your hand
'Cause you're my king and I'm your lion-heart

–Nanna Bryndis Hilmarsdottir & Ragnar Thorhallsson

1
PRESTON

"WHAT IF A dinosaur eats you?" Alice asks.

Well, isn't *that* an odd question. "Why in the world would a dinosaur eat me?"

She scrunches her nose and tugs at the sleeves of her nightgown, attempting to figure out how to articulate what she's thinking with the limited vocabulary of a nine-year-old. "'Cause it's America and Clara says America is dangerous and full of wild animals."

"Clara's a brat and likes to stir up trouble," I drawl, casting a passing look to Clara in the bed across the room. In response, Clara gives an indignant sniff, not looking up from her needlework. I continue, "America isn't any more dangerous than any other place I could be going. Besides, there aren't dinosaurs anymore. Remember the statues in Crystal Park? That's as close to dinosaurs as we've got."

"Did you know they eat cats and dogs in America?" Margaret pipes up from beside Alice. Damn it, I thought she'd already gone to sleep.

"They do not. Alice, don't listen to her; she's telling fibs again."

"It's true," Margaret insists. "You shouldn't go or they'll make you eat them too!"

I sigh. This is an argument I could be having all night. Sometimes there's simply no winning against so many headstrong younger sisters. "You three should be asleep, like the others."

Margaret pulls a face. "They only went to bed early so they could wake up before you. They're going to try to trap you in your room, you know."

"Margaret! You're not supposed to tell him!" Alice complains.

"Why not? It's not like it's going to work. He'll just break down the door like the boorish oaf he is."

"I'm going to show *you* boorish."

"Quiet, all of you," comes a voice from the doorway.

My shoulders relax a little as Emma, the eldest of my little sisters, steps into the room. She, too, has given me a bit of a headache over this whole trip, but she has maintained decorum better than the others. "Preston, you're the one who ought to be in bed with such a busy day tomorrow."

I smile and get to my feet. "You're right. I suppose I just wanted a little more time with these brats."

"You'll have plenty of time when you come back," she says, levelling a look at me. "Because you *are* coming back, of course."

"Of course. I promised, didn't I?" I duck my head into a nod. Not that I promised *when* I'd be back or that I'd stay when I did, but…

Emma opens her mouth to say something further but is interrupted by a knock upon the front door. All of us pause, looking first to the direction of the sound and then to each other, perplexed that we'd have a visitor this time of night. Mum and

Dad have long since gone to sleep, rising as early as they do. Despite the chaos of trying to wrangle my sisters into their appropriate beds, normally the rest of us would have already settled for the night as well.

"I've got it." I duck down and plant a kiss atop Alice's head and then Margaret's, before strolling past Emma. "Get them to sleep, would you? They'll be complete bears in the morning at this rate."

There are a few people I could have expected at this hour. A neighbour with some sort of urgent matter being the most likely scenario. Our little farm out in the countryside is hardly the sort to attract a random passer-by.

Who I do not expect to see when I open the door is Benjamin.

He's got a trunk on the ground beside him. His cheeks are flushed, his clothes rumpled, and his hair is soaked from the rain. It occurs to me that the gate at the road is locked for the night, meaning whoever dropped him off couldn't pull up close to the house. Benji not only had to haul that trunk over the gate but also dragged it down the driveway on his own.

And as the slew of emotions crashes over me at seeing his face, the only stupid thing that comes out of my mouth is, "What in the hell did you do to your hair?"

Benji's hair has been on the long side ever since I've known him. It got him a fair bit of unwanted attention at Whisperwood that he'd let it get to his shoulders, long enough to tie back. But it had been soft and beautiful and, most importantly, *he* liked it, so seeing him now with it cropped significantly shorter, only the slightest bit of curl at the nape of his neck and ears, is startling.

Benjamin's cheeks pinken as he lifts a hand to his face, reaching for a phantom strand of hair that's no longer there. "Is it horrible...?"

It's not. But it's also not *Benji* and I can't help but reflect on just how much I loved his hair, how much I loved reaching out to brush it back from his beautiful face. "It's...different?"

His hand drops back to his side, a small, embarrassed smile pulling at his mouth. "Father insisted it looked ungentlemanly and had me cut it."

"Everything that comes out of your father's mouth is shit," I blurt, wincing inwardly. Maybe it's being on my own grounds that makes me more brazen about speaking my mind on Franklin Hale, or perhaps I'm just so caught off-guard that Benji is here.

My remark makes Benji's smile widen a notch. "So I've noticed. May I come in? It's a bit cold."

Oh—hell, it is, and it's raining, and I'm just standing here like a fool, gawking at him. I bend to pick up that trunk and usher him inside. Benjamin sighs in relief as he slips out of his overcoat and turns to hang it up.

"I'm sorry for showing up unannounced. I know you're preparing to leave."

I close the door behind him. "It's all right. Is everything—"

A delighted squeal cuts me off. "It's Benji!" Alice comes barrelling down the hall from her room, launching herself at Benjamin with outstretched arms.

Benji laughs, dropping to a crouch just in time to catch her up into a hug. "Goodness! It's so late. I was sure you'd all be abed by now."

Alice clasps her tiny hands behind Benji's neck, hanging off him when he straightens up, and she gazes at him as though he hung the moon and stars themselves. "We were warning Preston about America. Are you here to comfort me?"

Benjamin strokes a hand over her hair. "Having him go so far away must be very frightening for you all," he murmurs, already taking her off to her room.

"Dinosaurs are gonna eat him!" Alice insists, sniffing as she shoves her face against his shoulder.

I roll my eyes, carting the trunk down the hall into my room and depositing it near the foot of my bed, right next to the other trunk of Benjamin's that I'm currently in possession of, in fact. The last time I saw him, after his mother had passed, he asked me to keep some of her belongings safe from his father, and I'd done so without a second thought.

I move to the door to listen to the girls in the neighbouring room. Well, Alice, Margaret, and Clara, anyway. Emma and Louise share the room directly across from mine, though often the girls will switch it up. Half the time Alice and Louise end up in my room, damned near crowding me out of my own bed.

I can only just hear the soft voice of Benjamin talking to my sisters and although I pick out a few words, he's speaking gently enough that it's impossible to decipher. At one point, Alice gets out of bed, and I hear a dresser drawer opening and closing.

A few moments later, Emma slips out of the room to return to her own, and Benjamin steps out after her, easing the door shut after calling one last *good night* to the girls. It figures they'd listen to him; every one of my siblings is utterly enamoured with Benjamin, thinking him lovely in every way a man can be. Gentle, smart, kind, nice to look at. Alice insists she's going to marry him someday. The first time she'd announced that at the dinner table, I'd laughed until my sides hurt.

When our eyes meet, I cut a small smile. "I've been trying to get them to bed for the last hour and a half."

Benjamin's eyes crinkle when he smiles back at me. "You ought to be resting too, I should think."

"I'm getting there. Can I get you anything? Something to drink, something to eat?"

"No need to fuss over me. I had snacks on the train." He rolls his shoulders back, reaching for his hair again—he's always messed with it when he's nervous. "Are you all packed to leave?"

I move out of the door to coax him in from the hall, not wanting our conversation to wake my parents (if Alice's shrieking earlier didn't already). "I am. I have to say, I didn't expect to see you here."

Benjamin tugs at his tie as he surveys my room, as though he hasn't been here many times before. He knows it almost as well as I do, likely. We've shared that bed many nights. He's penned letters home to his mother seated on it with me napping beside him. When Benjamin is here, I've considered this *our* room—we've spent some of the happiest days of my life in this space.

And now Benjamin is standing here again when I never thought he would be, because the last time we stood face to face, I had told myself I needed to let him go.

He'd made his choices. He wanted to lead the life his mother laid out for him, and I… I had to respect that, no matter how horrible a choice I thought it was. No matter how badly I wanted to beg him not to.

Benjamin takes a deep breath, shoulders slumping, and turns to face me. "I've quit my job."

I clearly did not hear that right. "Sorry?"

"I've quit my job," Benjamin repeats, ducking his head to stare at his feet. "I was hoping that…maybe there'd be room for one more on your trip."

I slowly lean back against the closed door, crossing my arms. "I feel like I've missed something." Something important, at that.

He wrings his hands together. "Yes. Um. Well, I've been thinking a lot. I had intended to follow Mother's last wishes because…it's what a good son ought to do, yes? But the more thought I gave it, the more I realised that Mother would have wanted me to simply do what made me happiest."

Despite myself, when Benji looks up at me, I feel my own expression beginning to soften and my heart catch in my throat. "And…happy means going to America?"

Benjamin manages a small smile. "Oh, well, I don't know. Perhaps I'll hate travelling. But I wasn't exactly happy where I was, and so… Why not, right? I ought to try something new. And if it's at your side…then…all the better."

I want nothing more than to take Benjamin into my arms, and I refrain because I don't know if I should. I've never known. There's always been that nagging worry in the back of my head that being too forward with him will ruin everything, that one misstep might fracture this relationship we've always had. Especially now, I'm so unsure of where things stand that it's almost paralysing.

"If you hate it," I say, "there's no easy way back. We could be stuck there for weeks, maybe even months." *Months* could be an exaggeration, but the boat trip alone across the Atlantic would set us back ten days in decent weather, and even I don't know many details beyond that once we actually get there.

I also think that Benjamin is far too cautious a person to not have thought about this already. Never have I known him to make a decision without mulling over every possible outcome— perhaps that's another reason I'm shocked he's here. And another reason why I had not previously pressed him nor asked him to accompany me. I have no illusions that this trip will be easy or something someone like Benjamin would enjoy.

He nods, long lashes lowering demurely as he takes a step closer. "Then we'll be stuck together, won't we?"

A blossom of warmth spreads through my chest. "I think I could live with that."

Benji smiles. "In that case, I presume we're departing early, so we really ought to get some sleep."

Not that I'll be able to sleep now, I think. This turn of events has energised me, and I want to grab him and dance about the room rather than go to bed. Instead of thinking of all the reasons Benji might come to sorely regret this decision, I'm thinking of all the good that could come of it.

I get to travel, I get to see a new world, and I get to see it with *Benji*.

He brushes a hand against my arm, such a simple, innocent gesture that he likely doesn't realise it makes my chest flutter. He has no idea the effect he's had on me ever since the day we met, when he'd been such a small, seemingly timid boy getting shoved into the dirt. I'd come to learn in the years since that although Benji is quiet, reserved, careful, non-confrontational, he is no coward.

But...sleep. Right. I leave Benji to change while I duck into the other room to fetch a spare blanket at his request. When I return, he's made himself at home in my bed. I had changed a while back before starting in on my siblings about going to sleep, so all I need do is blow out the lamp and slip beneath the blankets beside him.

I settle down and roll onto my side to face him. "Mum and Dad will be ecstatic you're going with me."

"Alice is pleased too," Benji murmurs. "Though she did sound perplexed why anyone would want to go along with 'stinky old Preston.'"

I whisper back, "It's only natural that she's angry. I'm taking away her fiancé."

Benji chuckles. "I shall have to try to find a nice gift for her while we're overseas."

"Something to make her permanently shut that sassy mouth of hers, perhaps."

"Terribly rude to speak of my fiancé that way," he teases with a smile. He scoots a bit closer. For warmth, I tell myself. That's all. "Now, sleep. We have a big day tomorrow."

2
BENJAMIN

MORNING ARRIVES WITH an invasion of Preston's sisters crawling all over us and demanding we wake before the sun has even risen. But there is a promise of food involved if we get up, and it would be wise for us to arrive at the train station early and with full bellies. I slip out of bed, sleepy-eyed and sluggish. Lying there beside Preston is so very warm and pleasant that I'm tempted to stay where I am and get a few more minutes of sleep—except that Alice and Louise are presently hopping on Preston, undeterred by his grumbles.

This is not unlike many a morning that I've spent in the Alexander household, though perhaps most of those did not come with quite an early wakeup call. This was a home away from home in many ways, a place where I felt appreciated, safe, loved. Mr. and Mrs. Alexander are kind people and although the girls can be a handful, I adore every one of them.

Preston finally drags himself from bed and shoos the girls out long enough for us to wash up and dress. I wait for Preston's back to be turned before I change out of my own shirt, not wanting him to lay eyes on the sizable bruising upon my arm.

The decision to leave London had not been an easy one, but I had taken it as a sign when I came upon Mother's favourite jewellery that had previously been lost to me. Something had quietly clicked in my head and I had known what I needed to do. I sold what I could, I resigned at the factory in which I worked, and I had hoped to clear out of my small flat before Father caught wind of what I was doing.

That did not happen.

He arrived yesterday morning like a storm, red-faced and furious that I would humiliate him by abandon the employment he'd secured for me. When I attempted to leave, he grabbed me, unaccustomed to being so blatantly ignored, and…well, the bruises are a testament to the ensuing scuffle.

I see no reason to let Preston see the marks. They'll only upset him, and surely they'll heal in a few days so I needn't worry about keeping them hidden long.

Bringing along entire trunks to America would be nice, but also far too much of a hassle for the journey ahead. We take only what can be fit into a pair of large rucksacks. It equates to a meagre few days' worth of clothing, toiletries, and the information Spencer gave to Preston regarding our client. Preston packed last night, but I find myself undoing most of it to re-pack it for him to make better use of the limited space.

Mrs. Alexander has quite the spread laid out for us this morning, along with a small satchel of snacks to tide us over on the seven-hour train ride to Liverpool. Breakfast is as loud of an affair as it always is here, accented by a tinge of sadness that colours the room. Preston acts as though nothing is amiss, but I know him better than that. He may be excited at the prospect of travel, but he's terribly attached to his family. Leaving them like this for weeks or months is likely one of the hardest things he's ever done. It is not the same as going off to Whisperwood for a term where they were always a train ride or a letter away.

I haven't had much of an appetite as of late, but I do poke at my food and try to force myself to eat what I can.

Melancholy pinches at my own insides. It's been an ever-present ache for a while now, ever since I last returned home and found out my mother had died while I was away. I will have no one to miss me when I board our ship for America and that feeling is depressingly isolating.

It isn't even *that* so much as…any time I have ever left home—for Whisperwood, for Preston's on holiday—I always *knew* Mother was there waiting for me. That she would be present at the station when I returned, ready with a smile and a hug and eager to hear all about my time away. She missed me fiercely, and I her, but she was always happy for me.

Mrs. Alexander brings a hand to rest upon Preston's arm and she smiles at her son. There's a quiet sort of pride in her eyes even amidst the sadness that her eldest child is going so far away. I miss that look from my own mother. I miss it so horribly that it feels unbearable at times.

As we prepare to leave, Mrs. Alexander and Preston's sisters gather around us both, full of tearful hugs. Alice, at least, seems to be keeping in mind what I said to her last night—that I would look after Preston and see him brought back home in one piece, but that she needed to be strong so Preston remembered her smile and not her tears. She keeps a stiff upper lip and does not beg us to stay. She hugs me just as tightly as she hugs Preston and asks, "You have it, right?"

I slide my fingers beneath the collar of my shirt and draw out the chain and crucifix she gave to me last night. A present from her Aunt Eleanor, she'd said, and insisted it would help to keep us safe. "I do."

Alice nods once, hugs me again, and manages not to weep as we depart.

We load into the wagon along with Mr. Alexander and Emma, who insisted on seeing us off. She was the only one Mr. Alexander would permit because he didn't want the theatrics of the younger girls at the station.

When we arrive, Emma remains seated. She's held it together thus far, but as we hop out of the wagon with our bags in tow, I notice how tightly her hands are clasped in her lap.

Preston leans up, catching her chin in his hand. "I'll be back before you know it, Emma."

She gives a bit of a sniff and stares at him, misty-eyed but still defying her urge to cry. "Please be safe, Preston. I have the most horrible feeling about all of this."

"You know Benji and I will look after each other." He leans in and kisses her forehead. "You're the oldest now, so it's up to you to keep an eye on everyone. Think you can manage?"

Emma scoffs. "I already manage it; you're as much a child as the rest of them."

I bite back a laugh and she catches my eye with a pleased smile.

Mr. Alexander is a quiet man. Dutiful, loyal, protective of his family, and impossibly kind. Still, I've never known him to be an overly affectionate sort, and Preston looks as surprised as I am when Mr. Alexander gathers us both up into his arms and squeezes tight.

"You'll do great. I'm proud of you both."

Tears prick my eyes and I blink them back, permitting myself to hug him in return. Perhaps I'll be missed after all.

When he draws back, he slips a few bills into Preston's hand, waving him off when his son tries to protest. "If you don't end up needing it, then get your mother something nice in America."

They depart, the wagon rumbling off down the street. Preston stares after them, mixed emotions playing across his face. No good thing comes without sacrifice and this trip is no different. I step up beside him, brushing my fingers against the back of his hand.

"They'll be all right, Preston."

He drags in a deep breath. "I know. Come on."

"WHERE'S THE FARTHEST you've ever travelled before?" Preston asks.

We've settled into a car—thankfully alone for the time being—with me closest to the window. Preston has pulled out the bag of treats from his mother, poking through it to see what she thought to pack for us. Pretzels, dried apple slices and berries, and some dried meat for Preston, seeing as I won't eat it. Being a vegetarian wasn't easy even back home. I suspect it's going to be even more of a problem abroad where our food options will be limited, but I am determined. The idea of ingesting anything that once had a heartbeat does nothing but destroy my appetite.

Preston offers one of the apple slices to me and I take it gratefully.

"Paris," I reply, chewing thoughtfully. "Mother took me to Berlin once when I was a baby, but I don't remember anything about it."

Preston no doubt recalls my trip to Paris. A summer or two ago, Mother had brought me along when Father requested she join him while he was there for business. Preston and I had both sulked about it because it had cut into the summer holiday we liked to spend together. I'd written to him often. There was plenty of time for it, after all. I spent so much of the trip there wandering through the city alone when Mother was otherwise occupied with Father.

Preston nods as though he suspected as much. "It was Whisperwood for me."

I smile. "Are you nervous to be going so far from home?"

"Me? I'm not afraid of anything."

"I didn't say anything about being afraid. Nervousness isn't the same as fear."

His nose wrinkles. "Sounds about the same to me."

I tuck the rest of the apple ring into my mouth and chew thoughtfully, turning my attention out the window. "Well, *I'm* nervous. It's a very long way from home. A whole new world to us, isn't it?"

"It's exciting. I can't think of anything worse than spending the rest of my years cooped up on a farm or someplace like London."

Not a sentiment I think I share, but, well. "It will certainly be an adventure," I admit.

And then I drop my head to his shoulder and close my eyes. We were up late and I've had a busy several days prior to showing up on Preston's doorstep. I could use the sleep.

I proceed to nap on and off for the remainder of the trip, using Preston as a pillow. In between catnaps, we chat and snack and watch the scenery pass by outside.

The train rolls into Liverpool many hours later. It's a leisurely fifteen-minute walk from the station before we spot the water and the ships and ferries lining the docks of the Mersey. This is my first trip to Liverpool, but the air has a familiar, overwhelming smell of fish and saltwater that reminds me of the docks in London.

We stroll down the seemingly endless line of ships, from sailboats to the massive passenger liners. The sheer size of them is a little overwhelming. As we stand there with our heads tilted back, taking one of them in, I ask, "Do you suppose one of these will be the one we take to America?"

"Maybe." Preston shields his eyes, squinting. "Huge hunks of metal out on the open sea... Looks like any one of them would sink like a rock."

I lean into him until our shoulders brush. An unconscious move, really, coming about due to my own nervousness, like I might somehow find safety in Preston's shadow. "Thousands of people make this trip all the time. I'm sure it's safe."

"People ride horses all the time, too. They can still kill you."

I bite my lower lip. My only real foray into swimming had been as a small child, still unsteady on my feet. It might very well be my first memory, toppling into the river and nearly drowning before a dock worker fished me out and returned me to my mother's arms. "Well, then I hope you know how to swim because I certainly do not."

He grins. "Not a clue."

My laugh is a nervous one. "I suppose we'll drown together, then."

His shoulder nudges mine. "No one else I'd rather drown with."

With a shake of my head, I continue down the road. We follow the instructions we received from Spencer about where to meet up with our client. The address leads us to a building not terribly far off and from the exterior, it looks to be nothing more than a standard small shipping and trading company.

When we step inside, a clerk glances up from his desk. "May I help you, gentlemen?"

"We're looking for Mr. Wilkerson," I say. "We've a letter from him. He should be expecting us."

Preston steps forward and offers out the initial letter sent to Miss Bennet, Spencer, and Esher. The clerk takes a look before recognition blossoms across his face. "Ah, yes, right this way."

We're brought upstairs to an office, this one much more lavishly furnished than the ground floor, although there is no escaping the fishy smell from outside.

"Mr. Wilkerson," the clerk announces. "I've got Mr. Spencer and Mr. Esher here to see you."

Oh.

I glance to Preston. Should we not correct him? He seems to be making no move to do so and I wonder if Spencer instructed him not to mention that we are, in fact, not who they think we are. Preston meets my gaze, looking just as uncertain as I feel, but then he shrugs.

Right then.

I feel guilty about the deception, but so long as the job gets done, what does it matter who completes it?

"Gentlemen," Mr. Wilkerson greets, rising to extend a hand. He's quite handsome, and younger than I expected although already greying a bit at the temples. "Thank you so much for coming. I know this is a huge undertaking, so I was fully prepared for you to say no."

Preston takes his hand. "We try not to turn away people in need if we can help it. Our schedule happened to be clear."

Mr. Wilkerson smiles pleasantly then turns to offer a handshake to me as well, which I politely accept. "Please, have a seat. I know my letter was a bit…vague, but that is because I need this matter handled with the utmost discretion."

I sit in one of the chairs before his desk and Preston takes the one beside me. "Is there a reason for that?"

Mr. Wilkerson steps back behind his desk and pauses. "The…peculiar nature of this item, yes. A few of the men who've handled it in the past reported odd occurrences. Seeing things, hearing things. *Haunted*, they say. Although I've not personally experienced anything out of the ordinary."

A haunted item. I wonder if Miss Bennett prepared Preston for the possibility of dealing with this.

Preston asks, "Is there any reason why this particular object might be haunted? Any questionable history behind it?"

Wilkerson holds up a finger. Then he turns and exits through a back door. When he returns a moment later, he carries a satchel in his hands. From inside it, he removes a box.

Not a large box, really. Large enough to hold a small stack of books, perhaps. It's carved from a dark red wood, its iron fastenings covering every seam. It would make it quite difficult to even axe open if someone wanted to get into it. Though the oddest part, really, is the lock. No key is required. Instead, there is a small set of dials requiring a combination.

The moment Mr. Wilkerson places the box upon his desk before us, my skin begins to prickle and my heart picks up speed.

Something is most certainly wrong with this box. Or whatever is inside it, rather. A low buzz of whispers begins to fill my ears, the edges of my vision darkening. My hands clutch at the arms of the chair, knuckles whitening.

"The contents need to remain a secret, I'm afraid," Wilkerson says. "I've gone through great lengths to obtain this. It was stolen from its rightful owner some time ago and I'm sending it home."

Oh, because *that* isn't suspicious. What would Spencer and Esher do? Insist on being told what the contents are? Does it ultimately matter?

Preston's smile is easy. "You can trust us to be discreet."

"It's appreciated. There are people who would very much like this back, so discretion will make this entire endeavour run much more smoothly." Wilkerson opens a drawer and removes a folder from inside, sliding it across the desk. "In here you will find everything you should need. A quarter of your payment upfront, as promised in my letter—the recipient of the box shall have the rest for you. Your boat tickets, a letter for an acquaintance in Boston to set you up with a good meal and a room when you arrive in America. I suspect you'll want it. And instructions on how to get from there to your destination in California. Mr. Michael Carlton is your final destination. His address is listed there to telegram him when you arrive in San Francisco."

He pauses then, studying us both.

"You are much younger than I thought you would be. I suspect neither of you have been across the Atlantic before?"

Preston is not the least bit daunted, of course. If there's anything he knows how to do, it's how to look and sound confident no matter what he's faced with. "No, sir. But in our line of work, we learn how to adapt to new situations quite quickly."

His demeanour most certainly puts Mr. Wilkerson at ease. "How about you?" he asks.

His question startles me into looking up from the box. "Ah—right. Yes. As he said." Wilkerson does not seem to notice the tight edge to my voice.

"Glad to hear it. The ship departs at dawn. I've taken the liberty of securing you a room at the inn across the street. Nothing overly luxurious, I'm afraid; mostly used by mariners making port, but the hospitality can't be beat."

"Thank you, sir. We should probably rest up before our journey." Preston rises to his feet.

I do the same. I take a small step toward the box, hands lifting, then hesitate. Why am I so frightened of touching it? Preston notes my reluctance and doesn't seem to think twice about picking it up. He slips it back into the satchel it came in.

Mr. Wilkerson sees us downstairs and outside, pointing to an inn across the road and a few doors down. Inside the inn, it smells even more strongly of fish than it did near the water. The attached tavern is alive and bustling with the noise of sailors and fishermen laughing and conversing and drinking. All I care about is fetching our room key from the desk clerk and heading upstairs.

The room itself is small and unassuming. Two beds on either side, a table with a washbowl, jug of water, and mirror, and a small table and chairs near the window. It reminds me a bit of our room at Whisperwood.

Preston heads to the table, removing the box from its bag and looking it over.

"Well? What do you think is in it?"

I hug myself, fending off a shiver. The whispers are still a hum in my ears. They grow louder when I step up beside Preston. "Nothing good."

Preston tips his head to look at me. "Hm?"

"You don't hear it? Feel it?"

A frown tugs at his face. He lifts the box, pressing an ear to it, eyes closed. "…No?"

I'm silent for a long moment, willing the anxious feeling in my gut to settle. "I suppose it doesn't matter. He did say others had experiences with it. Why else would he reach out to people who work with spirits?"

"A shame we don't have the time to bring this back to Aunt Eleanor and have her get a read on it. But you've got a strong sense for the supernatural; I suspect we can handle whatever it is." He grins. "Speaking of, which one am I, do you think? James or Esher?"

I chuckle. "Hmm, if he knew anything about them, then he'd have thought you were Spencer. Lighter hair. Confident, outgoing, charming."

"Afraid I don't know any poetry, though."

"I'm sure you could make some up. You're creative enough." I step over to the mirror atop the wash table, peering at my reflection. We could both use a wash after our train ride.

Preston flops down onto one of the rickety beds. "Um... The rose is red, the violet is blue, you've got a sweet face, I'd like to hug you?"

I pause, looking at him in the mirror's reflection, and then laugh. "See? You'd give Spencer a run for his money with art like that."

His grin positively lights up his face. It's been awhile since I've seen him smile like that. "Maybe I ought to alter my life goals then."

I make swift work of scrubbing my face clean, pushing my damp hands back through my hair. "We'll have a good seven to ten days aboard the ship. Plenty of time to get started on your budding poetry career. For now, let's see about nipping downstairs for some dinner."

3
PRESTON

DINNER IS A simple affair. Particularly for Benji, who won't eat the meat pies or dried jerkies the pub has to offer. He nibbles at a small helping of tomatoes and celery and sweet potatoes. Still, it's food and it fills our bellies well enough. We bring the chest along with us, deciding not to leave it unattended. If Wilkerson was right and people may be after it, well, it's for the best that we keep an extra close eye on it.

Once we've eaten and returned to our room, Benji sets to getting changed. I flop down onto my bed, which smells musty and of fish, but will do for a night. I pull out the packet of information we were given and spread the pages out across the mattress. "Ugh, reading."

"Like school all over again," Benjamin muses as he sheds his clothes. I make it a point to keep my eyes down, wanting to grant him some privacy. "Would you like me to read over it?"

Oh, would I ever. "You're a saint, Benji."

Once he's dressed, we swap places. Not that I had any interest in dragging along anything to sleep in, but Benjamin insisted I pack 'properly.' As he pores over the papers, he relays to me the most important of the information.

"We've got a cabin to ourselves on the boat. The trip ought to be seven to ten days from here to Boston... Then the train to San Francisco will take two weeks. That's going to be fun."

I wrinkle my nose at that last part. "Why can't we go it on horseback instead?"

"That would certainly turn our cross-country trip from two weeks into...well, significantly longer. Not to mention the bad weather, rough terrain, and bandits, I suspect." He glances up then, and I catch him from the corner of my eye watching me, lingering several seconds longer than I think he means to.

I catch his gaze and grin, folding my arms across my bare chest. "Still beats being stuck on a train for that long."

His cheeks redden and he swiftly drops his gaze. "I'll tell you what. After we've delivered the box, if you're still feeling that adventurous, we'll revisit the idea." Benjamin gathers the papers to tuck them back into their folder. "Five pounds says you're ready to go home just after the trip there."

I laugh, getting back into bed. "Ten pounds says I love it so much that I never want to leave."

He stills a moment then turns to me, head tipped. "Do you think that might happen?"

"Oh, I don't know." I tuck my hands behind my head. "If Whisperwood taught me anything, it's to not to try to play psychic with my own life." So much has changed since then. The friends I've made, the things I've encountered...the friend I lost. I certainly never would have predicted meeting someone like Benjamin.

This is what I've always wanted, isn't it? To travel? To see the world? So why today have I been plagued with such nerves and second thoughts? Why is it so difficult to leave now?

You know why.

I glance over at Benjamin.

Could I stay in America and possibly never see my family again? Could I stay even if Benji would not stay with me? I was prepared to leave him once, to put an ocean between us. It was quite possibly the hardest thing I'd ever chosen to do. I wonder if I could have gone through with it. I wonder if I had, how quickly I'd have come to regret it.

Now, if I found somewhere to settle down, if I had to watch him gather his things and walk out of my life, could I stomach it?

I watch him as he blows out the candles, sets the paperwork aside, and lies down. He rolls onto his side to watch me too. So very reminiscent of our time in Whisperwood, staying up talking long past curfew.

He says, "Fair enough. Plenty of America to see. I suspect it's very different from here."

I let my gaze roam back to the ceiling. I do wonder what led him to the decision to come with me. Benji's thought process has always been a mystery to me; he's a difficult one to pin down. He'd grown up sheltered, and while his mother was a lovely woman that I adored, it was clear to me that she influenced much of Benji's life. She fussed over him endlessly, worried about his well-being.

Yes, Benji has always been delicate. Gentle. Soft. It made me even more determined to look after him, to protect him, because the world can be a miserable place to people who are kind. It has a way of breaking a person's spirit and Benjamin is the last person in my life I would want to see that happen to.

Looking after him at Whisperwood was one thing. I wonder how well I'll do when we're abroad in a setting so unfamiliar to us both.

"Are you sure about all this, Benji?"

"I won't lie and say I'm not incredibly nervous, but that's just sort of my nature, isn't it? I'm confident this is the right thing to do."

That's so very much like him. He follows where I lead, no matter how many reservations he may have. I found it endearing once upon a time. Now, I just worry he's forcing himself to do something he truly does not want to do. "I promise, if you find it so disagreeable that..."

Benjamin shakes his head before I can finish the thought. "Everything will fall into place. If America isn't to our liking, somewhere else could be."

I like the insinuation that statement makes. That perhaps he just might stick around, stay with me, regardless of where we go. All the more reason to ensure I find somewhere he'll be happy, right? "Maybe we should visit them all anyway."

A soft smile tugs at his mouth. "Maybe China too, someday?"

He has a hand resting beside his face on the pillow, fingers curled. I wish we were close enough that I could reach out to take it.

I smile back at him. "Well, obviously."

He sighs, content, his eyes drifting shut. "I would like that. I'll need to work on my Mandarin. I've recently been told that I'm rusty."

A fair sight better than mine. All I know are a few words here and there that Benjamin has taught me. I'd be useless trying to converse in anything other than English or a sad stab at French. "You're a quick learner."

"Mm. I'll make you learn too. We can talk and no one will know what we're saying."

"*I'm* not a quick learner with things like that." Or much of anything, really, that doesn't involve me using my hands. I'm not so sure I'd have passed some of my classes without Benji's help.

Benji makes a soft sound that I know all too well. The one that says he's beginning to drift off. One of my favourite sounds in all the world. I smile to myself.

"Sweet dreams, Benji."

"Sweet dreams, Preston," he mumbles, and likely he won't even remember having said it in the morning, because his breathing has already evened out.

I've missed this. I've missed *him*. And even if we're kidding ourselves with this whole bloody affair, I'm going to hang onto this feeling as long as I can.

WE'RE WOKEN BEFORE dawn by a scheduled knock at our door. Or rather, Benji is. I don't budge because it sounds an awful lot like Mum's come to nag me awake and my brain doesn't fully register what it means. But Benji whimpers, slowly proceeding to drag himself out of bed, and that is what ultimately causes me to let out a groan and force my eyes open.

Beyond that, I don't complain. I may not enjoy being up before the sun, but I'm used to it.

As Benji sets to washing up and dressing, I remain seated on the edge of my bed, granting him space because there's not enough of it for us both to get ready at once. I lean back on my hands, watching him tiredly. It truly is like being back at

Whisperwood, with some subtle changes. We're older, for one. Benji's hair is shorter, no longer brushing his shoulders. I still have the strongest urge to run my hands through it.

As he slips out of his nightclothes to dress, I notice a glint of metal against his bare chest. A crucifix. Odd, really; Benji has never worn such things before. I'm just about to ask him about it when something else catches my eye.

Bruising.

It's not terribly fresh. A few days old, perhaps. Starting to morph from blue-and-purple to yellow-and-green.

A bruise in and of itself ought not to be anything particularly alarming. Things happen. People bruise. But it's the location—there upon his bicep—and the pattern of it that sets me on edge. As though someone grabbed him, hard, and did not let go. I can practically see the shape of fingers.

Anger surges brightly in my chest and I swallow it back. There could be any number of explanations for it, though I can't think of a single one that wouldn't enrage me. My knee-jerk reaction is to reach for Benjamin and gather him up, to ask if he's all right, but...

He's already slipping on his shirt and waistcoat, and for some reason it seems like it's too late and I find I haven't a clue what to say. We have a busy day ahead of us. Perhaps I should wait until we have a quiet moment more appropriate for bringing up a heavy topic he may not even want to discuss.

I catch Benji reaching up for his hair as though to tie it back, and he sighs. He moves away from the washbowl, granting me room to get up and start getting ready myself.

Rucksacks over our shoulders and the box-satchel beneath my arm, we head outside into the sleepy morning. The shipyard is far busier than I would have anticipated. Men hurry about, loading and unloading ships, fishermen prepare to head out to sea, and, of course, the passenger ships.

Benji keeps close to my side as we scan the ships. He lifts a hand and points. "That one's ours."

It's being loaded up with cargo as well, and plenty of other passengers are waiting in line.

"It doesn't look so bad," I offer, remembering his nervousness yesterday about being at sea. It's so massive, especially up close.

Benji bites his lip briefly before offering me my ticket. No one gives us a second glance as our tickets are checked and they gesture us on board. Passengers are funnelled along, directed where to go below deck.

Everything smells damp and fishy and humid, and below deck is no better. The halls are narrow and crowded and it takes a few tries to locate our assigned cabin. That we get our own space at all instead of being put into steerage is a blessing, so I don't want to complain.

Granted, our cabin is far from first class. It's even smaller than our room last night: a two-tier bed against the wall, a wash table, and nothing more. "I call top bunk!"

Benji laughs softly, stepping into the room. He closes and locks the door behind us. At least we can secure our things when we go above deck, including the box. "Not so bad, is it?"

"I've been in worse places." I toss my satchel on the top bunk and place our box beneath the wash table in the corner.

Benji takes a seat on the lower bunk, looking around, as though there's anything at all worth looking at. "Good, because we'll be spending plenty of time in here for the next week and a half."

KELLEY YORK AND ROWAN ALTWOOD

"No one else I'd rather be stuck in such close quarters with." I swing myself up onto the top bunk. I can't recall ever getting to sleep on one before. The novelty will wear off quickly, I'm sure, but for now it's fun.

I feel something bump beneath me and realise Benjamin is lightly kicking the top bunk above him. "I'll remind you that you said that."

I laugh, leaning over the edge to peer at him. "So long as I'm on top, I'm good."

He smiles. "It appears that you are, yes."

"It's a height rule, I think."

"That the taller person gets the top bunk? That seems backwards."

I stretch back out as much as my small mattress allows. "I don't make the rules, Benji. I just enforce them."

Benji chuckles. "You've never followed a rule in your life."

Well, *that's* not true. I've followed so many unspoken rules between the pair of us that it makes my heart hurt.

For a while, we alternate between chatting and dozing off, until we can hear men up on deck and someone in the halls calling out the final warning that the ship is about to depart. Any nervousness I feel is promptly shoved down as deep as I can manage.

"I suppose it's time for us to find out if we like sailing."

"Indeed," Benji murmurs, having trouble masking his own uncertainty.

I remind myself of the number of times people have made this trip. On boats far less safe than this, no less. Steamships are faster, safer than sailboats. Ten days is no time at all to cross the world.

Now that the boat is moving, I see no reason to lie around in bed. We venture back topside, find a section of railing towards the back of the boat that is unoccupied, and watch as Liverpool steadily vanishes into the distance. Most of the crowd upon the deck disperses quickly enough, once there's nothing to see but fog and an endless stretch of ocean in every direction. Benji, though, looks content to remain where we are, his head tipped as he breaths in the ocean air.

The view is lovely, but I can't help but grip the railing a little tighter every time wave rolls beneath the boat and my stomach rolls with it. The sensation is a difficult one to describe. It's not that I can feel the ship *rocking*, but I cannot quite seem to find my sea legs.

The moment I straighten up and attempt to turn around, for that matter, a wash of nausea sweeps over me.

"Preston?" Benji calls, concerned. "Are you all right?"

Not in the slightest. It's all I can do to whip around and lean over the railing to be sick. Not that I had anything for breakfast, but clearly no one informed my stomach. Benjamin, bless his heart, begins to rub my back until I've got nothing left to throw up.

"Well, now we know you get sea-sick. Come along," Benji croons, taking my elbow. "Let's get you some water and lie down."

He helps me below deck, where I continue to wobble on my feet and feel as though I might not be done getting sick after all. We make it to the cabin without incident and Benji leaves me there a moment alone. I slowly sink onto the bottom bunk, draping an arm across my eyes. Lying down seems to alleviate the sensation, at least somewhat.

Benji returns in short order with water. I know we only get limited amounts each day, but my mouth feels disgusting now, and when I sit up enough to take it and gulp it down, the coolness against my throat feels wonderful.

I finish off the glass and lie back. The mattress shifts with his added weight as he settles at my side.

"How are you feeling?"

"Not so bad so long as I'm lying down."

"Stay put then." Benji brushes the hair back from my forehead. "So...is that a no on boats?"

My face scrunches up. "Maybe I just ate something that didn't agree with me."

"Perhaps. Take it easy for now, hm? Get some sleep if you can. I think I'll venture topside for a bit longer, if you're all right on your own."

I wave him off, not expecting him to stick around if I'm nursing an upset stomach. He fusses over me a few moments longer, making sure that I don't need anything before slipping out of the room. Honestly, the silence is better and less embarrassing in the event that I throw up again.

Surely, I just need some time to adjust to being at sea. It'll pass.

IT DOES NOT pass.

In the days that follow, my seasickness does not wane, making it difficult to keep anything down. Benji assures me I'm not the only one. He enjoys being up on deck and there is apparently no shortage of people heaving the contents of their stomachs over the railings.

For the most part, though, Benji stays in the cabin with me. We play chess and cards, and he excitedly describes to me the dolphins and flying fish he's spotted out on the ocean. I scoff at first at the idea of fish *flying*, but as the trip wears on and I'm able to force myself out of bed to explore a bit, Benji eagerly takes me topside and I see precisely what he was on about.

They dart out of the water like strips of silver, glinting in the waning orange sunlight. Hundreds, maybe even thousands of them. It's certainly a sight to see, especially after five days of being cooped up in a cabin.

"Preston, look!" Benjamin grabs my arm and points almost straight down. The view of water rushing alongside the boat makes me momentarily dizzy, but then I spot the dolphins arcing in and out of the water.

It isn't even the sight of them that makes me smile so much as Benjamin's expression. His wide eyes, the way the sea-salted air caresses the hair back from his face. His cheeks have got a bit pink from spending time on deck in the sun.

I don't know how anyone could look at him and think he was anything less than perfect. How anyone could ever be cruel to him. Why any of these people around us would bother watching the sunset when they've got a personification of a sunrise right here.

Benji looks over and catches me staring. "What's wrong?"

It occurs to me that I'm smiling like an utter fool. "Nothing at all. Hungry?"

4
BENJAMIN

THE SHIP IS eerily silent at night. Quieter than home, quieter than Whisperwood. The few times throughout this trip that I've woken in the middle of the night, the silence has been almost unsettling. I would find myself unconsciously seeking out the sound of Preston's breathing to lull me back to sleep.

Tonight is just as quiet. However, I'm distinctly aware that something has woken me.

A shiver crawls its way down my spine. I pull the blankets up around me, face pressed into the pillow, waiting for the sensation to pass. Perhaps I had a nightmare that I don't remember and I'm simply shaking the remnants of it off.

Except it persists. Nagging. Pulling.

I roll over, staring into the room. I lean forward, peering over the edge at Preston, still sound asleep in the bunk beneath. Given his frequent seasickness, I ended up with the top bunk after all. Nothing seems to be amiss with him. He's sprawled on his back, ever so graceless, chest steadily rising and falling.

There is that tug again. An almost physical sensation of being watched, being beckoned.

I can just barely make out a piece of the satchel containing the chest peeking out from beneath the wash table. My pulse picks up.

Before I've realised it, my feet are on the floor. I do not recall moving or getting out of bed. Just as I am only vaguely aware of my legs carrying me across the short distance and bringing me to my knees before the satchel. I'm anxious to unveil the box for no reason at all. I just need to see it.

I slide the small chest out of its bag. With no proper lighting in the room, the wood looks almost black. My fingertips slide across the iron fastenings and embellishments, across the peculiar dial on the front.

Someone whispers against my ear, garbled, nonsensical. As though I'm listening to something from under water. There's pressure against my back and shoulders. Someone— something—is leaning into me, its arms around me. A cold embrace.

I cannot seem to move.

Open it.

The box needs to be opened.

I need to know what's inside.

A sudden startling, ear-piercing sound floods my ears. Not a scream. A *howl*. A wolf. One and then two until an entire chorus of howls seems to fill every corner of our small room and I cannot understand why it isn't waking everyone on the ship.

There's another voice beyond it all, far away.

"*—enji?*"

I try to open my mouth to speak, but nothing comes out.

"*Benjamin!*"

A stuttered gasp catches in my throat. I tear my hands from the box, whipping around to see Preston seated on the edge of his mattress. My eyes are wide and wild and I feel as though I've just been woken from the throes of a deep nightmare. "What?"

"What's going on? Are you all right?"

I blink once, opening my mouth, though no sound comes out. He starts to get up. I don't give him the chance before I'm scurrying across the floor and crawling into bed beside him. The confusion is evident in his voice and his face even as he gathers me into his arms. "Hey, hey, easy. It's all right."

I press my face into his shoulder. Shiver. My skin feels cold and clammy to the touch when compared to his. "There's something attached to that box."

He shifts, head turned to look. "Ah? What sort of something?"

"I don't know," I mumble. "I noticed it the moment Mr. Wilkerson brought it into the room."

"But… Is it a *feeling*? Or did you see something?"

"I thought I felt…something. I heard whispers. Howling."

"Howling?"

"Like wolves. I don't know. I'm sorry."

He hugs me to his chest and the tremors wracking my body begin to subside, slowly but surely. "No matter. Why were you messing with it anyway?"

"I… I don't honestly remember. I hardly recall getting out of bed." The memory of doing it is there, but not *why*.

Preston lays back, drawing me with him. "Whatever it is, we'll handle it. We'll get this job over with and be rid of it soon enough, hm?"

While carting it thousands of miles across the ocean and a country, yes. I know he's trying to comfort me, but it isn't quite working. Not when I still feel eyes on us from the shadows.

The bed is so small that it makes for tight quarters, but I'm not inclined to move and Preston doesn't appear to want to make me. I murmur a *thank you* as I nestle into his arms and go still. He strokes my hair until he drifts back off to sleep and I lie awake, listening to the silence.

I really hope we haven't got in over our heads.

WE SPEND ELEVEN full days at sea. Preston's seasickness never does fully subside, although it occasionally fades enough for him to come topside with me and enjoy the view. When we begin to see dry land in the distance, Preston perks up immensely. The last few hours of sailing toward port and docking drag at a snail's pace.

Preston looks like he wants to drop to the dock and kiss it. I flash him a smile at the relieved sigh he heaves upon setting foot on dry land once more.

From the docks, we're ushered into a building that smells far too much like sweat and unwashed bodies for my liking. Men with clipboards stand poised to question the passengers as they arrive. It does not go unnoticed that we're channelled into different lines—the first-class cabin passengers seem to bypass much of this process—and those from steerage seem like they will be stuck here far longer than Preston and me.

I also cannot help but notice that several families with skin as dark or darker than mine or whose English is not the best are being pulled aside for more intense questioning. It isn't the first time I feel nervous at the prospect of being singled out. I wonder if I will undergo the same treatment, if they'll notice the subtle differences in my skin tone or my dark eyes. But the man who comes to question us and look us over for any sign of illness passes me over without interest and we're instructed to be on our way. I feel a niggling sense of guilt that I'm permitted to go while so many others are held back.

Set loose outside the building, we stop on the side of the street to take our first real, proper look at Boston. It's so very different from home while not being that different at all, really. The buildings are taller, newer, the streets a bit wider. A flagpole sits in the very centre of the road, flying an American flag. It's much colder here than it was in Liverpool.

The most shocking bit, I suppose, would be the snow. It snows plenty enough back home in the winter, but the snow here feels so...*much*. Many of the horses are carting along sleighs instead of carriages and the people on the street are hunkered down, bundled up tight in furs and coats and scarves.

I fear we're underdressed for this weather. My wool overcoat is warm, but not much else on my person is and I suspect if I'm already feeling the chill then Preston likely is, too.

"What do you think, Benji?"

I shiver, readjusting the strap of my bag. "It's...ah, beautiful. Bit nippy, though."

"Just a bit," he agrees in amusement. "Where to next?"

I fish out the paper from my coat pocket. "Let's stop and ask for directions. The hotel ought to be nearby."

We nip into a nearby general store. While Preston asks the clerk where we're headed, I have a look at the goods for sale, noting all the differences and similarities between here and back home. Even hearing the conversations around us as we head outside and up the road is strange. I'm bombarded by a world full of accents that I've previously only encountered in passing. It's quite fascinating.

The Parker House Hotel is an impressive building. As we stand across the street, heads tipped back, gawking up at it, I'm *positive* there's been a mistake.

Preston shakes his head. "Check the address again. This can't be it."

I expected—oh, I don't know. Something more like the small inn we stayed at back in Liverpool. Something that suited our needs but no more. *This* place is grand. Five, perhaps six storeys, and the men and women I see coming in and out of its front doors are dressed far too finely to be of our ilk.

I offer him the paper. "No, this is it. The Parker House hotel. We're to ask for a Mr. Wilmer Cushman when we go in."

"If they even let us in the front doors," he jokes, adjusting his coat. Preston's wardrobe has never been impressive. Mine is hardly lavish either, but it's a sight more passable than his in such an extravagant setting.

We cross the street to head inside. The two doormen give us peculiar looks, perhaps on the brink of stopping us, but Preston walks by with purpose, not looking for a second as though he doesn't belong there. I stick fast to his side and try to do the same, though I do offer the men a polite smile.

The interior of the Parker House is even grander than the exterior. Gas sconces line the walls and when mixed with the crystal chandeliers hanging overhead the entire place is brightly lit, showing off the array of browns and reds and golds in everything from the panelled walls to the carpeting. Upholstered chairs sit in clusters of three and four about the massive lobby, some occupied by men and women conversing, reading, or simply waiting.

We approach the front desk side by side. The desk clerk doesn't seem terribly fazed by our travel-worn appearance and offers us a smile.

"How may I help you, gentlemen?"

I slide the letter from Mr. Wilkerson across the countertop. "We've been told to ask for Mr. Wilmer Cushman. He should be expecting us."

The clerk takes the letter and skims it. He excuses himself to disappear into a back room. When he returns, it's with another man at his heels that I can only presume is Mr. Cushman.

"Afternoon, gentlemen," Cushman greets, his voice the low and gravelly sound of a man who has smoked far too much tobacco. He looks us over before rounding the desk and thrusting out a large hand.

I take it without hesitating. "William Esher," I introduce myself. "This is my partner, James Spencer."

Preston smiles, a touch of amusement twinkling in his eyes. He gives Cushman's hand a shake as well.

"Glad you made it in one piece. Can't stand ships. God awful things. I'll be glad if I never have to make that trip." He sniffs and turns back around to the clerk. "Jeremy, room four-oh-two, please."

Jeremy the clerk fetches him a key from the numbered

rack and Mr. Cushman proceeds to escort us from the lobby to a door nearby.

The door, as it turns out, opens into a small mechanical lift. Oh! I've only seen these a few times, most recently in Paris. Preston halts abruptly, eyeing it with caution. Fair enough; the last time anything took his feet off the ground, he ended up seasick. I catch his elbow gently and give him a nudge. We step into the cart and the lift operator pulls a lever, bringing the rickety machine into motion. It's loud and unsteady, though aside from the initial dip of my stomach, it's actually quite fun. Preston flashes a grin over at me and I smile and wink at him in return.

"Are you the owner of this hotel, Mr. Cushman?" Preston asks.

"Just a manager," he grunts, sniffing and rubbing at his moustache. "Did Wilkerson tell you anything before sending you on your way?"

"Not much, sir."

"Ah. Well, figures. He's my wife's brother. We haven't seen each other in years. I'm honestly surprised he asked for this favour, in fact. He's unbearably polite, like all of you Brits. Never wants to ask for a thing."

I'm trying not to look amused as I raise an eyebrow at Preston, thinking that as charming as he can be, he is hardly what I would consider excessively polite.

The lift finally comes to a halt, and the operator slides open the door for us to step out. The hallway is a bit dimmer, but no less grand than the lobby. Every flickering sconce casts dancing shadows upon the gold-and-crimson carpeting and the dark wood panelling. Cushman escorts us to a door at the far end, unlocks it, and steps aside for us to go in first.

I venture in with Preston on my heels. My eyes widen. This far exceeds anything I would have expected to be offered to us on this trip. Every immaculate detail is a sight to behold, from the warm golds and bronzes, to each neatly placed throw pillow decorating the settee and the basket of fresh fruits and candies atop the table. A set of French doors opens into the next room, revealing a double set of beds. Another door leads into a room with both a tub and a toilet. I'm not certain I've had cause to be in any building with such new amenities. It's fascinating.

Cushman lingers in the doorway, arms folded behind his back. He doesn't smile, but he seems to seek our approval all the same. "Is it to your liking?"

Preston lets out a sound not unlike a stifled laugh. I've ventured into the centre of the room, eyes wide with barely contained excitement and awe. I swallow back a smile. "Yes, this will do nicely. Thank you."

"Excellent. I presume you'll be leaving first thing in the morning?"

"Not terribly early, no. I should think we'll enjoy sleeping in a bit."

He nods curtly. "Well, please help yourselves to dinner and breakfast in the restaurant downstairs, compliments of the house."

He's scarcely left the room before I've made my way across it and thrown open the drapes—crimson and shot through with gold embroidery. "This is incredible. Preston, come, look at the view!"

Preston moves to my side. We gaze out at the stretch of snowy city beneath us. It's a remarkable sight.

"Does this beat the lodgings in Paris?" he asks.

I look up at him. "This *far* exceeds Paris. Are you certain we can't just stay here a few days?"

"Lord, wouldn't that be nice." He draws back and we go to explore the rest of our room. The beds in particular look far too tempting to pass up. Preston drops his bag, places the box-satchel beside it, and flings himself onto the mattress. He sinks into the down-filled blankets and groans.

I linger in the doorway, toeing off my shoes and slipping my coat from my shoulders. "Oh, Preston. You're filthy and lying all over that nice clean bed."

He grins, folding his hands behind his head. "I'm staying right here until I can get a bath."

"Go on first, then. I'm feeling generous."

Preston hesitates, seeming to debate if that offer is worth getting up for. His curiosity over our fancy bathroom clearly wins out, because he gets to his feet and trots past me with a smile. A few moments later, I hear the water running.

In his absence, I dig through my bag for a clean set of clothing. A faint prickling slides up the back of my neck. I twist around, eyes falling right upon the satchel containing the box. The last thing I want is a repeat of that night on the boat. Hurriedly, I gather my clothes and retreat to the main room to wait outside the bathroom for Preston to finish his bath.

He takes his time and I don't begrudge him that. When he finally emerges, it's with a towel wrapped around his waist. I cannot help but let my gaze travel along his bare torso, the lines of his chest and shoulders and collar bones, and the way the droplets of water dot his skin. My cheeks grow warm and I divert my gaze, as though we didn't spend a school year and several holidays sharing a room and dressing in front of one another.

"At your leisure," he hums, brushing past me. The gesture seems almost intentional. The heat rolling off his damp skin makes me shiver as I inch into the bathroom.

A layer of condensation covers the mirror and the steam from Preston's bath still lingers. I draw myself an equally hot bath, undressing and sinking into the water with a sigh. It feels like it's been ages since I last had a proper wash in anything other than a bowl. I take my time scrubbing the weeks' worth of dirt, grime, and salt from my skin and hair.

By the time I finish, my skin is flushed from the heat of the water and I've grown remarkably sleepy. When I find Preston, he's scarcely bothered to get into a pair of drawers before sprawling out across his bed, and he's dozed off. I let him sleep while I dry off and dress. Only then do I lean over and poke a finger into his ribs.

"Come on. It's about time for dinner. I don't know about you, but I'm starving."

He grunts, making a grab for my hand. "If I lay on you, we won't be going anywhere," he mumbles. I chuckle, avoiding his attempts to catch me and prodding at him until he gets up and finishes making himself presentable.

We venture downstairs to take dinner in the restaurant. There's no question about it that I've never eaten in such a fine establishment. Given that Mr. Cushman said it was on the house, we only need to give Spencer and Esher's names to our waiter and then are able to eat our fill. For dessert, I order something our waiter refers to as the Parker House Chocolate Cream Pie and it is the most delicious, decadent thing I've ever had the pleasure of eating.

Rather than retire to bed immediately, we leave the hotel

to take a walk. It would be a shame to arrive in a new city and not have a look around. It's cold and the streets are flush with people hurrying about, unfettered by the snowfall. I hold my overcoat snugly around myself and stick close to Preston's side.

"Do you think all winters here are like this?" I ask. "With so much snow?"

"Maybe." He halts in front of a bakery window, admiring the cakes on display. "Everyone here looks used to it."

"I don't mind the cold, but this is a bit much even for me." I stop beside him, eyes widening as I lean forward to peer through the window. My breath fogs the glass. "Can we go in?"

He chuckles, even as he's opening the door and holding it for me. "Didn't you have your fill of sweets at dinner?"

"We don't travel abroad every day, Preston! What if they've got something unique?"

"By all means."

The aroma of chocolate and baked goods greets me upon entering, immediately bringing a smile to my face. As I peruse the display cases of pastries, candies, and pies, a wave of nostalgia and sadness sweeps over me.

I'm standing in Paris again, Mother's arm linked with mine. I can see her face so vividly. Her smile. Her eyes crinkling at the corners. She picks out a small tartlet and points out the truffles to me. They're one of my favourite sweets.

Preston touches my back, pulling me away from the past and to the present. My chest aches.

"What looks good?" he asks.

I swallow hard, trying to regain my bearings. "Ah. Those, there."

We come away with a bag of truffles and fudge, walking in the snow near the boardwalk. I alternate between eating my sweets and tipping my head back, tongue sticking out to catch the occasional snowflake. Preston, however, has been oddly quiet.

"Say, Benji…"

I make an inquiring noise, popping another truffle into my mouth.

"Are you all right? That is…" A pause. "I noticed your arm the other day."

My steps falter ever so slightly in the snow, just a hitch in my movements. I say nothing at first, facing straight ahead, keeping my expression carefully unreadable.

I had tried to keep the bruises hidden. No sense in worrying him. No sense in bringing up something I would just as soon forget about.

"If you don't want to talk about it…" Preston begins.

I roll closed the paper sack containing the rest of my candies. "There isn't much to say. Father and I had a few words when he found out I was leaving."

Oh, how the tension practically radiates off him. "Bruises aren't exactly words, Benjamin."

Silence.

What do I say to that? It's done. Over with. I likely will never see Franklin Hale again. He's as good as dead to me and I do not care to revisit any memories in which he's present.

Preston heaves a quiet sigh. "We don't have to get into it. But I'm here, if you need me."

"I know. Thank you, Preston." I turn a smile his way, though it's a little tight round the edges and I know it.

I suspect Preston knows me too well to be fooled.

5
PRESTON

A KNOCK UPON the door startles me out of a dead sleep because *of course* I'd be woken. I'd been looking forward to my first solid night's rest in a while and having that interrupted makes me open my eyes and cast a sullen glare in the direction of the door. What bloody time is it? Maybe someone has the wrong room.

They knock again, louder. Benjamin stirs in the other bed. I don't want him to wake up too, so with a sigh, I fling back the blankets and get up to answer it.

A curly-haired man with dark eyes stands there, hands clasped behind his back. He blinks at me once, as though surprised that I—what, actually opened the door?

I squint at him. "Can I help you?"

"Good morning. I was told this room had a wake-up call scheduled for Mr. Spencer and Mr. Esher."

I run a hand down my face and sigh. Without really thinking about it, I grumble, "Wrong room."

A pause. "I'm terribly sorry, sir."

With an apologetic smile, he turns away and I shut the door. Well, I had not asked for any wake-up call, but here we are. Benji is still sleeping though, and I have half a mind to crawl into his bed, which is undoubtedly warmer than my own.

I scrub my hands over my eyes and shuffle across the room, pausing at the table. The bag containing our cargo sits upon it and I find myself reaching for it, to slide it out and have a look. The early (very early) morning sunlight glints off the iron fastens. I pull out a chair and have a seat.

Ever since I woke that night to find Benji in a near trance-like state staring at the damned thing, I've been trying to keep a closer eye on it. Still, I get no supernatural feelings from it—not that that means anything. Even Aunt Eleanor has said Benji is far more sensitive to these things than I am. If Benji says he senses something about this thing, then I believe him wholeheartedly.

I scoot closer to the table and place my palms flat against the sides of the box. Eyes closed. Focusing. In the quiet of the early morning, without a rocking ship to distract me, surely I ought to sense *something*.

Nothing. Just wood against my skin and me feeling incredibly foolish.

I open my eyes.

A woman's face, mouth agape, hangs just in front of me.

She screams. Ear-piercing. Dragging blades down my bones.

The chair clatters to the ground as I scramble away. A shout catches in my throat. But she's gone, just as suddenly as she appeared. The room is silent and still again.

My heart is racing. What *was* that? Or should I ask, *who* was that? What the hell is inside that box?

Benji never could properly convey to me what he saw or heard. Any time I've asked, he's tried, but ended up shaking his head and looking away. He had said it was a feeling more than anything, and now I can understand what he meant. I could describe that I saw a woman, that I heard her screaming, but I could not have said what she looked like.

No, that's not entirely true. She looked like *agony*.

I advance to the table, grabbing hold of the box again, willing the woman to return and bracing myself for it. This time, I think perhaps I feel an inkling of *something*, but beyond that...nothing.

"Preston?"

I turn to see Benji standing in the double doors of the bedroom, his hair adorably sleep-tousled.

"Good morning," I say, careful to keep my tone easy and light as I let go of the box. "Why are you up so early?"

"I thought I heard..." He shakes his head. "I don't know. What are you doing?"

"Some staffer mistakenly thought we wanted to be woken before the sun was fully up." I sigh, turning to upright the fallen chair. "Why don't you go back to sleep?"

"Not sure that I can." He casts a wary look in the direction of the table as he crosses the room to me. "Did you...see something?"

After seeing him so shaken from his encounter, I really don't want to worry him. But I also know Benjamin has gone so much of his life being unable to discuss the things that he sees with anyone that pretending I saw nothing might do more harm than good.

"I saw a woman. Just briefly. Not getting anything now, though."

Instead of looking shaken by this revelation, Benji seems relieved. "Did she say anything?"

"Not a word. Did she speak to you?"

"I think she tried, but…" He shivers, hugging himself and turning away from the box. "I couldn't move. Felt like I couldn't breathe."

I can't help but place a hand against his back, rubbing small circles between his shoulder blades. "Do you think we ought to try to communicate with her? Going to be quite a long trip if she's popping up as she likes."

"We aren't Esher and Spencer, Preston. Do you think we're experienced enough to try without making it worse?"

Shrug. "Esher loaned me a book of his notes. I'd wager there's enough in there to walk us through it. Haven't looked at it, though."

Benji cracks a small smile. "Of course you haven't. I'll give it a read on the train."

Oh, thank God. "Have I told you lately that I appreciate the way you spare me from having to read anything ever?"

"You have not, but after all these years, it goes without saying. Now, since we're up anyway, let's see about breakfast and purchasing our train tickets. We've got a long journey ahead of us."

WE LEAVE THE hotel early and when we drop off our key at the front, we are presented with an envelope containing a note informing us we have pre-purchased tickets waiting at the train station. I had expected the cost would come out of our own pockets, so it's a pleasant surprise.

However, upon arriving at the station, I find we are not as lucky with the train as we were with the boat. First-class seating is limited, and so the tickets waiting under not-our-names are second-class. Ordinarily this would not make me bat an eyelash. We've both travelled by train plenty back home, often seated near strangers. I'm quite good at making acquaintances with anyone I sit near, in fact.

The transcontinental railroad is nothing like the trains in England, though.

We're ushered into the cars in an orderly enough fashion, but then crowded in along with several others—families and individuals alike. Among them, there's a friendly Scotsman who smells strongly of bourbon, who keeps trying to chat up a Chinese woman with three little ones clinging to her skirts. She smiles weakly at him, but by the uncertain look on her face, she's having trouble keeping up with his heavily accented English.

The inside of the car is lined with benches that convert into cots, with a single water closet at the far end. It stinks of sweat and smoke, and that much is not unlike home. For the next two weeks, we will be sharing our daily living, sleeping, and eating space with these people, all while dealing with a box that may be haunted. Sounds like a grand adventure.

I keep the bag with the box slung about me at all times, even when the strap begins to make my shoulder ache. With the multiple conversations, the sound of the train roaring down the tracks and away from Boston, Benji and I do not try to speak much for the first few hours. He stays pressed to my side, hands in his lap, quietly observing the people around us. Near lunch, he leaves me long enough to investigate the dining car but returns largely empty-handed after seeing how expensive the food is.

As the sun begins to set, the atmosphere aboard the train shifts drastically. What began as a buzz of excited, anxious energy swiftly diminishes into an irritable sort of exhaustion, exacerbated by the cramped spaces and crying children and language barriers making communication difficult. The din of voices amongst the other passengers dies down as the sun vanishes, and people begin to crowd into the seats and bunks to claim their place for a spot to sleep.

We're lucky enough to snag a set of bunks at the far end of the car, close to the door. They're not really large enough for two people to fit comfortably—though Lord knows plenty of people are trying—so Benji decides to take the bottom cot while I plan to take the top.

Then I see him pause, looking back to a row of seats across the way, at the mother with her three children as she tries to wrangle them all into one small bunk. It would appear she plans to sleep on the floor with the youngest in her lap; there's no room for them all on the thin mattress.

It takes me only a second to predict what Benji's going to do, and it makes me smile. He crosses over to crouch down before the woman, speaking to her softly in Mandarin. Her eyes widen a fraction, confused, then flick to the bed where he points. Then gratefulness and relief overtake her features and she says something to him in return. I think I recognise the repeated phrase as *Thank you*. See? I've picked up a few things in my time with Benji.

As the woman and her youngest child take up residence in the bottom bunk, I flash Benji a smile and gesture to the top.

"Is it all right?" he asks sheepishly. "It's going to be cramped."

"I've never minded sleeping in close quarters with you," I tease, pleased by the blush that crosses his face. He hauls himself up to the bunk, closest to the wall, and I follow.

Close quarters indeed. We're forced to lie on our sides in order to fit. And, face-to-face, Benji is so very near that it makes my heartbeat pick up as I study all the familiar lines of his face. I miss his long hair even if just for the excuse to reach out and brush it back from his dark eyes.

He smiles, lashes lowering. "Will the box be all right down there, do you think?"

"Not much room for it up here," I point out. I tucked it as far back against the wall as I could, where no one walking by would even see it. They'd have to get through our shoes and rucksacks first. Besides, having it up here would put us both in constant contact with it and now I'm not so certain I want that any more than Benji does.

The car has grown eerily quiet inside, offset by the loud clattering of wheels on the tracks and the wind howling outside. Thankfully, with our proximity, I can still hear Benji even when he whispers.

"What do you think California will be like? As cold as Boston?"

"Not really sure. Bigger, I suspect. Hopefully a bit less snow."

He makes a noise of agreement, and then he shifts carefully to roll onto his other side. It makes for a better fit as he inches against me, his back to my chest, and after a moment of debate, I slowly allow an arm to fall across his middle. Surely plenty of people are curled up close, men and women alike, for warmth and comfort. Besides, shy of standing on the bottom bunk to look at us, we aren't easily visible.

Maybe I'm just making excuses because I want to hold him. I allow my face to turn enough to let his hair tickle my jaw and I breathe in deep. He still smells of soap from his earlier bath. Lying there with him, the rest of the world drops away, leaving just Benjamin and me.

I've often thought about what life could be like for the pair of us. I've thought of following in James and Esher's footsteps with the whole spirit-hunting thing. I've thought of travelling all over the world, maybe living in each place for a few months, working until we had enough money saved to travel to the next destination. I've even thought of simply remaining on the farm, taking it over someday, and even that doesn't sound altogether horrible when I picture Benji there with me.

He's the one thing in my life I cannot envision myself without. Lord knows I tried when I thought he'd be running off to marry and to suffocate himself in some stuffy factory job. It never worked. Every scenario I tried to imagine was like a blind spot in my mind and Benji always somehow found his way into those scenes regardless, no matter how unrealistic they were. I envision myself miserable and alone, and there he is, knocking on my door with a smile that lights up the world around him.

Years of sharing a room has me knowing the precise moment Benji drifts off to sleep. The way his breathing evens out, the tension that eases from his shoulders, the way he snuggles back into my arms and tugs the thin, flimsy blanket up to his nose. He is resting easy, our haunted cargo seems to be behaving, and I believe I will enjoy his nearness for however long I can have it.

THE WRATH OF WOLVES

IT'S STILL DARK when I wake to a hand clamping across my mouth, and Benjamin's wide, dark eyes inches from mine. I inhale sharply, startled. Reflex has me wanting to ask what he's doing, but the palm over my mouth and the finger he holds to his own lips keeps me from speaking.

At first, all I hear is the roaring of the train. Benji slowly withdraws his hand from my mouth and points toward the nearby door leading from our tram into the next. There, I can make out a conversation, barely audible.

"Tellin' you, we searched this place high and low. Ain't no sign of 'em," a man's voice grinds out, low and gravelly and very American.

A woman responds. Her voice is softer, more difficult to hear. "He verified they got on this train. They didn't just up and vanish. What about the box?"

I hold my breath.

"No sign of it, but—"

"Did you check *everywhere?* Bags, cargo?"

"What, y'want us to just start rootin' through everyone's belongings?"

"That's exactly what I want you to do," the woman says, exasperated. "Do it now when they're sleeping, just don't get your fool selves caught and tossed off the train. I don't even care about Spencer and Esher so long as you find the damned box."

Brilliant. We've got two people—or more, as the woman mentioned others—on our trail. We were warned it might happen, but for whatever reason, I had thought our client was simply overreacting and this job would go off without a hitch. So much for that. How in the hell did they find us on one of many trains crossing the country?

I weigh our options. I could hop out of this bunk and confront the both of them head-on. But two against one, not knowing how many others are working with them, likely won't end well for us. Besides, what would I do? Throw them from the train? Wake every other passenger in the process?

Option two involves trying to get a look at the pair of them and hoping we can lay low and avoid them for the rest of the trip. They're looking for James and Esher, not Benji and me.

As I start to move, Benji grabs hold of my arm. I give his hand a reassuring squeeze, close my eyes, and sluggishly roll over to face the aisle. The voices go quiet for a moment, but I settle, feigning a sleepy sigh, and they seem to decide my supposedly sleeping form is no threat.

"Get on it," the woman finally hisses, followed by the sound of the tram door opening and closing as she leaves. Her companion is still present; I hear him swear and mutter under his breath as he begins to shuffle down the aisle. When I dare to crack an eye open, I see him crouched near the bunk opposite ours, cautiously beginning to root through the contents of another passenger's bag.

My heart leaps into my throat. All he needs to do is turn and happen across our bag beneath the lower bunk, and he's got our cargo.

Benji has got his fingers curled into my shirt against my back. His breath falls against the nape of my neck as he whispers, "Don't…"

I grit my teeth. Shift. Stretch out and feign a yawn. The man startles into an upright position and I slide from bed, pushing a hand through my ruffled hair. When my feet hit the ground, it's a touch too loud, and I wonder if it may have woken anyone else. Good, more attention means this bloke won't be likely to get far in his search.

Christ, he's a big gent. I'm built sturdy and strong, but this man makes me feel small with his broad shoulders and thick arms. He scowls down at me, heavy brows furrowed, and I return the look of displeasure with an easy smile.

"Oh. Sorry, mate. Everything all right?"

He grunts in response, averting his gaze. He must know he looks terribly suspicious standing in a car he has not occupied at all today and with someone else's belongings in hand.

"Just lookin' for the john," he mutters, letting the bag fall to the floor. He pushes past me for the opposite exit. Well, that was a bit too close for comfort.

Benji sits up, clutching his chest as though to keep his heart from leaping out of it. "*Preston.*"

"It's fine, lay back down." I crouch to retrieve the box from beneath the bottom bunk and find myself almost eye-to-eye with one of the Chinese woman's children, wide awake. I grin, give her a wink and hold a finger to my lips to signal her to keep quiet, which makes her smile. Then I fetch our bag and haul myself onto the top bed.

Benji is lying down again, but his features are scrunched up in concern. "Honestly…"

"Don't look at me like that. What was I supposed to do?"

His silence suggests he's got no better answer.

We're already cramped for space, but we wedge the box beneath the covers down by our feet. There truly is no real way for us to avoid it completely, and I just hope that Benji will be able to sleep with it so close by.

Once we've settled again—somewhat less comfortably than before—I finally meet Benji's worried eyes.

"What now?" he whispers.

"What *can* we do? We keep the chest hidden and we lay low, I suppose."

"For two weeks?"

"They don't know who they're looking for. Even if they get their heads out of their arses and realise James and Esher aren't aboard the train, they've got no idea who has their cargo."

He bites his lip. This is, I suspect, far more than he anticipated having to deal with on this trip and I'm horribly regretful for that.

He says, "We could get off at the next stop and board the next train that comes through town."

That's a possibility, and yet we wouldn't have any idea when the next train runs. It could be a day; it could be a week. That's assuming they had any room for two more last-minute passengers.

"Suppose they let us off at the stop long enough to find out when the next train comes through?" I offer.

Benji closes his eyes and sighs, bringing his forehead to rest against my shoulder. It's as good an idea as any, and really the only one we've got. Barring getting onto another train…

We had better get very good at making ourselves invisible.

6
BENJAMIN

I FEEL WE'VE SCARCELY moved in the several days since we boarded the train. My joints ache from the inactivity, from sitting so much, from sleeping in such cramped quarters. Even though Preston and I enjoy being close, I think we're both quite tired of having absolutely no space to do so much as roll over.

Mostly, though, we're exhausted.

We take turns napping throughout the day because neither of us sleep well at night. Whether it's because we've got the chest crammed at our feet or because we spot that man lurking about the car now and again, eyeing everyone with suspicion, I'm not certain. He's not come through at night again, but that doesn't mean a thing other than that he and his companions are likely occupied searching through other cars first.

We've had plenty of stops and while we sat there, eyeing the doors and the passengers who both came and left, neither of us moved to disembark ourselves. The stops were short, crowded, and I was not confident if we got off that we would have a viable option for what to do next. The next train could roll through in a matter of hours or a matter of weeks and then what? We'd be stuck in a town we didn't know with limited funds and a client waiting for us in California.

One such stop is at a station directly on the border of Indiana and Illinois, where the carman announces we will be paused for nearly an hour should anyone wish to get off for a spell. Preston stands, flashing me a smile. "We might as well stretch our legs and grab a bite to eat since we'll be here awhile, yeah?"

I rise to my feet, joints aching in protest, and I hesitate, looking to the bag that had been sitting between us. Preston scoops it up and slings it over his shoulder, and together we file off the train with the other passengers and onto the station platform.

It's a much larger station than anywhere we've stopped at thus far. Multiple trains are crammed along several tracks and the platform is so busy that it's difficult to make sense of where we're supposed to go. In the end, Preston seems to follow his nose and I follow Preston. Not far from the queues at the ticket counters, we locate a string of vendors selling everything from newspapers to trinkets to food.

Knowing it may be awhile before we have another stop that we feel comfortable getting off at, Preston purchases a few meat pies, some dried salted bacon, and two sandwiches. I peruse the pushcarts, having difficulty finding much in the way of meatless food selections.

Just as I'm paying for spice cake and a cup of ginger beer, a nagging sensation draws my attention toward the crowds near our train. The man from the first night is difficult to miss with his hulking stature and stark blond hair. He's far enough away that I'm not overly concerned about being spotted, but I lower my head all the same.

This is going to be exhausting, worrying ourselves sick aboard this train for another seven or eight days.

I find my way back to Preston to give him a nudge and a nod toward the man. He looks, frowns, then says, "I'll be right back. Wait here." He nips over to the nearby ticket booths to wait in the queue.

I wrap my hands about my drink, trying to watch the man by the train without making it obvious that I'm watching. My heartbeat is picking up.

The howling has returned.

Fainter this time. So faint that I almost think I'm imagining it.

When Preston returns, I've taken a seat near some of the vendors and have finished off my cake.

"Next train to San Francisco comes through tomorrow evening," he announces.

That isn't so bad. "Any idea if there will be available seats?"

"No telling until it rolls through." He sits beside me. "They said it's coming from New York, and those tend to be fairly packed from here to Nevada."

I bite the inside of my cheek. "So… Either we take the risk or we keep our heads down. What's it going to be?"

Preston scratches a hand through his hair with a sigh. "I think we keep our heads down, honestly."

Something feels unsettling about that decision. It's wrong and I do not know why. The howling has grown louder. I squeeze my eyes shut, willing it to silence.

"Benji? What is it?"

The sound begins to fade just a bit. I exhale. "I don't know. Something tells me we should stay and take our chances here."

He rolls his shoulders back. "There's, what, two or three hundred people aboard this train and a handful of them? We can handle it."

Oh, I want to push back this time. I'm normally so content to let Preston take the lead, to simply follow where he goes. It's far easier allowing someone you trust to make all the important decisions, to not have to feel guilty if it turns out to be the wrong choice, and yet… I find myself looking back to the ticket booths.

I don't like this one bit.

And yet I relent with a nod and we board the train without another word of protest from me. As we take up a seat, the blond man boards not long after. I notice the way he pauses, the way his gaze seems to linger on us a moment longer than is necessary.

Lord, I hope we haven't made the wrong decision.

EVERY CITY AND countryside we travel through is blanketed in snow. Inside the car, everything is hot, humid, and smells of sweat, so that when a window is cracked, the feel of the frigid outside air and rain and snow is welcome against my face. Sometimes I press my cheek to the glass; it seems to be the only way I've been able to sleep the last two nights.

Preston fusses over me, over my lack of sleep and, more often, my lack of food intake. It's true that without meat on the menu, I'm largely surviving off bread and a bit of fruit. Vegetables aren't a luxury available on a cross-continental train. Hardly a filling diet. But it is what it is and the idea of ingesting meat has not yet begun to sound even remotely better than having near-constant hunger pangs in my belly.

We pass through the remainder of Illinois and Iowa, and then into Nebraska. At times, the train crawls at a snail's pace, put off by the influx of snow. More than once, we stop altogether while section hands scramble to shovel the tracks.

Somewhere in Nebraska, we brave the cold again just to get away from the cramped offerings of the car. Everything aches. I miss the trains back home and I could cry for a proper cup of tea.

Preston is sleepy-eyed and sluggish beside me. "This is almost worse than the ship."

I'm inclined to agree. At least there, we had privacy and some semblance of space.

"A few more days," I say gently. "That cart there has got rolls and coffee."

He casts me a most unimpressed look. "Will you really not try to eat something proper while we're stopped? Look—that cart's got boiled eggs."

"I'll be fine once I've bought some more bread."

"You've been surviving off of bread, Benji."

"So have many of the other passengers, if you haven't noticed. It's likely all they can afford."

He opens his mouth and pauses, looking sheepish that he had not considered such a thing. "I'm afraid I can't feed them all, but I can feed *you*."

I touch a hand briefly to his arm. "I'm fine, trust me. I'll stock up on snacks here."

We walk the narrow platform for a few minutes, just to work some feeling back into our limbs and restore our food supplies--although I *am* growing quite tired of bread and potatoes. The station is maybe a tenth of the size of the one back in Illinois and significantly less crowded. I don't believe anyone disembarked the train who does not intend to continue to the next town. The vendors are still plentiful, probably grateful for the business to come through such a small stop.

Before long, the whistle sounds and the attendants begin calling for departure within five minutes. Preston and I make our way back to our car, ensuring our tickets are still on our person, although the attendants recognise our faces by now.

Yet as we near the train, the increasingly familiar sound of wolves pierces the air.

I halt dead in my tracks, clamping my hands about Preston's arm. I see the blond man near our car again. This time, he is not alone.

Beside him stands a young, dark-skinned woman in similar trousers and shirt and coat as the man's, with a Stetson hat atop her head. It isn't the sight of her that has me frightened, though.

It's the hulking shape of a dead man directly behind her.

"Christ, Benji, you look like you've seen a ghost," Preston says.

I can scarcely hear him above the howling. I can scarcely hear myself speak, for that matter. "There, by the train."

He follows my gaze. "What? What is it? I see him."

"We need to go," I say, urgently, yanking his arm as I step back and away, annoying the crowd around us as they try to file past where we're holding up the line.

"What are you talking about—"

"Preston, *please*, not back on the train!"

Thank the Lord above he doesn't try to argue with me or reassure me that things are fine. Maybe it's the look on my face or the panic in my voice, but he relents, allowing me to pull him back through the crowd.

I don't stop until we've crossed the station, circled round the back of a ticket booth. There, Preston drags me to a halt, which might be good because I'd likely haul him halfway across town otherwise.

"Benji, *stop*. Breathe. Talk to me."

I slump against the side of the booth, pressing a hand to my chest as though it will do anything to still my racing heart. "That woman... You didn't see it?"

He glances over his shoulder. Frowns. "I just see that man from the tram, and a woman with him. What am I missing?"

I open my mouth, close it, at a loss for words. Then my ice-cold fingers catch hold of his hand and I turn him back in the direction of the train.

Miss Bennett did this once before. She told me I could, too. She told me my presence alone was enough to help others see what I see, right? So I focus, I concentrate, staring at that woman and her ghost.

The sensation is peculiar, like a wet, sheer cloth being pulled over us. It's a queer feeling that I pinpoint as having experienced seated at Miss Bennett's table with her holding mine and Preston's hands. Her touch, her abilities, had opened our eyes to seeing more than even I have ever seen.

Now, here in the middle of the train station, with my inexperience, I'm not certain how much Preston is able to see. Everywhere I go there are shadows and shapes at the edge of my vision, ever-present. Now and again I see more tangible forms lingering about in the shadows and I have learned to pay them no mind, to pretend they aren't there. As Mother always told me to do.

But this spirit is different. It isn't malevolence I get from it, no, but the way it lingers near that woman, attached to her like a second shadow, is unlike anything I've seen before.

And I can tell by the look upon his face and the tightening of his hand that now Preston can see it, too.

"Preston, can you hear the howling? Can you see it?"

His voice cracks. "Yes. I see it. Whatever *it* is."

He releases me. The woman casts one last look about the platform before trailing after the other passengers, with the blond man on her heels. A faint flicker of worry settles as the attendant calls again for last-minute stragglers to board. We're supposed to be on that train.

Taking stock of our situation, however... We've got our bags, we've got the chest, and we've got funds to purchase new tickets. God willing, in a few days we could be on another, safer train on our way to California without having our pursuers breathing down our necks.

I remind myself of this as the train departs, rumbling away down the tracks. Only once it's disappeared into the distance—and the howling fades—am I able to fully relax. I slump against the ticket booth, head tipped back, a sigh escaping my lips. Preston levels a concerned frown my way.

"All right now?"

"Yes. Sorry. I just... I've never seen anything like that. I've never seen a spirit *attach* itself to a person." I pause. "If a ghost can latch itself to an object, I suppose there's no reason it couldn't do the same to a person." I try to shake the unease of whatever it was we just witnessed. Preston squeezes my shoulder.

"Seems to be the case, doesn't it? But she's gone now, hm? And we've got some new things to worry ourselves over. Like where we're going to stay until the next train with open seating comes through."

"Right. Sorry about all this." I bow my head.

Preston promptly nudges my chin back up to look at him. "Hey. Don't ever apologise to me for following your gut. I'll trust it over most anything else any time. All right?"

It's a reassurance that I desperately needed. As I gaze up at him, our eyes locked, I can tell that he means it. He trusts me. He trusts that if I push, it means it's something important. I only hope that my concerns aren't unfounded, that my sudden, inexplicable panic doesn't result in needless frustration and difficulties for us now.

Preston allows me to linger a few moments longer, just to settle my nerves. We circle around to the front of the ticket booths to address a sleepy-looking attendant. The next train comes through in two days' time, barring any delays. I wince, but Preston shrugs it off and asks if there are any lodgings nearby for us to pass the time. We're directed to the only place in town to stay, which is a small inn just up the road.

When I had imagined America, it was with significantly more deserts, ranchers, and Indians. Significantly less snow. The wild frontier, so to speak. Bellporte, Nebraska is small, undeveloped, and although there is snow on the ground here, it's mostly slush and chunks of ice. It's cold out, but the sun overhead feels lovely on my face as we walk down the dirt road.

The inn doesn't even have a name outside, simply an old wooden sign hanging cockeyed above the door that reads, aptly, *Inn*. Through the door is a small lobby, with a restaurant off to our right just past the stairs leading up to, I presume, the rooms. The entire place is relatively silent and devoid of people. Preston and I exchange looks before he steps up to the counter and rings the call bell atop it. A wobbly-legged woman emerges a few moments later and greets us with a toothy, kind smile.

"Can I help you boys?"

"We'd like a room for two nights, if you've anything available," I say, as though this place looks like it would be full.

She snags a key from behind the counter, placing it alongside a guestbook that she slides over for me to sign. "Passing through, eh? Missed your train?"

I reach for a pen. "Does it happen often?"

"Often enough. Out in the middle of nowhere like this, we don't get many visitors otherwise." She shrugs, extending an open hand. "Two nights will run ya fifty cents. Dinner's served around six, but that's an extra fifty each. Lot of the locals gather for music and drinks, if you're into that kind of thing."

I rifle through my rucksack, procuring money to place into her hand for both the room and meals. "It sounds lovely. Thank you very much."

She smiles in a way that suggests she finds my polite demeanour refreshing. At my request, she also fetches us a jug of water for our room. Lord knows the pair of us could use some cleaning up.

There is nothing remarkable about our room upstairs. It's draughty and small, and given its placement, I would guess it's directly above the pub. Not a problem for us at the moment, but it might be later if the gathering locals get particularly rambunctious.

Still, it looks like a piece of heaven right now. Preston falls onto a musty-smelling bed with a groan. I collapse into the bed opposite his. After more than a week of sleeping on a train cot, it's delightful. Neither of us move for the better part of ten minutes. When I lift my head to look over, Preston's eyes are closed.

A nap doesn't sound bad, but I pick myself up to make use of our washbowl. There was little in the way of staying clean aboard the train. Not when we were cramped alongside several other human bodies for twenty-four hours a day.

After I've cleaned up, I drape my shirt across the foot of the bed and take a seat. The bag containing the chest sits on the floor nearby. Howling aside, we've not had any further issues with it on the train, which is peculiar, although not unappreciated.

I steal a glance at Preston, ensuring he is good and well asleep. My hands are clammy and a touch shaky as I reach for the bag and slide the box from inside, placing it on the bed before me. The intricate metalwork was done with great care, and the wood is polished and lovely. Whoever made this did so with a good deal of craftsmanship. Along with the dead woman attached to it, I'm even more curious as to what's inside.

That curiosity is enough to overcome my nerves, it would seem.

I slide my fingers along the three small dials on the face of the box. Each one contains a series of pictures engraved into it—four in all. A bird, a wolf, a dog, and a sheep. To unlock it, I would need the correct picture combination. Wolf, wolf, sheep? No. Bird, wolf, dog? Also no. If I were truly determined, I could go through every single combination to figure it out. Tedious, but plausible.

But what then? What good would it do us, beyond potentially annoying our client when we deliver the box if they realise that we've been snooping?

Sighing, I place the box back upon the floor and lie down. It's been a tiring couple of days and I suspect it will only continue to get more hectic. For the time being, I try to push the thoughts of ghosts and haunted women out of my head and catch up on some much-needed rest.

7
PRESTON

DREAMS OF HOME drift in and out of my consciousness, but it's the howling that draws me from my nap some hours later. My eyes flutter open, puzzled by the sound. When I turn my head to check on Benji, he's stirring, frowning as he lifts a hand to scrub at his face. By the time he opens his eyes, the howling has stopped.

Damn that box.

When Benji had told me about the howling the other day, it had sounded so peculiar and I couldn't grasp why a ghost, of all things, would be projecting such a sound. But then I heard it for myself at the train station, and now it feels ingrained into my ears.

Perhaps this time, I was dreaming about it. That's all.

"Good morning, sunshine," I greet.

A sleepy smile tugs at his mouth. He pushes himself up to sitting. "What time is it?"

"About time for food, according to my stomach." I pause, listening. "By the sound of it, some of those locals we heard about have started arriving. We could mingle a bit, throw back a few drinks along with our meal?"

Benji cracks a smile. "You're just looking for an excuse to drink without your sisters lecturing you."

I sniff indignantly. "That's not it at all! But if we're going to be stuck here anyway and with no need to rise early tomorrow, I should think we deserve to enjoy ourselves tonight."

"Of course, of course. Let's at least make ourselves presentable then."

After a wash, shave, and a change of clothes, I'm feeling markedly more human. Growing up on a farm as I did, being dirty has never bothered me much, though perhaps Whisperwood did instil some sense of "civilisation" into me. Just as it taught me to watch how I speak, to sound *proper*— something I still stumble over from time to time, especially when I've been home a while—or how to dance and which are the correct utensils for each course of a meal. I learned all these things not because I cared to personally, but because I knew the financial burden it placed on my parents to send me to Whisperwood and I didn't want them to think their struggle had been for nothing.

Benji, on the other hand, grew up with tutors and schools that taught him these things from a young age. Whisperwood had two sorts of boys: those who were from poor families who pinched and saved to send their sons to a boarding school in hopes they would someday climb the social ladder, and those from well-to-do families who had got into so much trouble that no other school would take them. The two sides were always at odds. The rich boys looking down on the poor boys, the poor boys thinking the rich boys were stuck-up pricks.

But Benji… He never looked down on Frances and me for how we spoke or ate or anything else. He was patient when I struggled with my studies. He was kind to everyone he spoke to, never thinking he was better than anyone. He was gentle and patient and easily pushed around by others—and Frances and I both felt an overwhelming need to protect him, to ensure nothing and no one tarnished that shine of his.

I did not want the world to get a hold of Benjamin and ruin him.

"Do I look all right?" he asks, smoothing a hand down the front of his waistcoat. As always, he manages to look put-together despite our travel weariness. I've not even brought along a proper waistcoat as I left behind anything that didn't seem necessary, so the pair of us look very mismatched indeed. It makes me smile. "Dashing."

We tuck the box far beneath one of the beds and lock the room behind us, with Benji pocketing the key. It seems less suspicious than carting the damned thing around with us.

When we descend the stairs, the pub is already quite full of bodies. Men and women, a few children scurrying about, talking and laughing with a familiarity that makes me feel quite a bit on the outs. I suspect most everyone here knows one another, and I wonder how they feel about travellers passing through. An inn this may be, but clearly the bulk of their business is this, right here.

For that matter, all the tables appear to be occupied, but we locate a few lone seats at the counter to take up. Dinner consists of roasted beef and veal, bread, cheese, cabbage and fish. Benji offers me his meat and fish in exchange for my cheese and cabbage, and I look over at his plate with some sympathy because it really does not look at all appetising.

The meat is overcooked and the trout on the burnt side of crispy, but it's the best damned thing we've had aside from Parker House's upscale menu. Benji's must be edible enough because he eats every bite. What a relief, given how little he's had the last few days. He does, however, swiftly wash the boiled cabbage down with beer.

The beer isn't altogether horrible. By the time we've got through our meals and a few cups, we're full, content, and more than happy to converse with our neighbours.

The gent next to me is named Robert, and within ten minutes of knowing the man, I've heard all about his wife, four children, and his ailing mother-in-law for whom he's just waiting to kick the bucket.

"So you—where'd you say you're goin'?" he asks, as though just remembering I am not, in fact, a friend he's known for years.

"California," I say. "San Francisco, to be exact."

"California, eh. I went out there once—back in the forties. They said gold was all over them hills, though I never found a bit of it. But it helped me meet my Marnie, so I s'pose it wasn't all bad. Though it also brought her mother along…"

He peers down into his now-empty cup, squints, and slams it down on the counter while waving down the barkeep for another. Then he becomes distracted by a friend who comes along to chat, leaving me to my own devices again.

Benji has long since moved off elsewhere in the room. Normally, in a group setting, the pair of us would stick close together because Benjamin relied on me to carry a conversation, wherein he could interject his opinions quietly without being the centre of attention. It's peculiar to look to my side and find him not there now. I spot him sitting at a table near a window, chatting with two doe-eyed women who seem utterly fascinated by whatever he's saying.

That's Benji for you. He's disarming and soft-spoken, and I've yet to see him speak to a woman that didn't find him absolutely darling. Once upon a time, I found that endearing and amusing.

Now, when I see one of the girls rest a hand on his arm, an ugly, jealous little snake slithers its way round my heart and squeezes.

I turn back to the counter to flag down another drink. Maybe I've had a few too many already. Perhaps the alcohol is the cause of such an unpleasant feeling.

Or perhaps it's that I've almost lost Benjamin once and now I haven't a bloody clue where the two of us stand. I had thought I knew that whatever was between us was unspoken, unconsummated even, but that we just *knew* and we were all right with that. I could have gone all my life as we were back in Whisperwood, but then his decision to take up a job and possibly marry some girl he hadn't even met turned the world on its head.

He came back to me, I remind myself. It's still just Preston and Benjamin and I've no reason to be jealous.

And yet after I've got another drink in my hand, I find myself weaving through the tavern to Benji's table. I swing a nearby chair around to casually situate myself between Benjamin and the girl whose hand has not left his arm. The flicker of a frown passes over her face. My physical interjection requires her to budge over.

"There you are!" Cheerful, easy. I place the mug in front of Benji since his looks about empty. "Thought I'd lost you for a moment there."

He casts me a small smile, almost curiously. "Sorry. I was just telling these two young ladies some stories of Whisperwood."

The girl on Benji's other side—bronze-skinned and dark haired and lovely—leans forward. "Haunted, he said. That true?"

I nod gravely. "Very true. Couldn't walk down a hallway without seeing ghosts."

"No need to exaggerate," Benji muses. "Really, it was only in our third year that it started to get unbearable. We had a friend—"

"A friend who is now a ghost hunter, I feel I should add."

"Ghost hunter?" the girl to my right gasps, seeming to have forgiven my earlier intrusion. "How's that work? How d'you *hunt* ghosts? Not like it's a rabbit or something."

I grin. I learned the answer to that well enough from James and Esher and Aunt Eleanor, and what I don't know, I can certainly make up.

For the better part of an hour, we sit there with the two women—and eventually a brother to one of them who joins us—while spinning stories of ghosts and our haunted school. I include James and Esher and Frances, even useless Edwin Davies, though I'm still sour over him ditching us the night we needed him the most, so perhaps I use him as a comedic plot device. I highly doubt any of this would be quite as entertaining were the lot of us sober, but it's fun, it passes the time, and it feels good to relax with Benjamin at my side.

That is, until he murmurs something that sounds like *I'm getting some air* and leaves the table. When he hasn't returned after a few minutes, it occurs to me he went outside on his own and it's dark and unfamiliar and...

I excuse myself from our little gathering, thanking them for keeping us company and head out the front doors. The cold is biting and I left my jacket in the room, so my immediate thought is that Benji is going to be freezing out here too.

The street is a bit muddy from rain and melting snow. On either side of the hotel is a general store and a tailor-plus-shoemaker's shop. Directly across from me, a row of small cottages, a bakery, and a sheriff's station. All the windows are dark and the buildings are silent this time of evening. And trees. I see plenty of trees, crowded in among the buildings, stretching out into woods that go on forever.

What I do not see is Benji.

I head down the inn's few steps and venture down the road to the right. It isn't a particularly long stretch before the street gives way to dense forest with only a narrow dirt road disappearing into the trees, worn down by years of feet and horse hooves. But still no Benji. I start back the other way. As I come to pass the inn, I spare a look left, into an alleyway, and catch sight of Benji leaning against the wall and gazing up at the sky. Relief unknots the anxiety in my chest.

"All right?" I call as I head his way.

Benji straightens up a little too quickly, a bit unsteady on his feet after so many drinks, and he gives me a small smile that seems...off, somehow. Tired. Perhaps being drunk doesn't sit well with him. I've never seen him have more than a drink with dinner before.

"Yes, sorry. I just needed a breather." He slouches back again. I lean against the opposite wall, hands folded behind me.

"I'd have come with you, you know."

"You were enjoying yourself."

"I thought you were too."

"As I said, I just…needed some air." He looks down at his feet, scuffing his heel against the dirty alley ground. "You should go back in. Talk. Drink. Have fun."

Something *is* off, I think. And it isn't the alcohol. "What's wrong?"

He shakes his head, flashes me a smile. "You worry too much. I'm perfectly fine."

I frown. "No, you're not. Something is bothering you."

"*I'm fine*, Preston."

The words aren't angry, not exactly. But they're sharp at the edges, blunted only by the way Benjamin seems to wince in immediate regret that he allowed them to slip past his lips at all.

We stand in silence, Benji staring up at the sky, me staring at my feet, feeling suitably chastised and wondering at this tension in the air. I feel I've done something wrong or that something has happened to upset Benji and I'm somehow the cause of it.

At the risk of annoying him further, I venture carefully, "I'd like to try to fix whatever is bothering you, but I can't if you don't talk to me."

And I don't only mean here and now and this. I mean…everything. Every day. Benji never asks me for a damned thing—and I wish that he would. I think of the bruises on his arm or how after Frances' disappearance, Benji fussed over everyone else but never seemed to give himself time to mourn. The only time he's ever come to me was when his mother died and even then, his grief had been far more reserved than I'd anticipated it would be. He still always had a smile when I caught his eye, even if he looked miserable when he did not realise that I was watching.

He hurts and he faces things alone and when I find out after the fact that he's endured something horrible all by himself, it breaks my heart.

Benji sighs. "You can't always fix everything, Preston."

Such a response indicates there is, in fact, something that *needs* fixing. I lift my chin, prepared to push the subject, likely because my alcohol-addled brain doesn't seem to realise it's wiser to shut up.

However Benji's attention seems to have shifted, his gaze no longer wandering the sky, but instead pinpointed at a spot far above my head.

"Benji? What is it?"

"A woman," he says, slowly. "In the window."

Frowning, I turn around and look up.

Indeed, there is the shadowy form of a woman above us. Aside from the outline of her figure and the slight tip of her head that suggests she is specifically watching *us*, I cannot make out many details.

"Yes, that is a woman, I think." I look to Benjamin, brow cocked. "What about her?"

Benjamin meets my eyes. "Preston, that's *our* window."

THERE IS NO graceful way for two half-drunk men to make a mad dash up a flight of stairs. I'm amazed we don't trip over one another and end up with a broken limb. I reach the door to our room first, though in my hurry I forget we've locked it and I slam into it rather painfully. Benji scurries over, fumbling for the key in his pocket while I rub my sore nose.

He flings open the door and we stand there, staring into the darkness. It was locked and no human being could have scaled a flat outside wall to get in through the window.

"The box," Benji whispers.

I move past him, casting furtive glances to every shadowy corner, and drop to my knees to reach beneath the bed and drag out the box. I heave a sigh of relief.

A hand touches my shoulder. I look up to see Benji beside me, staring across the room with an unwavering, wide-eyed gaze.

"Do you see her?" he whispers.

I rise to my feet, box gripped tightly. I expect to see nothing, as so often happens.

Except I *do* see the woman in our room, standing near the door as it creaks closed. She looks every bit as dead as any of the ghosts at Whisperwood, long, dark hair a tangled mess, and everything about her looks *wrong*, the proportions of her face slightly warped, her fingers too long, the whites of her eyes pitch dark.

The same screaming woman from the Parker House Hotel. She truly did follow us all this way.

No, she followed the box—or whatever is inside of it.

Heart racing, I take a step forward. "What do you want from us?"

She opens her mouth, a yawning chasm of inky blackness. Somewhere in the distance, a wolf howls, followed by another, and another. The words that escape her lips are garbled and hoarse, uttered in a language I do not know and do not recognise at all.

"We can't understand you," I press, keeping my voice steady, level. James said that was important—not to display fear. "We'd like to help you, but you have to speak with us."

"Is it this?" Benji asks, stepping up beside me. He takes the box from my hands and lifts it. "Is this what you're after?"

The woman's mouth snaps shut. Her face turns, studying the chest in Benji's hands. In the blink of an eye, she stands before him and he shivers as she places her hands over his and leans in to speak.

"The wolves are coming."

She vanishes.

She does not fade, does not walk away, she's just…gone. Benji sucks in a sharp breath, shudders, and drops the box onto his bed. He turns away, rubbing his hands and arms as though trying to shake a chill.

I cross over to shut the door fully, noting the cold spot in the room right where the woman stood seconds ago. My pulse appears to be slowing itself. It isn't fear that I feel when I see the ghosts—not truly. At least not for myself. Even years ago when I stood at Nicholas Mordaunt's gravesite, exhuming his bones, staring into his eyes before James and Esher managed to lure him off into the school, any fear I had felt was centred around the fact that Benji was there, and that *he* might get hurt.

Father always did say I lacked much of a survival instinct.

"'The wolves are coming,'" I repeat quietly. "What does that mean?"

He sits on the edge of my bed, tucking his hands beneath his thighs, shoulders hunched. "I don't know. It could be gibberish for all we know."

"The howling we've been hearing must mean something. But if the wolves aren't real—how could they be, trailing us across an entire continent—what are they? Some metaphorical thing? Some ghostly echo?"

When Benjamin has no answer to my questions, I pick up the box, staring at the dials on the front. Initially, I began this journey thinking that it didn't matter to me one bit what its contents were, but now, all things considered...

I take a seat, hunch over the chest, and begin turning dials.

"What are you doing?" Benji asks.

"What's it look like I'm doing? I'm going to get this bloody thing open and find out what's in it."

WHEN I SLEEP, it's slumped back against the rickety headboard with my chin dipped to my chest, so that when my eyes open, I have the most ungodly crick in my neck. The box sits in my lap, still locked.

I groan and press the heels of my hands against my eyes. Although my head is not aching much, my eyes are dry and my tongue feels two sizes too large for my mouth. I could kill for a glass of water.

Beside me, Benji is still asleep. He tried to stay up while I spun the dials in succession, working out every single possible combination that could be created. Eventually his eyelids began to droop and the exhaustion coupled with the alcohol dragged him into sleep. Now and again, he shifted and whimpered, taken by dreams, and I would reach out to touch his shoulder or stroke his hair until he settled again.

And, damn it all, I went through every combination, *twice*, and still the locks remain in place. The lid has not budged. There's something I'm missing. Some secret to opening this bloody thing but I can't locate any sort of other contraption, keyhole, or dial that appears to be out of the ordinary. Whoever closed this wanted to ensure that it was not opened again.

Sighing, I move the box to the floor and slide further down on the bed, allowing myself to relax. In the light of morning, everything from the night before feels like a blur and far less urgent. Then again, sobriety likely also helps, even if I can't quite get a proper thought in my head just yet.

Benji stirs before long, sitting up with his hair an adorably chaotic mess. Sadly, he's quick to run his fingers through it to tame it. Then he turns to look at me with a groggy smile. "Your poor eyes are bloodshot. Did you sleep?"

"A bit," I mumble, scratching a hand down my jaw.

"No luck with the box, I see."

"None at all. If I could locate a hammer and chisel, I bet I could get the bloody thing open."

"Then we really wouldn't get paid for our work, I think." He presses the backs of his fingers to my cheek and his skin feels so pleasantly cool that I find myself leaning into it. I hope this means whatever he was cross over last night has stopped bothering him. He adds, "Why don't you try to get some more rest and I'll see about fetching us some breakfast?"

The idea of him traipsing off while that ghost is speaking nonsense about wolves and danger has me instantly on edge. "Quite all right. I can go with you."

Benji's mouth presses together and for some reason it looks as though he may object, but… "As you wish."

The tavern cook conjures up a half-arsed breakfast for us, little more than bread with a bit of gravy. Shortly thereafter, we drag ourselves squinting and grumbling into the sunlight, into a small but busy market square toward the train station.

Many of the vendors are selling furs, blankets, and dry goods. Nothing fresh will grow this time of year. We purchase some beans and a small sack of salt. By some grace of God, we find a woman willing to part with some potatoes and turnips, which ought to stay good so long as they're kept cool. Jars of preserves are too likely to get broken, not to mention we don't have a whole lot of room to pack much else, so we make do with our meagre findings. The rest of the day, we remain in our hotel room, fussing over the damned box and trying to decipher the ghostly woman's message.

We know she didn't mean *actual* wolves. Was it possible, then, she referred to the people from the train who were after us? What would a ghost know or care about that?

"Plenty of ghosts cared about Headmaster King," Benji points out. "And about Nicholas Mordaunt."

"You think she's trying to help us?"

"It's a possibility. I get a lot of fear and anger from her, but not malevolence, really."

Suppose that's a bit comforting, isn't it? Ghosts are shit at communicating. Never can seem to get a straight answer out of them about much of anything.

Toward nightfall, we attempt to speak to the woman again. Even though the room grows icy cold, she never shows herself.

But as we drift off to sleep that night, we hear the wolves howling in the distance.

8
BENJAMIN

WE ARRIVE AT the train station an hour early, ensuring we in no way will miss the next train coming through. Which means a fair bit of sitting, especially as it's running an hour late. But we soon find ourselves in possession of two first-class tickets—a miracle that they have any seats available—and it's with much gratitude that we board the train and enter our private quarters in a sleeper car, with its own sliding door. It's small, yes, but we won't be cramped alongside anyone else, nor will we need to concern ourselves with someone snooping through our things.

"Say," I begin as I stash our rucksacks on the top bunk. "I've been trying to figure it out, but have come up empty-handed... How did that woman and her companions know we would be on that particular train?"

Preston takes a seat on the edge of the mattress. "I've been thinking that over too and I haven't the foggiest. They knew James and Esher would be on board—but not about *us*. Could they have got a hold of the route we planned to take to California?"

"All the way down to the specific train we intended to take?" I frown. "Possible, but how? Why?"

"I've got no answers to any of this, I'm afraid. Though if we encounter them again, you had better believe I'll knock one of them senseless to find out."

My expression sobers. "The sheep really ought not to antagonise the wolves, Preston."

THE DAYS ARE the easy part.

Preston and I talk, we sleep, we watch the scenery change—mountains to forests to plains to mountains again—and we play a great deal of cards with a deck we received from a kind attendant. It's with amusement that I watch Preston desperately search for my tells when I'm bluffing about the cards in my hand; I'm oddly good at these sorts of games.

But in the dead of night when sleep eludes me, I find myself staring out the window into the darkness and thinking…

How much I miss my mother.

Oh, I *want* to be enjoying this trip. And I *am*, truly. I'm enjoying Preston's nearness, these long stretches of uninterrupted time with him. We never seem to run out of things to speak of. I do not tire of *him*, only the lonely dark hours wherein I toss and turn and struggle to find sleep.

I cannot help myself. I still find my thoughts wandering to the past. I think of sitting across from Mother on a train, of the soft sound of her voice. I remember being a small boy, frightened by a thunderstorm and burying my face into her skirts as she stroked her hair and sang to me.

I remember arriving home to find her absent from the station, and Father's voice, so cold and indifferent, telling me that she had died.

My mother was ill and dying and her only son was not there to look after her. I don't know how to forgive myself for that. The guilt of it threatens to drown me.

These moments, these long nights, are so difficult because I don't have Preston awake to save me from my own thoughts. Still, I cannot say even the nights are all bad. No more worries about being found out or waking to find someone stealing our cargo. Four nights in, we even brave leaving our cabin in favour of the dining car to spoil ourselves with a drink or two and some company.

I'm grateful when Preston ceases tiptoeing around me like he's afraid I'm still upset with him. Truth be told, our first night in Bellporte had less to do with him and more to do with my own sense of shame and worry. I had thought speaking lightly of our time at Whisperwood would be fun, but then—

Then Preston had to go and bring up Edwin Davies.

Davies, who had been my friend, of sorts, when I first arrived on school grounds. And who had subsequently proven himself to be a rather horrible friend who could not keep secrets. A flaw which ended up with Oscar Frances dead at the hands of Headmaster King and Mordaunt's ghost.

Davies hadn't truly bowed out of helping us that final night because he was afraid. He'd left because I told him to. As much as I felt Preston and Spencer deserved to know, it's a secret I've carried with me these last few years.

And for a while, listening to Preston speak so sourly after Davies, hearing how much it still affected him, that secret simply felt heavier than it had in some time. He doesn't ask after my little episode, though, and hopefully it'll stay that way.

It takes us nearly a week to make it to San Francisco after a particularly gruelling trip through the snowy mountains. To see signs of life again is exciting. As much as I may have enjoyed the quiet time with Preston, I'm excited to see our destination. On the train, I spoke with a San Francisco resident who was returning home after a trip out East, and he regaled me with stories of the views, the rolling city hills and impressive buildings, the ships coming and going into the harbour all hours of the day and night. I'm not so certain it will be anything out of the ordinary from back home, but it's charming to hear someone speak of their own home in such a fashion.

Granted, when the train rolls into the station, it's nearly full dark outside so we won't be seeing much of anything exciting. We've obtained a list of several lodgings in the area and although the hour is late, I've no doubt we'll find one to our liking.

With my bag over one shoulder and Preston carting along the box-satchel, we disembark onto a dimly lit, over-crowded platform and try to make our way along with the crowd for the exit. All I can think about is finding a hot bath, a hot meal, and a warm bed for the night, and revisiting what needs to come next after a solid night's sleep. A bit of exploring, perhaps, if I'm lucky.

As we near the marked exit, a prickling sensation drags itself up the back of my neck, along with a howl of an ear-piercing pitch that has me coming to an immediate stop. Out of reflex, I grab Preston's arm in an iron grip, choking on a plea for him to stop.

He starts to ask what is wrong with me, but then he hears it—he sees it—too. Not just the howling, but the woman and the blonde man from before. They're standing just outside amongst other families and individuals, as though they're simply eager to greet their loved ones arriving home.

"Christ Almighty," Preston whispers. He catches my elbow, yanking me closer to his side. We have no choice but to keep walking; the crowd is so dense that it may work to our advantage. "Keep your head down, Benji. They still don't know they're looking for us, right?"

Oh, Lord, I certainly hope not.

I swallow hard, dip my chin, and focus my attention straight ahead, purposefully disregarding the man, the woman, and the ghost that clings to her.

We've just got to get past the exit, down the road a way, and all will be well. Meanwhile, I lecture myself: of course it would have been an easy matter for them to check in with the next few trains coming from Nebraska. We would have been wiser to wait another day or two, or perhaps to have taken another, more roundabout route.

We squeeze through the exit. I can see Preston glancing at them, likely debating if he could take the two of them if need be. The blonde man is a head taller than Preston, built like the side of a barn. I know Preston is quite skilled in a tumble, but I'm not so sure my money would be on him in that fight.

I have never paid so much attention to how quickly or slowly I'm walking in my bid to not draw attention. Preston slides the bag with the chest from his shoulder over to mine, no doubt to free his arms in case it does come down to fists. He keeps his hand upon my elbow so as not to lose me in the crowd.

When we pass directly by our stalkers, it's harder to ignore the spirit attached to the woman than anything else.

Maybe she isn't watching me, but *he* is. I can feel his eyes boring into me like needles.

Just a few more steps. I think we've made it.

Until a large bloke with a string of little ones at his heels bumps into us from behind and Preston loses his grip on me. I immediately lose him in the crowd as people push around and past me and I feel like a fish swimming up current. I stumble and someone catches my arm—to help me, is my first thought.

I look up and find myself face-to-face with the hulk of a man from the train.

He smirks. "What's the hurry, boy?"

My heart about leaps from my chest. I smile, nervously, praying that Preston has not gone far. "I think I'll give you two seconds to let go before I scream."

His grip only tightens, that smirk twisting into a sneer. At least until Preston shouts, *"Let him go!"* from somewhere nearby. The sound distracts the man just enough that I can yank my arm free and make a run for it. He grabs for me, fingers grazing the back of my coat in a narrow miss.

Preston barrels through the crowd. He gives me a push when he reaches me. "Go, go!"

We fall into rapid step alongside each other, pushing for the street as swiftly as we can.

"Sid!" I hear the blond man bellowing behind us. "Over there—the Oriental kid's got the chest!"

Preston reaches for the bag, but I pull it back against my side and order him to keep running.

The woman's voice rings out above the crowd: "STOP! THIEVES!"

I almost do stop out of sheer confusion before realising her tactic is to get someone else to stop us before we get too far ahead. Oh, blast it all. It's causing people to stop and look about, eyes turning toward us as we make a mad dash for the street. Two men half-heartedly try to step into our path and are swiftly knocked back as Preston shoulders past.

I am not as lucky.

A stranger snags the back of my coat, dragging me to such an abrupt halt that my shirt collar strangles the cry I try to give out. Unwilling to be taken so easily, I squirm in his grasp as one of his arms locks around me. Preston seems to appear out of nowhere, taking a swing and slamming a fist into the bloke's face. With an unholy howl, my captor staggers back, gripping his nose. We do not wait around to see how long it slows him down.

We round the corner of a neighbouring building, tearing down the roadside. I've not had to do this kind of legwork since drills class back at Whisperwood, and it shows. By the time we've reached the corner at the far end of the street, we are red-faced and winded, and I'm developing a cramp in my left leg.

But a glance back shows the woman and the blond man not far behind us and so we keep moving, rounding corners and ducking down side streets to lose them. Surely in a city of this size, they cannot possibly trail us forever.

That cramp begins to work its way up into my side until I stagger, stumble, and hit the ground on my knees as I struggle to catch my breath. Preston, winded but still standing, takes me by the elbows and hauls me to my feet before we duck between a pair of buildings.

"Pretty sure I could take the pair of them on, you know," he pants.

I double over, hands upon my knees. "Remember… Remember when you promised…to give it at least a few seconds…of thought before rushing into danger?"

He bites back a breathless laugh. "I did think about it the entire run here."

I pin him with an unimpressed look and drag in a few more deep breaths. "I think we ought to stash the box somewhere and come back for it. At least that way, if we're caught, they won't get a hold of it."

"Stash it? Where?"

We're presently standing in a narrow alleyway, not even wide enough for two people to stand abreast. I spot a few doors, rubbish bins, and old crates, but nowhere safe enough to stow something valuable.

Except, maybe…

I point across the street to a set of apartments. "There. The roof, up those stairs." I don't wait for him to object or agree. I pop my head out from the alley, glance both ways, and cross the road at a brisk walk. Preston dogs my heels, anxiously.

I scurry up the fire ladder to the rooftop of the four-storey building while Preston keeps a lookout below. The burn in my limbs and my lungs has begun to subside to a tolerable ache, and I hope I'm up for more running if it comes to that.

The rooftop is anything but empty. Some tenant who resides inside has placed a slew of potted plants everywhere, which is excellent to suit my needs. It means I can move to the far corner of the roof and tuck the satchel behind a row of large ferns where no one is likely to notice it without rearranging the massive clay pots.

A metallic clang rings up from the bottom of the alley.

Preston, signalling me that we need to go. But as I begin to descend the ladder, Preston hisses up at me, "Stay put! Don't move 'til I get back!"

He disappears out onto the street before I can tell him what a horrible idea that is.

Oh, I'm going to have many unpleasant words for him later. Still, there is nothing I can do but linger there on the ladder as three figures go rushing past the entrance of the alley. I wait, count to ten, and cautiously continue my descent. I step out onto the road again. My heart is racing as though I were the one running.

What do I do now? Do I go after them? If they catch Preston, I need to make certain I know where they take him. This city is far too big to risk losing track of him.

I take a step back and look up at the apartment building, taking a good, long moment to commit the surroundings to memory and take in a street sign. I'll need to know how to get back here later, after all. Then I turn to jog after the others, uncertain where they may have turned.

A pair of gentlemen at an intersection are able to direct me down a street and from there, I am just in time to spot the blond man and another, shorter but stocky man dragging Preston into another alley.

There are three of them now. There could be more. I cannot risk going in swinging and hoping for the best; if we're both taken, what then? And what will they do with us when they have us? If it's true that all they want is the box then surely they won't harm us. That wouldn't get them any closer to their goal.

The box doesn't matter right now. Preston's well-being matters.

I cannot let them take him away without me.

9
PRESTON

I PEER AROUND THE corner, spotting our pursuers heading our way. The woman and the blond, accompanied by—oh, hell, that bloke I popped in the face at the station. He's got a bit of tissue or cloth shoved up his nose, though it's covered in blood. Good.

We've trapped ourselves here. The only way out of the alley is the way we came in. I act without thinking beyond that I need to lure them far enough away from Benji and the box so they aren't found. What are the fools going to do, kill me on a city street? It may be dark out, but the streets are not empty.

I know the exact moment they spot me. I don't dare look back, but I hear the pounding of footsteps coming up behind me at the bottom of another sharply angled hill before something heavy slams into my back so hard it sends me sprawling to the ground and knocks the air from my lungs.

I choke in a deep breath. Someone plants a shoe against my side to roll me onto my back and I am now staring up at three faces. Judging by the pleased leer on the blond man's face, it's safe to say he's the beast that knocked me off my feet.

"Get 'im up," the woman snaps, pointing to a nearby alley. Both the blond and the man I hit—dark-haired, with a sparse moustache—each grab one of my arms and half-drag me out of the street before we can draw too much attention. I swear under my breath, praying that Benji stays put and does not try to play hero. I like to think he's smarter than that, but it's not as though we've been in a situation like this before.

The blond shoves me against the side of a brick building and holds me there by the front of my shirt.

"Americans are so brutish," I rasp. "Not even a hello, how do you do?"

His free fist connects with my jaw.

"That's enough." The woman nudges him aside and he releases me. I sag against the wall, peering down at her. I cannot see the ghost attached to her, but I can feel it. The way the hair on my arms stands on-end, the prickling of my skin, the sudden coldness. She peers up into my face, unblinking and unsmiling. "Where is the box?"

I drag my tongue across my teeth, tasting a smidge of blood. "What box?"

The corner of her mouth twitches. "Look, I don't really care to watch Hugo here beat you bloody, but I ain't above letting him do it, neither. I don't give a whit about you or your buddy; we just want the damned box."

"You're certainly welcome to search, but I promise I do not have it."

"Nah, but your friend does. Where'd he go?"

I shrug. "We tossed the box into the bay. Really not worth our time and effort; we've already got paid for half the job anyway."

"I'm telling you, Sid," Hugo growls. "Let's just snap his neck and find the other one—"

The woman named Sid silences him with a stormy look before returning her attention to me. Then, she turns away and heads for the street. "I'll have Louisa bring the carriage around. Then we'll see 'bout rounding up the other one."

A few moments after she departs, everyone is silent, and I dare not risk an escape attempt while both my captors are watching me so intently. But the moment I hear commotion out on the street, and the woman's voice shouting—"I've got him!"—panic overtakes me.

Benji. They've got Benji.

Hugo makes a grab for me and it spurs me into action. Like hell they're going to take me quietly, especially if they've got Benji too.

But for as much as I've prided myself on my size and strength, I am, apparently, no match for a man much larger than myself accompanied by another man of moderate size. I plant my feet firmly into the stone ground, pitching my weight back. The moustached man loses his grip, but Hugo's remains iron-clad and determined.

I twist left, right, and my jacket comes loose, sliding off my shoulders and rendering me able to break free.

I make it four feet down the alley before I hear a resounding *crack*. Pain blossoms across the back of my skull, and…

I WAKE CONVINCED I've been tied to the back of the carriage and dragged through the streets. Without the use of my hands, I can't touch the back of my head, but it throbs something fierce. My eyes are heavy and refuse to open at first, even to the sound of voices. I force myself to look, to take stock of the room around me.

It appears to be some sort of small shipping warehouse, as it smells strongly of fish and salt. Close to the bay then, I suspect. Before my vision has even fully cleared, I know that I am surrounded by Hugo, the other man, a woman I do not recognise, the girl from the alley...

And Benjamin.

That certainly brings some clarity back to my foggy-headed mind.

Like me, Benji is bound with rope to a support column, arms pinned to his sides. If that wasn't enough to infuriate me, Hugo stands before him, bowed down, their faces inches apart. Hugo's is several furious shades of red.

"Listen, you little shit, I *know* you can understand me."

And that *look*, that chilly, detached expression upon Benji's face takes me back to the day I met him at Whisperwood. The look he gave to the boys tormenting him. A look that said he would not cower beneath the cruelty of others. He stares back at Hugo, unflinching, opens his mouth and replies.

In Mandarin.

I pick up only a few of the words and I would daresay he's reciting a biscuit recipe. I bite my tongue to keep from laughing aloud.

The moustachioed man and the other woman—I presume this to be the aforementioned Louisa—linger nearby, observing the interrogation and how poorly it's going. As for the dark-skinned girl, Sid, I spy her seated atop a stack of crates, her hat resting on one drawn-up knee, and looking almost as amused as I feel. When Hugo whirls around to look to her for guidance, she shrugs.

"Told ya, wait for Crane. He'll get him to talk."

Crane. Another person in this group of bandits? Their leader, perhaps? Good. I know who to beat to a pulp for doing this to us.

"Hey," Louisa says, tipping her chin in my direction. "The other one's awake."

Sid rolls her gaze to me. "What about you, boy?"

"Oh, don't look at me. I barely know my alphabet."

Hugo looks half a second away from hitting me again. He very well might have too, if the door did not then swing open from somewhere behind me. Everyone is silent and I hear footsteps but cannot turn enough to see who it is.

"Well?" comes a voice.

Moustachioed-man and Louisa scuff their feet a bit. Before Sid can speak, Hugo, terribly full of agitation and bluster, points at Benji and me both like a child tattling on its sibling.

"They won't fuckin' talk, Crane!"

Finally, this Mr. Crane strolls into view. And he is…nothing at all remarkable, really. Younger than I anticipated for some reason. I'd not place him any older than his late twenties. He's tall, lanky, with a head of dark curly hair. Even his clothing is that of a working man: his boots are travel-worn and the sleeves of his dusty shirt are rolled to his elbows. No waistcoat. A shotgun hangs from a strap on his back and another, smaller gun is holstered at his hip.

Still, as unremarkable as he is, something about him feels oddly familiar, and I cannot place where or why or how.

No. Wait. Yes I do.

The Parker House Hotel. The staffer who came to our door in the early morning hours…

Crane stops in front of Benjamin, studying him. Benji stares back, defiant, but something in his gaze wavers now, something akin to fear. I see his throat move as he swallows hard.

Crane says in a voice that is most certainly English and not American, "Take this one back to the train station. Have him retrace his steps and locate the chest."

Hugo gives an indignant snort. "That one insists he don't speak a lick of English, but I heard 'im at the station."

With a roll of his eyes, Crane looks over to Sid and nods in my direction. She hops down from the crates and crosses over to me, sliding a revolver from her hip. My throat goes dry. If they had wanted to kill me, surely they would have already. But there's what my brain says is logical and what my racing heart says when I'm staring down the barrel of a loaded weapon.

"We only need one of them, yeah?" Sid says.

Benji falters, his eyes wide. *They're bluffing*, I want to tell him, except even I'm not so sure.

Sid presses the gun to my temple. Benji chokes out a horrified sound. "No, *no*, I'll take you to it!"

I draw in a breath and hold it, halfway expecting her to still squeeze the trigger. But Sid holsters the gun and turns to Crane. He gives a wave of his hand.

"Go on, then. You heard me."

"All of us?" Hugo asks, scowling at me. "You wanna be alone with that one?"

"I'm sure he'll be a terrible threat, tied up like he is. I said get going."

The four of them untie Benji. Hugo gives him a rough shove toward the door when he stops to steal a frantic look at me while I'm glaring daggers at Hugo for laying his hands on Benjamin.

Somewhere behind me, the voices fade and the warehouse door slams shut, leaving Crane and me alone in the dusty lantern light. The only windows are high above us and through the dirt-encrusted glass I can tell it's still dark outside. I was not unconscious long enough for it to become morning.

Crane sighs, pushing a hand back through his messy hair, and strolls over to crouch in front of me. Not close enough that I could slam a foot between his legs, damn him. Up closer in the poor light, with him staring straight at me, I realise this completely unremarkable man has the most remarkable eyes. And not in any sort of good sense, either.

They're dark. Not in the way that Benji's are dark, the colour of gunmetal. Crane's are the sort of dark you see when staring into a lake in the dead of night. They swallow up everything, even my own reflection. They look wrong in ways I don't have words to explain.

He tips his head, studying me in the same way I'm studying him. Finally, "So, what's your name?"

I have half a mind to spit at him. "Edward the Seventh."

"Would you like to try that again?"

"Alice." I flutter my lashes for added effect.

Crane heaves another sigh, rolling his reflectionless eyes toward the ceiling. He stands again, turns away with his hands upon his hips.

Then he slides the revolver free, turns, and fires.

The sound ricochets off every metallic surface in the room, making my ears ring. A sting of pain blossoms on my left bicep.

He shot me. He bloody *shot me*.

"The next time," Crane says slowly, "I'll do that to your friend, and it won't be just a flesh wound."

I swallow the lump in my throat. The shot had skimmed off the side of my arm, a minor flesh wound, but it still burns like hell. I manage a startlingly calm response.

"You touch him and then my name isn't going to matter because you'll be fucking dead."

"Not in much of a position to be making threats, are you?" Crane taps the gun against his thigh. "Perhaps we got off on the wrong foot. I know you aren't James Spencer or William Esher because I've met them. Frankly, I don't give two shites *who* you are. What I do care about is that chest. It's urgent that I get a hold of it, return it to its proper owner, and then you two can go traipsing back to England."

I grit my teeth. He's *met* James and Esher? When, where? Not that that information is going to do me much good right now, though it does clear up a few things. He came to our hotel room to claim the box and was thrown off when it wasn't James or Esher who answered.

"Rightful owner," I hiss through gritted teeth. "What makes you think you've got the rightful owner? According to our client, that box was stolen and *we're* returning it home."

"Well, we've got ourselves a case of one man's word against another, don't we? But your client is dead now, so I'm not so sure he'll be speaking up about much of anything."

I still, eyes widening. "What?"

Crane gestures at me with the revolver before holstering it. "Don't give me that look; wasn't me. But Wilkerson was responsible for the theft of that chest, so really, he deserved what he got."

If they've been to Wilkerson's, if they hurt him, that could explain how they got hold of all our information. Our hotel name, the boat... But still, it doesn't make sense that they also obtained our train information, does it? They would have needed to get that from someone at the Parker House Hotel, and...

Nothing is quite lining up and I doubt Mr. Crane is going to be kind enough to fill in the blanks for me.

"*If* he stole it, it was only to get it back to its rightful owner!" I insist.

Crane scoffs. "Whatever helps you sleep better at night, mate. Just thieves stealing from thieves. I think the pair of you haven't got a clue what you're carting around in that box."

We should have broken the damned thing open back in Nebraska. "Can't say that it matters. And to be quite honest, Mr. Crane, regardless of whether what you say is true, you've taken my friend and me hostage so right now I'm having difficulty thinking of much to say beyond 'go fuck yourself.'"

"Fair enough. Can't fault you there." He shrugs, folds his arms across his chest. "Perhaps you'll feel differently after a few days with no food and no sleep, though. As I said, all I'm interested in is the box. Not your lives, not your backstories, or why you're here instead of them... Just what belongs to my employer."

He walks past me, and I hear the door open and shut.

I swear into the darkness and pray that Benji is having better luck than I am.

10
BENJAMIN

RATHER THAN LOAD me into the same carriage we arrived in, we walk the distance to the train station. My legs ache in protest and the only small blessing is that Sid has had no choice but to untie my wrists. Parading me through the city bound would no doubt attract attention. Oh, but they're certain to flank me on all sides, though. Sid to my right, Hugo behind me, Louisa ahead, and the moustachioed man, whose name I've gathered is Philip, to my left. Even if I could break free, I'm not so certain I could outrun them.

But that doesn't mean I'm not looking for my opportunity to try.

At the station, Sid turns to me. "All right. You had the box when you left here. Where'd you go?"

"It was all such a blur," I insist. "We were being chased, you see. Made it quite difficult to know where we were going."

I *do* remember, but I'm not about to lead them straight to the chest. Hugo growls in warning, and I thank God there are people around even this late at night because it may be the only thing that keeps him from striking me.

Sid breathes in slowly, mustering her patience. "Yuh-huh. Take a guess, then."

I run through the options in my head. They know which direction we started out running in, and if I lead them the wrong way, they'll know it. I need to take them back to where we lost them, and from there…

Then what? I can only keep them traipsing about the city on a wild goose chase for so long. What I need is a distraction, if I can get even two of them to be otherwise preoccupied…

"This way," I relent, nodding down the street Preston and I fled to hours ago. I begin to lead them, retracing our path, eyes darting about. We're nearing the apartment buildings now, too close for comfort. If they're smart, they'll know we were halted near here and that this is likely where the chest was stashed.

I stop near a fenced-in building, hesitating. "This might be it."

"Might?" Hugo asks.

"Might… It was in a bush behind a fence. But it was dark. I don't know that I remember which one."

Sid rolls her eyes, then looks to Philip and nods. He hauls himself over the fence and begins to pick through the brush on the other side.

"I don't see nothin', Sid!"

"Well, of course not, it's dark," I say. When Sid shoots me a needle-eyed glare, I do my best to look chastised. "I told you, it might not be the right one. We'll have to keep looking."

And look we do. Five blocks and nine different fences and bushes later, I can tell even Sid is beginning to lose her patience. Excellent. They're getting tired and irritable, and it also means they're getting careless.

Fence number ten involves Hugo hoisting Louisa up to the top to drop down on the other side. There's a resounding crunch of a body landing in a particularly prickly bush, followed by a pained yelp that makes Hugo snicker.

A second later, it's followed by the barking of a very large, very angry guard dog.

Sid darts forward, Hugo all but tossing her to the top of the wall so she can reach down for Louisa on the other side. "Girl, hurry it up! Come on!"

All of this is good and fascinating and working out nicely, except Philip still has hold of my bicep. Loosely, though, as he watches the scene before us and seems to have forgotten that I'm there for the time being. I study his profile, the bruising about his nose…

I almost feel bad for what I'm about to do.

Almost.

The heel of my hand connects with his already delicate and injured face. He chokes on a yowl, releasing me, and I'm free to make a run for it even as Philip is swearing and alerting his distracted companions.

I do not stick to the streets. I dart down the nearest alley, scrabbling up a fence at the end of it. As many twists and turns as I can take to make them lose my trail in the dark. Finally, I heave myself up a fire escape and huddle outside someone's window, panting and willing the flare of pain and exhaustion to ebb.

It seems to have worked. Ten, fifteen minutes pass by. No sound, no pursuers chasing me through the night. I've lost them. I'm a bit lost myself, too, but I remember where the box is, and how to get to the warehouse from there. And that was the entire reason I let them take me in the first place.

Which means all I need now is the nearest police station.

11
PRESTON

I COULD ALMOST sleep like this if left alone long enough. If it weren't for the ache developing in my arms from being bound and the vast amount of worry coursing through my veins…sleeping just to pass the time might not be so bad. Crane returns at some point, though he does not speak a word to me, and I suspect he settles somewhere near the door. Perhaps he's doing some sleeping of his own. I ponder singing, loudly and off-key, just to annoy him. If I've got to be uncomfortable then he should, too.

Locked in here, I also have little concept of time. I don't know how many hours pass, but it's got to be two, perhaps even three. Is that good? Bad? I can imagine Benji not making this easy for them and while that thought has me proud, it simultaneously makes my pulse quicken in fear of what that lot would do to him to force him into cooperating.

When the door finally swings open again, the warehouse comes alive with several voices talking at once. I wince at the assault on my senses, trying to twist around to see them.

"Philip was supposed to be watching him—"

"—I had him, I swear I did—"

"And we looked all over—"

"Christ almighty, *be still*," Crane snaps. Like obedient dogs the group falls silent, but the tension is palpable. "Now, who wants to look me in the eye and tell me you lost him? A boy half your size?"

Sid clears her throat. "Ah, yeah. He was leading us round in circles awhile, saying he couldn't recall where he'd stashed it. In a bush, but didn't know which one, just that it was behind a fence. He had us climbing every damn fence we saw."

"So he wore you down then took an opportunity to slip away. I don't know whether to be impressed with him or furious with the lot of you."

I want to laugh. That's my Benji, capable of outsmarting most anyone. And I hope that intelligence has him retrieving the box and finding somewhere safe to hide. Granted, our rucksacks are in a heap nearby which means he hasn't got any money on his person, so he won't be able to get far. But if anyone can figure out a way around that, it's him.

Hugo appears before me, red-faced and scowling. "All right, you got ten seconds to tell us where that box went."

I start to shrug. Pain zips through my sore arms and my smirk turns into a grimace. "Would love to tell you at this point, mate. Really, I would. But see, I wasn't there when he hid the thing, so you may as well let me go."

"Or I can spend some time breakin' each of your fingers until he comes back for you," Hugo snarls.

"He doesn't know anything and we are not here to perform torture for the sake of torture," Crane drawls from nearby. "Leave him be. His friend will return for him."

Ah, so someone's got a bit of civility about them after all.

Will Benji come back?

Christ, I hope he's wrong about that.

I CAN SCARCELY feel my arms and hands; the ropes and my positioning has rendered them numb. I desperately want to sleep, but the steady hum of activity around me and the nervousness in my gut makes sleep impossible.

The group takes turns watching over me. Two of them remain outside on the perimeter at all times, while one stands guard inside. Whoever's turn it is to sleep goes, I think, off to the carriage—the same one I was dragged here in.

Sometime shortly after dawn, Sid takes a seat near my side, offering out a piece of bread she brought back from a nearby bakery, still warm enough that steam wafts from it when she breaks it in half. I turn my nose up at it, which does little more than make her roll her eyes.

"Be stubborn about whatever you want, but refusing food seems like the kind of stubbornness that leads a man to an early grave."

"Not quite so much as being taken hostage, shot, and threatened with beatings, I should think."

She snorts, cramming another hunk of bread into her mouth and muttering around it. "You ain't dead yet, big guy."

True enough. But that doesn't mean I'm going to make any of this easy for them while they decide my fate or while I wait for an opportune moment to escape.

I study her as she eats. I can almost feel the ghostly eyes on me, the cold trickling across my skin because of its nearness. Should I mention it? Would she tell me, even if I asked and she knew? Perhaps she's utterly unaware of the creature's presence.

In the end, I keep my mouth shut. Sid takes her leave, not offering me food a second time. Which is a shame, because I probably would have taken it; my stomach is growling loud enough.

In Benji's absence, I try to think of what he, James, or Esher, would do in this situation. James would no doubt craft some entirely mad and brilliant scheme to sneak free. Esher might nag his captors to death. Benji would... Ah, hell. He'd probably charm them into letting him go, brokering some kind of bargain.

But I've got no bargaining chip without that chest and it's not as though I would hand it over even if I did. Not even for a commitment to my job so much as to spite these people. I also lack Benji's sweet face or James' charm to talk my way out of this.

So I sit, sullen, annoyed with myself that I have found a situation that I cannot punch my way out of, and think that I would kill for a hot cup of tea, a hearty meal, and a damned toilet.

The warehouse has settled into a state of lethargic quiet for the time being. Crane, Hugo, and Louisa depart to begin the search for Benji anew, which leaves me alone with Philip and Sid—who seems to be the only one Crane has any real faith in. Hugo, it seems, is kept closely watched because of his tendency to lose his temper.

The bloke I punched at the station is named Philip. He's a quiet man who does what he's told and keeps his head down. Not much of a threat there, I feel. Louisa is steadfast, steely-eyed, and something about her feels dangerous even if she would look harmless enough in a crowd.

And Sid... I can't quite get a read on her. Every now and again, I swear I can see the flicker of shadows around her. A hand against her shoulder, a face just above hers. Her ghostly guardian. She's the only one who bothers to try to speak with me, but as it is, I prefer to keep my mouth shut and even when she does goad me into talking, I only respond with as taunting a reply as I can think of.

Shortly after Crane and the other two have left, Philip settles atop some crates nearby with a small book, while Sid slouches by the door and watches the sky through the windows. I'm about to start gnawing at my ropes out of sheer frustration.

The sound of a fist beating against a door jars us all upright. Not the main door, no, but another one on the opposite side of the small building. Sid is on her feet in an instant and Philip lifts his head to look to her for instruction. She squints, hesitates.

"This is the police! Open up!"

Oh, well, I might be saved after all.

Sid swears under her breath. "Get him out of here. Back to the carriage or somethin'. And keep him *quiet*."

She perches her Stetson onto her head and stalks to the door, unlatching the deadbolts and opening it up. She steps outside, however, rather than allowing the officers to get a peek inside. Philip, discarding his book, scrambles up and over to me, cramming a handkerchief into my mouth before I can shout for help. Disgusting. I have no idea where this has been!

With frantic hands, he then unties the outermost ropes binding me to the column. One step closer to freedom, but my wrists are still bound behind my back. I could potentially take him, off guard like this...but not just yet.

He's stronger than he looks, however. He grabs my arm, hoisting me to my feet. He wastes no time nor care in marching me to the main door. We step outside and I blink rapidly, the sunlight almost an assault after sitting in a dimly lit warehouse for God knows how long.

As soon as I can orient myself, I plan to slam him into the wall of the building and make a run for it. My legs are tingling as feeling returns to them, and I will them to function properly to get a safe distance away.

Philip escorts me round the other side of the building, close to the docks and the water and where the carriage awaits. Just faintly I can hear Sid and the police conversing around the back of the building. Damn it all—I'm *so close*.

Philip reaches for the carriage door. I see a flash of movement, likely even before he does. The door flies open, slamming into his face and his nose, which is still swollen and bruised, and sends him back with a startled cry. Benji darts out from the carriage, catches hold of the larger man by the front of his shirt and shoves him toward the edge of the dock. Philip recovers quickly, plants his feet, and makes a grab for Benji. I take the opportunity to slam a shoulder into his, which does the job of sending him staggering back that last step off the dock and into the water.

"Am I ever happy to see you," I say. Or…try to say. It comes out more like *Mm mmmph mm mmmn mm!"* and Benji lets out a nervous laugh and yanks the cloth from my mouth.

"I'm so sorry I took so long. But let's chat later. We need to hurry."

"Our things are inside," I start as he ushers me back the way I came. "We won't be going anywhere without our money."

Benji stops, bites his lower lip, and gives me another push. We halt near the front door and he says, "Wait here and keep a lookout," before ducking inside.

I swear under my breath, praying Sid hasn't managed to get the police to go away and is lying in wait in there. But not a moment later, Benji is joining me again with our bags.

There's no time to even get my hands untied. We just run.

Running like this is a bit trickier than I would have anticipated. We get several blocks down the docks before I have no choice but to stop and allow Benji to fuss a moment before he can get the knots undone. As they fall away, I let out a noise of relief. Proof of my capture is embedded into my skin where my wrists have been rubbed raw. Benji takes my hands in his, turning them over to examine the rope burns. Then his eyes travel up and widen.

"Your arm, it's bleeding—"

"It's just a scratch." I manage a tired grin. "You're a sight for sore eyes, you know."

His expression softens, although worry still lines the edges of his smile. "Did you think I wouldn't come back for you?"

Before I can answer that, a grizzled man rounds the corner of the building and startles at the sight of us.

"Oi, what're you two doin' near my boat? Go on, git!"

He waves a fist in our direction. Laughing, we hurry off, at a slightly more leisurely pace now. It's broad daylight, we're putting a fair bit of distance between us and my captors and...oh, I do wish I could see the look on big old Hugo's face when he realises that we've outfoxed him.

Crane, though... I think I can do without seeing that man's ire.

WE CHOOSE THE first hotel we see when we feel we cannot walk any further. Seeing as my coat was lost in the initial scuffle last night and there's blood soaking my shirt sleeve, Benji removes his wool coat and drapes it around me. It's far too small for me to wear properly, but it does the job of hiding my arm.

The hotel attendant must see his fair share of people in as sorry a state as us, because he doesn't so much as blink when he hands over a room key and says for an extra fifty cents apiece, he can have meals sent up. Yes. I'll gladly take that.

The rooms have only one bed here. Benji sits me on the edge of it and tugs at my shirt until I remove it. Then he studies the bullet wound with a worried frown. It's a bit deeper than I originally thought, but not so bad that it's in need of stitches.

"There's a shop just across the road. I'm going to see if they've got bandages and something to clean that with."

When he moves away, I catch his wrist. "No, no going out alone."

He covers my hand with his own. "Easy. It's just right there. You can watch me from the window, right?"

I force myself to relax and release him, glancing to the window. "Be careful."

"Me, be careful? You're the one who managed to get kidnapped and shot all within the space of twenty-four hours." Benji swings on his coat again and departs with a chuckle.

I do indeed watch from the window as he crosses the street and disappears into the store, and again when he remerges.

Our experience thus far in San Francisco has not inspired me to relax, it seems.

Benji returns with a roll of bandages, some rags, and a bottle of alcohol. I eye the latter.

"That's for drinking, I hope?"

"I sincerely doubt it would taste any good." He props one knee on the mattress and dips his chin, silent as he opens the bottle to wet one of the rags and sets to cleaning my arm. He needn't tell me that it's going to burn. I know damned well it will.

But watching him does take me back to Whisperwood. This is hardly the first time Benji has bandaged me up—although previous times have involved things such as a busted lip or scraped knuckles and not so much a gunshot wound. I abstained from getting into too many fights at school, knowing it distressed Benjamin to see it, but I still saw my fair share of injuries from one source or another.

Benji's eyes flick up to me. "What are you smiling for? Doesn't this hurt?"

"A bit. I was just…remembering. You used to do this often."

He scoffs, but I see the corners of his mouth edging upward. "I would much rather this be a scrape from a rugby match."

"Are you regretting coming along yet?" I ask, watching him carefully. I expect the answer to be a hesitant, polite distraction from the topic. Or to at least be an attempt to soften the blow. This trip has certainly been more than either of us anticipated.

But Benji, beautiful Benji, does not miss a beat.

"Not at all." He looks up to meet my eyes. "I regret that we're faced with more obstacles than I had hoped for, but I'm getting what I wanted out of this."

"Which is…?"

"You."

Oh, if words could melt a man's heart. Never in all my life have I wanted to kiss Benjamin as much as I want to right now. To just take his face in my hands and tell him how darling he is, how I can't begin to imagine this trip without him.

Yet as I lift my hands to do just that, Benji scolds me, "Be still, Preston," and I realise he's still quite focused on the task of bandaging my arm.

I swallow back a sigh. He's going to be the death of me.

He finishes his work and relocates his supplies to the top of the nearby table, oblivious to the way I cannot take my eyes off him. When someone knocks at the door, we both still, hesitating a heartbeat because we're still so rattled from the events of the last few days. I shake it off quickly and stand to answer it. It is, of course, just a member of staff delivering us a rolling cart with dinner, drinks, and a fresh jug of water. I thank him and draw the cart inside.

As ravenous as I am—as I think we both are—we take our time to enjoy the food, of which there's plenty. Nothing compared to the Parker House, but leagues above our lodgings in Nebraska. I had quietly let the front desk clerk know that we would be grateful for anything not-meat, so Benji has more of a selection this time: a fresh salad and some fruits, grey pea soup, and baked potatoes stuffed with sage and onion, along with a dish of some kind of pudding topped with flummery for dessert. Seeing Benji's eyes go so wide at the spread makes it worth it that aside from some eggs, there's nothing in front of us he won't eat.

The meal leaves me full, content, and lethargic. By the time I've had seconds and downed a mug of beer, I'm prepared to crawl into bed and sleep the rest of the evening away. Benji seems inclined to let me. He clears the food, leaving the cart in the hall (although he keeps hold of his bowl of pudding), and draws the blankets up around me. I'm so exhausted I do not bother to argue. Sleep, breakfast, then we can decide what to do with that stupid—

My eyes fly open. I bolt upright.

"Benji, where's the box?"

He places a palm flat against my bare chest and shakes his head. "It's still safe where I left it. I'll be heading out to fetch it once you're settled."

Oh, as though *that* statement is going to put me right at ease. I close my hand over the top of his.

"You're what? You're going to get it, *alone?*"

He blinks, as though the answer is obvious. "Yes? You need to rest."

"You can't be serious. It's the middle of the night and those...whoever they are, are probably still out there looking for us!"

"All the more reason for me to do it now, while they're likely as tired and worn out as you are and while I have darkness on my side."

"Or, hear me out, we wait until morning when the sun is out and there are other people on the street."

His eyebrows lift. "There were plenty of people at the train station. That didn't stop them."

He has a point, but not one I care to hear.

"You aren't going alone, Benjamin. It isn't safe." I release him and start to slide back out of bed, disregarding how leaden my limbs feel. "I'm going with you."

Benji draws back, lips pursed, studying me. "No, I don't think so. We rented this room so you could rest and get your strength back. I'm better off than you right now, I know where the building is, and I can nip over there and be back before you've even realised that I'm gone."

Christ, I'm developing a headache. Since when has Benjamin ever ventured off into something dangerous on his own? I was always with him. That's just how it's been.

I rise to my feet, looking down at him. "I don't know why you're being difficult, but the answer is no."

A crease forms between his brows. "I wasn't asking your permission, Preston."

"I wasn't implying—"

"You sort of were, really. I'm not a child. I can choose to do this and I'm confident in my ability to do it alone."

I stammer, frustrated. "Yes, well, I think it's foolish to go gallivanting off on your own!"

"You would do it without a second thought."

"That's me, Benji! I've always done things like that. You're the—the responsible one. The *sensible* one."

"And I am, sensibly, saying that I feel it's smarter for me to go now on my own than risk giving them a chance to regroup and plan tomorrow. Why do you act as though I cannot look after myself?"

"Because you never do!"

The words tumble from my lips along with miles of regret the moment they do. I have never thought of Benjamin as a prideful man, not by any means. But the hurt that registers across his face just then makes me flinch. I sink back down to the edge of the mattress.

We are both silent and still, taking in what's just transpired. After a spell, I grasp for words.

"Benji, I'm sorry. I didn't mean that."

"Yes," he says, softly, not looking at me. "You did."

I try to swallow the lump in my throat. This is uncharted territory. We don't fight. Ever. Never in all our years have we had any real argument aside from trivial disagreements over silly things. But ever since Benjamin's mother passed, something has shifted. The foundation beneath our relationship has tilted, leaving us both off-balance.

Just moments ago, we were sharing a tender moment, and I've mucked it all up.

Benjamin straightens himself, smoothing a hand down the front of his rumpled shirt and waistcoat. He says, "I'm going out. Alone. Please get some rest." His voice permits no room for argument, and it's the closed-off tone I've heard him take with many people over the years—with the boys who shoved him into the dirt and called him names, with the people who realised his heritage and turned their noses up at him—but a tone he has never taken with me before now.

Every inch of me screams to stop him as he walks out the door, afraid it could be the last time I see him. Hugo and Crane and the others could run him down like the hounds they are and he would be defenceless against them.

And if I were to tell Benji I thought as much, I suspect it would not make this problem any better.

It's true that I have always viewed Benjamin as someone

who needs to be looked after and protected. Someone too gentle and incapable of defending himself. How many years have I spent, holding him close to my side where I could protect him, where I could fix whatever went wrong?

You can't fix everything, he'd told me.

Well, I sure as hell don't know how to fix this.

12
BENJAMIN

THE SAN FRANCISCO streets are freezing and fog-filled, making navigating in the dark harder than I anticipated. If I get lost, I'll never hear the end of it from Preston.

Our disagreement has left a poor taste in my mouth. I got the last word in, I got my way, and yet I feel empty inside. Was I being unreasonable? Am I needlessly stepping into harm's way? I feel my reasoning behind this is sound, and yet, Preston pushing back so vehemently has me second-guessing myself.

No, I'm making the right choice. I'm simply not used to making choices at all, much less making them and pushing back against resistance. Preston needs to rest. The longer the box remains in its hiding place, the longer it gives Crane and his people time to find it—or to find us. We need to contact the box's recipient and hand it over. After that, what happens to it is out of our hands. Quite literally.

The streets are quiet, but I pass by plenty of people. The further from the hotel I go, however, the emptier it becomes until it's just me, walking alone in the fog, distracted by the occasional shadow that moves from the corner of my gaze. I shudder, tugging my coat tight around myself.

A gust of wind howls between the buildings and far up ahead, I notice the shape of someone standing on the corner. Even encased in fog, I'm familiar enough to know that what I'm looking at is nothing alive.

The skin along my arms and the back of my neck prickles. What was a bearable chill is now almost choking. The howling has returned, louder and more insistent than before. I clutch at my chest to calm my racing heart.

It's a woman, I think. Whatever she is, she appears to be facing me although all I can see is her silhouette. When I stop, she turns. Disjointed, broken, she skulks out of view, around the street corner. I exhale, my breath visible in the air. Yet my legs are already moving, directing me after the woman, somehow aware that I'm meant to follow her.

I turn the corner and spot her again, still up ahead and barely discernible in the dark and mist. And again, she vanishes around a corner.. As I hurry to catch up, I realise some of these buildings look a touch familiar. I'm no longer feeling quite so turned around.

In the end, the ghostly figure leads me right back to the apartment building. Whatever fear I had been harbouring dissipates into relief. I scale the ladder to the rooftop, moving carefully past lit windows where the inhabitants inside might wonder at a stranger sneaking past their homes. The box in its satchel is right where I left it with no signs of having been disturbed. With a sigh of relief, I sling it over my shoulder and start back down to the alley.

When my feet hit the cobblestones again, a whisper of air caresses the side of my face and I whirl around. The woman stands in the shadows at the far end of the alley, watching me through milky-white eyes. I force myself to stand my ground. She brought me here to retrieve the box; she must know we're only trying to return it to its rightful owner.

"Can you tell me your name?" I ask. Not that I truly expect an answer. I dare a slow step forward. "We want to help you, but you've got to show us how. Can you do that? Can you show me what it is you want?"

She opens her mouth, although no sound comes out. In the blink of an eye, she goes from being twenty feet away to being two inches from my face, and she grabs me, her hands clutching my shoulders so tightly I can feel the bruises forming. I gasp, instinctively trying to jerk away, but she holds fast.

A flicker of a memory presents itself in the forefront of my mind, a memory that I realise is not my own. It's of an ocean, a beach untouched by humans, stretching toward the sunrise in stunning hues of wine and cider.

And another memory, this one more disjointed than the first. Footsteps. Running.

Hands around my throat.

This is how she died. This woman who has followed us from England halfway across the world. She died running, trying to escape something or someone, and she was caught. Someone strangled her to death.

I choke on a scream.

Or is that only in the memory-that-isn't-mine? I cannot be certain. I only know that the world is black for a few seconds and I cannot breathe.

When I open my eyes, I'm lying on the damp cobblestones, staring up at the sky...and the woman is gone.

13
PRESTON

SLEEP COMES IN fits and starts. I toss and turn, waking at every small sound in hopes that Benjamin has returned. But the room remains silent and still for the better part of three hours, and I've begun to wonder if something has gone wrong. Perhaps Benji got turned around, did not know where he was going after all. Perhaps he encountered Crane and his group and was either taken hostage or is on the run from them as we speak.

No amount of trying to think of other things works to clear my head. If I'm not dwelling on all the terrible things that could have happened to Benji, then I'm dwelling on our earlier conversation and how horrible I feel for it.

It's one thing to want to protect a friend. It's another entirely to tell that friend you think they're useless at protecting themselves. Especially, I realise grimly, right after that friend rescued *you*.

I owe him an apology. But is it proper to apologise for something when I have not changed my way of thinking? Benjamin has never been good at fending for himself. The day I met him, he was face-down in the mud, not fighting back. And that's how it was all through Whisperwood. Even his own mother... I recall the first time I ever visited Benjamin at his home in London. Ms. Prichard was delighted for the company and the first time she got me alone, she had asked, "Is Benjamin really all right at school? I worry about him. He's such a delicate boy and I know how cruel others can be…"

I had given her my word I would look after him, but it didn't quite stop there. For as much as I adored the woman, Ms. Prichard largely managed every major decision in Benji's life. He sought her permission for most everything he did, fretted over how she might react, revolved his world around looking after her for the rest of his life. Never have I heard him speak of what *he* would like to do. It always came down to what his mother wanted for him, what she hoped he would become.

It was why he'd been willing to give up whatever it was we have—or had—to stay in London near a father who despises him, working a miserable job and potentially setting himself up for a marriage that would never make him happy. That had cut me deeply and the taste is still bitter in my mouth.

I stare up at the ceiling in the dark, mulling these things over, transitioning from worried to frustrated to angry to sad, then back round the loop again. When the door finally opens and Benji's soft footfalls enter the room, I'm cycling back through worry, and the relief of him being returning unharmed has me heaving out a heavy breath and closing my eyes.

He's safe and he's even got the box—I hear him place it upon the table. Perhaps tonight, when we're both so exhausted and on edge, is not a good time to reopen this topic. We can sleep and start fresh tomorrow after we've had a little time to clear our heads. It will give me a bit longer to sort out what I ought to say; the last thing I care to do is upset him again. Or to say something further that I'll regret.

I stay attuned to the sounds of Benji moving about the room. Undressing. Sliding into the bed beside me. His skin radiates a chill from being outside and he nestles down beneath the thin blankets and curls in on himself. He does, however, remain very prominently on his side of the bed, careful not to encroach on mine. I want to roll onto my side and wrap my arms around him, but would the touch be unwelcome right now?

The ground is still most definitely off-balance beneath us.

If we aren't going to speak, then there's little left to do except try to get some sleep. Even my constant thoughts can only keep me awake for so long through my exhaustion. One moment I'm certain I will never sleep again and the next, I'm opening my eyes to sunlight streaming in through an open window, curtains fluttering in a chilly ocean breeze, and the smell of food greeting me.

I sit up slowly and with a wince. My arms are still sore and the gunshot injury throbs a bit, although the bandages have held nicely. Benji is seated at the table before a spread of breakfast foods, sipping at a cup of coffee. He meets my eyes, steady, and with a smile that makes me wonder if everything last night was all some horrible nightmare.

He greets, "Good morning. I thought you'd wake hungry."

Is this better or worse than him still being cold to me? "Quite. How long have you been up?"

"Just an hour or so." He gestures to the food as I relocate to the chair across from his. Just as I had tried to be accommodating and provide him with vegetarian meals the night before, he seems to have ensured a selection of meats for me. The scent of bacon alone makes my mouth water.

As I tuck in to eat, I remain vigilantly aware of Benjamin and his body language. He's relaxed in his seat, reclined, legs crossed, gazing out the window at the city as he enjoys his coffee. His own plate is already mostly empty. Did he eat without me because he's angry? Or was he being considerate by allowing me to sleep? He's quiet but no longer aloof and angry. It would truly be simple to play along and go about our business as usual.

I would be doing us both a great disservice if I did that, I think.

"About last night," I say, after I've wolfed down a fair bit of my breakfast, enough that my stomach has stopped protesting. "I... I owe you an apology. For what I said."

Benjamin hmm's into his cup, dark eyes flicking to me. "No, you don't."

I lower my cutlery with a frown. "I do. It was unfair and I—"

"You said what you meant, Preston." His tone is firm, but not unkind. Not that I could ever picture Benji being unkind to me. "It wounded me, of course, but sometimes the truth does that."

"It wasn't true. You aren't incapable of looking after yourself."

"Hm, maybe. But I haven't proven that much and you were only going off my past record." He shrugs, takes another sip, and places his cup aside with a sigh. "You and I both know I've looked to you to protect me ever since we met. There is no sense in ignoring that. You stepped in and frightened off those who sought to do me harm and you attempted to shield me from anything unpleasant. I was so used to Mother doing that, that I don't think I even noticed it until after she was gone and I was truly left on my own for the first time."

I find myself slouched forward, elbows gracelessly upon the table as he speaks. He's barely spoken of his mother this entire trip and now that he is, he does so casually, as though she's merely back at home waiting for us rather than dead.

It may be the wrong time to ask, but since he's being so open... "What happened with your father, Benjamin?"

One corner of his mouth twitches. His brows draw together briefly, then smooth out again before his gaze shifts from the window to me. He sighs.

"I informed my employer I would be leaving. Rather short notice, and I was apologetic, of course. The work may have been unduly boring, but he was a decent man and he paid me fairly enough. But still, it got back to Father quicker than I'd have liked it. He caught me just before I left for the train station to see you."

"And I take it he wasn't pleased."

"To say the least." His smile is tight, almost bitter. It isn't the sort of smile that suits a face as sweet as Benji's. "He called me all manner of unflattering names, of course. He ranted about how ungrateful I was, how foolish. How I'd made *him* look foolish. The idea that he had no power over me sent him into a rage. Perhaps, in a sense, he was saddened to see me go. I was the last piece he had of Mother...the last thing he thought he had control over."

"Did he really love her, do you think?"

"I think he loved the idea of her. Someone complacent with what he felt like giving, someone who relied upon him for everything. He never had to fear losing her." He sighs again, hooking a finger into the handle of his coffee cup and peering into its empty bottom. "Not that it matters how much or little he loved her. If someone's love hurts you, what good is it? That is not the way I would ever want a man to love me."

Something in that statement feels like a heavy stone in my belly. "…Your arm."

He blinks. "My arm?"

"The bruises."

"Oh. Nothing of consequence, I suppose." A pause. His fingers tap the outside of his cup in debate, perhaps about how much he wants to reveal to me. "He couldn't keep me there with words, so…he grabbed me."

I sense there is more to that he isn't sharing. Words that were exchanged, even. I can envision Franklin Hale, taking Benjamin's arms so tightly that they bruise, shaking him and shouting in his face. I swallow back the guilt and the anger. I should have been there for him. I never should have left.

"You're doing it again," Benji murmurs.

My eyes pinch shut. "Doing what?"

"Blaming yourself for not fixing one of my problems. Stop that."

"If I had stayed…"

"Do not make me regret telling you, Preston. I would have been humiliated having you there, handling my battles with my own father for me. It was something *I* needed to do for myself." Another pause. His hand comes to rest atop one of mine, startling me into opening my eyes. "And I did it. So here we are."

I study our hands. His fingers are long and slender. He's never raised a hand to anyone or anything. Never lashed out in anger. He is nothing like his father. Benji's hands are gentle hands, the sort to care and tend to, never the sort to hurt.

I can't get the image of Hale confronting him out of my head because I was not there. I can't put an end to the scenario without knowing what Benjamin said, what he did, how he managed to leave. And yet—it isn't my story to know, I cannot go back in time to rescue him from it, and I think that is the point Benjamin is trying to make now.

You can't fix everything, Preston.

My hand turns so that I can wrap my fingers around his.

"And so here we are."

OUR NEXT STEP is reaching out to our contact. We have his address, but we were instructed merely to contact him when we reached San Francisco, not to go showing up at his door. Benji pens a note to send out, after which point, all we can really do is wait.

Benji returns from placing the telegram and he joins me at our small table where I've sat staring at the box the entire time he was gone. Crane's words are still rattling around my head, leaving me unsettled and with so many questions.

Benji permits me to sit in silence a bit before he asks, "All right?"

"Yeah," I mumble. Sigh. Run a hand over my face. "No. I don't know. Something Crane said has been nagging at me."

"Ah?"

"He said, 'we're all just thieves stealing from thieves.' What do you suppose that means? Are we just transporting stolen goods from one bad person to another? This box—

whatever's inside of it—has got some spirit attached to it for some reason. I guess I'm just not convinced we're doing the right thing."

His lashes lower, dark eyes surveying the box, our travel papers beside it. He makes a soft click with his tongue. "Well, then I suppose the only option is to try to find out what she wants."

"We tried that already. She wouldn't speak with us."

"I doubt Spencer and Esher give up after one failed attempt. If we followed some of Esher's notes in his book that he lent you, we may get some sort of answer out of her yet." He leans down to open his bag, retrieving Esher's notebook. The one I couldn't quite get through but I'm certain Benji has read four times over by now. "Besides, she may be a little more inclined to communicate this time."

"What makes you think that?"

"Because I saw her." He pauses, considers, and adds, "Vaguely, anyway. When I went to retrieve the box. I think she understands we're trying to help, and she wants to tell us how to do it."

"You *saw* her? Did she try anything? Why didn't you tell me?"

He shrugs. "We had other things we were dealing with. It slipped my mind. Do we want to try this or not?"

I bite at the inside of my cheek. James had told me about his and Esher's little foray into summoning spirits. It worked for them, but they'd been nervous about it. Benji and I are hardly as experienced as they are, and with Benji's sensitivity toward ghosts... But he's staring at me intently, almost daring me to say no on his account. He's aware of the risks and willing to try it anyway.

Not that he waits for my permission. He places his hands against the box in the same way he did the night I woke on the ship and found him in his trance-like state. I swallow back a protest. Should it happen again, I'll be right here to snap him out of it. I come to rest my hands over his, noting how chilled they are, and close my eyes as well, hoping that I can see or hear whatever it is that he does.

"We're here to help you," Benji says. "But you have to show us how."

I open my eyes again to darkness.

It's only midday, yet the sunlight seems to have been smothered in inky blackness. Outside our windows, there is nothing. Gooseflesh rises across my skin. Benjamin exhales and his breath fogs before him as his fingers twitch beneath mine. Somewhere in the darkness behind him stands the shape of a woman. Her neck and limbs are twisted as though broken. Her mouth does not move, but I can hear her regardless. Garbled whispers brush against my ear and I struggle to make out the words.

Somewhere outside, the howling returns.

Benjamin's eyes snap open. The sunlight begins to peek through the darkness, gradually illuminating the room once more like a second sunrise. Our gazes meet. I do not know if we heard the same thing, if we *felt* it, but suddenly...

I know how to open the box.

"Three birds," Benji says breathlessly.

I slide my thumbs across the dials, directing each of them to the image of the long-legged bird. A combination I had tried multiple times before, except this time I know that I must now press each dial in as though it were a button. The middle one first, then the left, and then the right. The entire mechanism gives a satisfying little click and pops out half an inch, enough that I can twist it like a latch until the lid pops open.

Sunlight catches on fabric, wads of silver-coloured silk packed into the box for padding. Benji is watching me, palms still pressed flat against the sides of the smooth wood, waiting for me to make the first move. I take a deep breath, reach inside, and carefully pull out the topmost object, swaddled securely within the fabric, and unwrap it. My thumb slides across a smooth surface, largely unmarred save the occasional odd, thin, suture-like markings. I stare down at the object, seeing it plainly, but my mind is not quite catching up with my eyes. I know what it is, but disbelief is a difficult thing to cast aside.

But I am most definitely staring down into the empty eye sockets of a human skull.

I barely refrain from dropping it, although I do abruptly place it onto the table. Benji stands, moving around to my side.

"Is that…"

"The reason why our cargo is haunted?" I rasp. "I would say so."

His eyes go wide. "But…why? What is the point to transporting human remains?"

"I haven't a clue. Wilkerson said it was to return it to its rightful owner, though who *owns* a body?" A pause. "Perhaps we're returning it to the next of kin. A means of laying her to rest."

"Why would she have been stolen in the first place? None of this makes any sense." Benji extends a hand, fingertips brushing across the top of the skull. He then gathers it up, so achingly delicate, cradling it in its swath of silver fabric as though it might crumble to dust in his grasp.

"We can ask these questions until we're blue in the face, really, and it's not going to do us a lick of good. I think we should…" I trail off, distracted by the sudden subtle shift in the air. A chill coasts along my skin and up my spine. Benji has gone so deathly still that I tip my head back to look up at him. "Benji?"

His lashes are lowered over his dark eyes, almost sleepily, lips parted ever so slightly as he mouths something to himself that I cannot make out. Clutching the skull to his chest, he pivots away from me and begins to head for the door. I lurch from my seat before he can get too far, catching him by the shoulders.

He stops, does not fight me, but he also doesn't register that I'm there.

I've seen this before. Years ago, with Esher at Whisperwood. With him, it was different. He'd had the milky eyes of a corpse when he walked out of the hall and into the cold, and Benji still looks very much like himself. Just a sleep-walking version.

This must be the woman trying to communicate with us. I may not be a professional ghost hunter like James and Esher or a medium like Aunt Eleanor, but I know enough to realise that if I want answers, I may have to listen to them in whatever form she wishes to give them.

With a grimace, I release my hold on Benji. He steps away, proceeding as though he'd never stopped.

I follow him into the hallway, down the corridor to where a set of stairs leads higher still. A sign begs no admittance except by staff, but Benji bears it no mind. He ascends the steps, pushes open the hatch at the top, and crawls up and onto the roof with me on his heels.

Our hotel is not a terribly tall building compared to several others we've seen in San Francisco. However, it stands just tall enough that we've got quite a view of the surrounding streets and the bay in the distance. Sunlight catches on the water, making it almost blinding if one looks at it too long. It would be a beautiful sight, the sort that would be lovely to watch a sunset over.

Admiring it is not on my agenda at the moment as I follow Benji to the edge of the rooftop. He stops there, the toes of his shoes just to the ledge. He cradles the skull to his chest with one hand, lifting the other to point off into the distance.

"*There.*"

"There, where?" I step up behind him, not touching, but close enough to grab him should he venture any closer to plummeting several storeys down. "What are we looking at, Benji? The docks? The water?"

When he speaks again, it is both his voice but not. As though someone is speaking the same words right alongside him from lips I cannot see. Yet the language is neither English nor Mandarin, and every syllable is utterly foreign to me. Can Benji understand any of it? He speaks it fluently now, as though he came into this world with the words on his tongue.

My heart is running a mile a minute. I bring a hand to rest upon his back.

"Benjamin, I need to know what's happening. What is she wanting us to see?"

A pause. He breathes deep.

"The sea."

He looks at me. No longer do I see Benji's clear, dark eyes. I am staring into the hazy eyes of a corpse, and the voice coming from his lips is no longer his own.

"We all return there someday."

He steps off the rooftop and into the open air.

I almost anticipated it. Almost.

The moment he moves, I lock an arm around his middle, hauling him back even as an inhuman shriek tears from his lips. Benjamin fights me like a wild animal, thrashing, kicking his legs back into my shins. His arms remain locked fast around the skull.

Small as he might be, he's stronger than he looks. I stagger back, not resisting when our legs tangle and we hit the rooftop in a mess of limbs. With one arm fastened tight around him, I reach with the other, snagging a fistful of silk and what I think and hope is the skull within it, and yank it from his grasp.

Benjamin drags in a shuddering gasp and goes boneless in my arms.

We lay there for a spell, chests heaving. He draws himself up to sitting, running a hand back through his tousled hair. Thank God, his eyes are normal again, alert and wide and confused. I sit up, placing the skull aside and out of his reach. "Christ almighty. Are you all right?"

"Yes, I…" He blinks once, looks to the skull and back again. "I… I'm so sorry. I don't know what came over me."

"The ghost, I presume. Wait—do you remember coming up here?"

"I remember all of it," he admits, brows furrowing.

Well, that's new. When Esher was possessed, I recall him not remembering a thing after the fact. Aunt Eleanor did say Benji had some sort of special talent for all of this, didn't she? This is perhaps what she meant.

He doesn't look shaken so much as disoriented, but I still find myself reaching out to touch his hand. Almost out of reflex, he wraps his fingers around mine and tries to smile.

I ask, "Those words you were saying, what were they? Do you remember?"

"I recall speaking them, but I couldn't tell you what they meant. I don't even know the language, just that it felt...old."

"Lovely. We've got a multilingual ghost who fancies the ocean." With a sigh, I rise to my feet, keeping hold of his hand to draw him up with me. I retrieve the skull, turning it over delicately in my hands to ensure it wasn't damaged during our tussle. Everything seems intact.

Benji steers his gaze ocean-ward. "It isn't just that. It was... I felt this *longing*, Preston. Like every inch of my being—of her—needed to find its way there. If she's unsettled because her remains have been separated and lugged about in a box across the world, perhaps she needs to be returned somewhere to be laid to rest."

A sound enough argument, and yet... "Which ocean? Any of them? There's an awful lot of them in the world." I look down at the skull in my hand. "I wonder how she died."

"She was strangled," he murmurs, without missing a step. "I felt it last night when I saw her, and again just now. She was trying to escape from somewhere, or someone, and they caught her as she fled."

I think back to how Benji struggled when I grabbed him from behind and wonder if that was the spirit's doing. If it brought back the memory of fighting for her life. And I wonder again, are we returning her to someone who will do right by her remains, or are we merely passing them off from one thief to the next?

If we permit that to happen, what sort of people does that make us?

"Could we just go to the water here, then? The bay?"

Benji presses his fingers to his forehead like he's staving off an oncoming headache. "I... I don't know. I couldn't sense that much. I just knew I needed to be near the water."

I puff out a heavy breath and then shiver. "Well, we've already sent for our client. I'm not so sure we've got a good case for backing out now."

"No, I suppose not."

Lapsing into silence, we crawl back through the hatch and return to our room. I do not want Benjamin to put his hands on the skull again any time soon, so I immediately return it to its box.

Standing over it and glancing inside, I see something that gives me pause. The skull was not the only thing in there. I reach in, pushing aside more fabric, and pull out two small, leather-bound notebooks.

"We wanted answers," I say to Benji. "Maybe we've got them after all."

I offer them out as he hurries to my side, then place the skull back into the box, folding the silk over the top. Benji unties the first journal as he takes up a seat, head bowed, beginning to pore over the pages with such focused intensity it makes me smile. I pull up a chair beside him and take the other book to flip through it.

The outside is generic enough: dark brown leather, worn from use. The first page contains a stamped image of a circle with the silhouette of a wolf's head within it. The rest of the pages are filled with small, scribbled writing, difficult to make out. For that matter, the longer I stare at it I realise it isn't in English, although I don't know what the language is. Amidst the paragraphs of condensed text, notes are scribbled into the margins, symbols and sketches take up pages and corners and anywhere else there is room. The same girl appears throughout the book, doe-eyed, thin lips, a round face. She couldn't be any older than Benji or me.

And then there are the symbols. Odd markings and etches within circular patterns, unlike anything I've seen. Something fires in my memory. James told me about their last job with Reverend Thomas and the state of things in the cellar beneath his home. James recalled the symbols he saw there, painted upon the walls, but that they were too smeared to really make out. He knew nothing about them other than they were likely tied to whatever organisation the Reverend had referred to. *The Order.* I tap my finger against the page and look up.

"Do you recognise this language, Benji?"

"German…I think. I could be wrong." He glances over. "My book has all those peculiar drawings, too."

"Did Esher have anything like them in his notes?"

"No, nothing like this. But I think they and your aunt would be interested in the contents of these books."

They would. Except we've got our client meeting us in a little over an hour to collect them.

We could take the items and flee, just steal back to England without a word. What would that mean in the long run? They think James and Esher are playing courier here and it would not be difficult for a disgruntled client who *really* wanted to get their hands on these things to track the pair of them down. I cannot put their lives or reputation in danger.

I retrieve a pen and Esher's notebook from our bags and flip through until I find where his text ends and empty pages begin. Laying the two notebooks side by side, I hunch over, and begin to copy the symbols, exactly as I see them.

Benji looks up. "What are you doing?"

"They'll want to see these, right? We don't have time to copy down every word, but every bit helps. Keep reading. See if you find anything of importance."

We sit in silence for the following hour. Benji reads while I copy every symbol and drawing I can, attempting to let my hand uncramp now and again. My fingers have begun to ache. What little is in English seems to be of no importance. A few dates, a few names. A location or two.

I'm halfway through the book. Benji is just about done with his, but I know he's had to skim through much of it as the writing is so bloody small. I flip through several pages, scanning for any words that jump out, searching for more drawings. The same girl appears a few more times, along with the occasional face I don't recognise.

Except one.

I stop, staring into the illustration on the page. There are two of them, one next to the other. But it's the one on the right that catches my attention. Curly-haired and wide eyes... Except here, they're lighter, shaded as though intended to be blue or green or something bright.

"Look at this." I turn it around to Benji. "Is this Crane?"

He leans over. Frowns. "I don't know... Perhaps? I didn't get that good a look at him in the warehouse."

"It's the spitting image, except the eyes. Crane's got these dark, intense eyes. Not like these." I look to the adjoining page and press a finger to the text. "And here!" Amidst the German writing is a name: *Nathaniel J. Crane.*

"Copy that bit down," Benji instructs. "We'll see about having it translated later."

I duck my head to begin doing as I'm told. But I've only got halfway through the page before footsteps creak on the floorboards outside our door, and someone knocks.

We exchange looks. Do we ignore it? Try to push off the meeting just a bit longer? Do we throw ourselves out the window or under the bed? All sound like appealing options. We could just keep the items and hand over an empty box, but what if they know how to open it and check while we're standing right here?

Benji looks to me to make a quick decision. Damn it all.

I shut Esher's notebook and leap out of my chair to cram it beneath the mattress. Benji scurries to get the other books back into the box with the skull, closes it, and fastens the latch once more. I smooth a hand over my hair, straighten my shirt, and step to the door to answer it.

There is not one, but three gentlemen standing in the hallway. The first is a lean, broad-shouldered man with a thick moustache and a full beard, with a Stetson perched atop his greying hair. The hat looks a bit out of place with his otherwise tidy suit, and yet somehow it works for him. Behind him are two men in bowlers and clothes more befitting a rancher than a gentleman. Nothing about their demeanour suggests they're here for any reason other than to act as hired muscle.

I can only presume our gentleman in the hat is our cargo's recipient, Mr. Carlton. He greets us with a charming grin as one of his men shuts the door behind them.

"Evening, gentlemen. I'm Michael Carlton. You must be Mr. Esher and Mr. Spencer."

"That would be us," I agree, stepping forward to extend a hand. Carlton takes it and gives it a firm shake. "I'm James Spencer, this is my partner, William Esher."

"Pleasure. I'll admit, when Wilkerson told me he had two ghost hunters carting along such precious cargo, I was a little concerned. But here you are. I trust everything went without a hitch?"

I steal a glance askance at Benjamin before smiling. "No problems whatsoever."

We step aside, gesturing to the box upon the table. Carlton's eyes widen a fraction as he steps over to it, bringing his hands to rest on its lid. He runs his fingers along the locking mechanism, almost fondly. Then, he turns back around and snaps his fingers, and the taller of his two companions advances to retrieve the box. Carlton returns his attention to us, sliding an envelope out from the inside of his coat pocket and offering it to Benji.

"The remainder of your payment, as promised. Go ahead. Count if you'd like; I won't take offense."

Benji, too polite even on a bad day, only smiles fleetingly and holds the envelope tightly in his hand. "Quite all right."

Carlton waves him off. "You English folk, always too nice for your own good. I could tell you I'd shorted you twenty dollars and you'd probably still smile and say thanks."

"Manners are a burden, sir," I say, smiling tightly.

"Indeed they are. So, tell me…" He tips his head, surveying the both of us closely. "Did either of you open the box along the way?"

My stomach damn near twists itself in two. Surely he has no way of telling. No seal that was broken, no evidence left behind.

"No, sir," Benji says. "Although, I'll admit, we've been quite curious about its contents. Might we ask what's inside that's so special?"

It could be my imagination, but Carlton seems to relax at this answer. "Just a few old books. Manuscripts. One of a kind, at that."

Interesting. "Mr. Wilkerson told us we were hired due to some supernatural activity. Any idea why a few books would have something spiritual attached to them?"

Carlton turns his appraising gaze to me. I'm not the best at reading people anyway, and his face is as locked up tight as that damned box. "Reckon there's many reasons, son. The one who wrote them died rather tragically. Could be his spirit following them around."

Except the spirit we saw was most certainly a woman, and we know for a fact her ghost was attached to the skull, not those books. I wonder if this man has no idea what all the chest contains, or if he knows and refuses to share the knowledge. Either way, it's suspicious.

He drags his tongue across his teeth. Some of the good humour has left his voice. "Any further questions?"

Benji's voice is just as disarming as his smile. "No, sir. Thank you for satisfying our curiosity."

Carlton seems to relax. He tips his hat, turns, and leaves the room. As soon as we're alone again, I latch the door, not feeling safe until there's a locked barrier between us and him. When I turn around and slump back, Benji has relocated to the window to peer outside, perhaps waiting to see Carlton and his associates leave the building. Even from across the room, I can see the worried lines of his face.

"Benji?"

"I don't feel right about this," he murmurs.

I sigh. No, I don't either, if I'm going to be honest. "Do you think he was telling the truth? Do you suppose he has no idea about the skull?"

Benji shakes his head. "I'm not certain, but he was not telling us the full truth, either."

"How do you know?"

"Just…a feeling. I don't know. Something felt off. Even the books themselves… We were told they were stolen from their rightful owner. If the person who penned them is dead, who would the rightful owner be? Next of kin? He didn't seem terribly torn up by receiving the haunted possessions of someone related to him."

As I move to the window and look outside, I can spot Carlton and his associates making their way to a nearby carriage. One holds the door for Carlton, and after he's settled inside, both silently get into the driver's bench and pull out into the road. The sound of hoofbeats hangs in the air long after they've vanished from sight.

No. This does not feel right at all.

Benji retrieves Esher's notebook from beneath the mattress. We sit hip-to-hip on the edge of the bed, looking over the notes I took. Toward the end, my handwriting became something frightful as my fingers had begun to cramp up and our time ran short.

"Don't suppose you know anyone who speaks German?" Benji asks.

I chuckle. "Not off the top of my head, but I'm sure we can find someone. If not here, then back home."

His mouth downturns. "That's a very long ways off, it feels." He stops on the page containing Crane's name, placing a finger beneath it. "Although, Crane himself might have answers. If his name is in that book, then he may be interested in seeing this."

"Oh, right. Ought we just to wander around San Francisco looking for him and see if he's feeling partial to us after the whole kidnapping thing?"

"No need to be testy." He cracks a grin. "And no. I suspect he'll be cross that we delivered our cargo."

I shrug. "Then all there is to do is bring this information home again. See if Aunt Eleanor can't make some sense of it."

Benji dips his head, studying the page before him. The way he chews at his bottom lip tells me this is bothering him still, and I hate to admit it's likely to eat at me too.

"Your mind is racing, I can tell," I say. "Talk to me."

He hesitates. "The ghost. The woman. I know what it felt like in those few moments she was here—the loss, the anger, the sorrow… Preston, for just a few seconds, I felt what it was like to *be* her. She deserves to be put to rest."

Damn it all; I should have just kept the contents and given them an empty box. I'd be willing to bet money that Mr. Carlton does not know how to open it. It won't stop him from cracking through the wood if he wants in desperately enough, of course, but it would have bought us time.

In frustrated silence we pick through the notes, but nothing else jumps out at us as being relevant. It's gibberish on the page until we find a translator, and even then, it could very well be nothing. I must admit, I'm almost curious enough to want to track down Crane after all.

We crawl into bed. What ought to be a night of relief that we've succeeded in our work and can return home has a shadow cast over it in the form of that woman. At half past midnight, I look across the room and see Benji still wide awake, his eyes locked upon me.

"I can't sleep," he says. He doesn't need to say why.

With a sigh, I rub my hands over my face. "Neither can I."

"I know it's difficult to explain, but I don't think those things belong with that man. The woman wanted to go to the ocean. Even if we cannot have the notebooks…"

I study the various patterns in the wood of the ceiling. Look hard enough and you start to see faces. I make out one shape that looks like a wolf. After a spell of silence has passed, I say softly into the darkened room, "Just the skull, then. That's what we need to retrieve."

A sigh from the other side of the bed. "What, we just show up at his home and ask for it back?"

"Yes. Maybe. Christ, I don't know." This entire job has been one big bloody headache. How much easier would it be to call it quits now and go home? We did what we were paid to do. James and Esher's reputation will remain untarnished. Surely even they would say that it isn't possible to put every spirit to rest. We can't fix everything, I remind myself again and again. Why do I feel as though we've done the wrong thing?

14
BENJAMIN

I DREAM OF THE water. Not of any ocean here, but the River Thames back home near the docks of London. Preston stands beside me, my head resting against his shoulder as we watch oranges and reds bleed through the clouds and fog as the sun sets. We would watch the stars come out, and neither of us would say a thing because we didn't need to.

I'm even dimly aware of it as it's occurring—*Ah, this dream again; I like this one.*

Somewhere in the distance, across the water, a haunting sound reaches my ears.

"Do you hear that?" I ask Preston.

Dream-Preston opens his eyes. "Hear what?"

"That sound." A pause. "Like wolves."

"I don't think we have wolves in London, Benji."

"But we aren't *really* in London," I press. The sound is louder now. Piercing. I wince, bringing my hands to my ears. Preston's mouth is moving but I cannot hear him over the howling.

I wake with a gasp upon my lips. When I open my eyes, there's a gun two inches away from me and Sid's scowling face behind it.

"Oh," I manage hoarsely, the wolves still a distant echo in my ears. "Good morning."

THE WRATH OF WOLVES

"Get up," she says, tone clipped. I comply because I would rather not be shot so early in the day.

Preston is upright beside me, staring up at Hugo's hulking form at the foot of the bed with a pistol aimed in Preston's direction. Sid seems far less likely to shoot me than Hugo is to shoot Preston and I'd rather we not give him a reason to get trigger-happy. Seeing as Preston is not the best at keeping his mouth closed, a feeling of dread is already making itself known in the pit of my stomach.

"Where's the damned box?" Sid asks.

Preston and I exchange looks.

"Gone," Preston says. "Delivered to our client."

Hugo's sneer turns into a snarl. He steps forward, jamming the barrel of the gun against Preston's forehead. "Guess there ain't no reason to keep you two alive anymore, then."

Preston grits his teeth, unflinching, but in those fractions of a second I see the tension slithering up his spine into his shoulders and the fear flashing behind his eyes.

"We opened the box!" I blurt.

Hugo stills. He and Sid turn, their full attention now on me. Preston looks about ready to launch himself off the bed to try to wrestle that gun from Hugo's hand; I pray he does not try.

Sid purses her lips, considering this new information. "What's in it, then?"

I lift my chin, defiant. "You'll never find out if you kill us. You need our help if you want it back."

Her mouth twitches, a glimmer of annoyance registering across her face. "You're gonna help us, huh? Why would you do that?"

"Because we need you, too." I hold up a hand and slowly slide out of bed. As I inch over to the other side of the room, Preston frowns, questioning, but wisely remaining silent and permitting me to do the talking. I crouch to the rucksacks on the floor, retrieving the papers where I scribbled my copies from the notebooks. I leave Esher's notebook where it is; I don't want to risk them taking it. "We copied down just a bit of what was inside of the box. It isn't much, but I believe Mr. Crane would be particularly interested in its contents."

Hugo starts, "I don't give two shits about what Crane—"

Sid brings a hand up so abruptly it startles him into silence. She steps forward, gun lowering, and she snatches the papers from my outstretched hand to skim over them. Judging from the frown on her face, I suspect she does not speak any more German than we do.

Finally, her dark eyes lift to fixate on us. "Books, then? That's what's in the box?"

"Notebooks," I agree. "And a human skull."

That seems to catch their attention. Sid looks back to Hugo, whose face has gone a peculiar shade of pale. He's finally lowered his gun, at least.

"A skull?" she repeats. "Whose?"

I remain silent. When she pivots her attention to Preston, he follows my lead and presses his lips together, sealed tight. We shouldn't reveal more than we must in order to get her cooperation. I've given them just enough information to make her curious.

When it becomes apparent to her that we aren't going to speak further, she sighs, turns, and adjusts her Stetson. "Get dressed. We'll let Crane decide this one."

Wonderful. Though I'm unsure if I mean that sincerely or sardonically. Crane is clearly the leader of this group, but it also means he can choose to kill us as quickly as he can help us. I glance at Preston as he slides from bed and whispers, "I hope you know what you're doing."

I do not. Not in the slightest. But if it gets us out of this room alive, then it's a step in the right direction.

So long as it isn't leading us into something far worse, that is.

We aren't left alone for any length of time. Hugo and Sid stand there while Preston and I dress and gather our things. I suppose we ought to be grateful they don't make us leave our belongings behind for the hotel owner to confiscate.

At the door, Sid holsters her pistol inside her coat. Hugo tucks his into the waistband of his trousers, then turns to me, gripping my face between his calloused fingers. For half a second I'm reminded of Father, looming over me and snarling obscenities in my face, and I almost give into the urge to kick this buffoon in the shin.

His attention is on Preston, however. "Fair warnin'. You try to run and I'll snap this runt's neck. Clear?"

There's a fire behind Preston's heated stare. "Crystal."

I scowl. Now is probably not the time to be annoyed that anyone present thinks Preston is the one who could escape while I stayed helplessly behind. But if they want to forget that I'm the one who previously slipped out of their grasp—*and* rescued Preston—then fine. Their underestimation will help us in the end.

We're marched out of the hotel and onto the street where a carriage is waiting. Louisa sits atop the driver's seat, not so much as giving us a second glance. I steal a look down the street. There are a few casual morning strollers wandering through, but it's early yet, the sun has barely risen, and I suppose we are not in an area where many will be out walking at such an hour.

Still… Should I shout for help? Should I make a run for it? I think Hugo would leap at the chance to hurt either of us. Besides that, I rather do want to speak with Crane about the contents of that box. The skull, most of all.

Silence it is, then. For now.

Hugo shoves at us impatiently until we slip into the carriage. He and Sid crowd in together across from us and I fit myself against Preston's side, both for his comfort as well as my own. I clutch my bag to my chest. I've given over my half of the notes; I'll not let them discover and take Preston's half—or Esher's writings—without a fight.

They seem unconcerned that we're able to see out the windows, and thus have some vague idea of where we're going. At least, I can spot the docks as we pass, the moored ships and sailors milling about, preparing for their day in the fog. It's so thick in this area it's almost smothering. It's a miracle our driver can even see where she's headed.

I take the opportunity of sitting in silence for the duration of the ride to watch Hugo and Sid, studying their body language. Although the bench they're seated on could squeeze a third person between them, they sit as far apart as possible. Sid's posture is relaxed, while Hugo's shoulders are rigid and tense and he rarely takes his eyes away from the passing scenery.

Can some part of Hugo sense the ghost that clings to her, even if he cannot see it? It hovers near her even now, not always a discernible figure but ever-present. Sid's shadow seems darker; where it casts on the coach around her, there are vacant corpse eyes staring back out.

But, no, I don't think that's why he keeps his distance. He simply doesn't like her. Then again, he does not seem to like much of anyone. Perhaps it's the authority he despises, and although Crane is their leader, Sid appears to carry some sort of rank among them, as well. I could use that, potentially. Hugo is quick to anger. I learned from my harassers at Whisperwood that angry men are much easier to outsmart.

We arrive at a small, unassuming building just a block inland. It appears to be some sort of unused office or storefront, with a *For Sale* sign hanging on the front door. Most of the windows are boarded up. Someplace our captors think they'll not be disturbed.

Louisa climbs down and opens the door for us, and we file out and into the building. The sun has finally started to come up enough to chase some of the fog away, but everything is so boarded up that the sunlight does little to cut through the dusty darkness.

This appears to be where they've set up camp for themselves. There are bags near one wall, along with some provisions. In the centre of the room stands a table where Crane and Philip are seated, hunched over, engaged in a game of cards by candlelight. The latter quickly looks up, game forgotten, but Crane scrunches his nose and lays down his hand.

"Three Aces. Told you, I'm good at this."

"No, you're not. You cheat," Sid says, venturing further into the room until the candlelight spills onto her heart-shaped face.

Crane straightens and tips his head to peer at her, hands spread wide. "I'm an angel." Before she can argue that, his attention drifts to us. "Dare I ask why they're here?"

"They delivered the chest," Hugo announces, shoving the heels of his hands into our backs so hard that Preston and I both stagger forward a step. Preston's jaw clenches. I grab hold of his arm to steady his temper.

Crane lets out a long sigh, tossing the remainder of his cards to the table as he stands. "Well, that's bloody fantastic. Suppose we've got to go get it now, don't we?"

"And then what?" Preston growls. "Deliver it back to your *master*? Do you even know what's in it?"

Crane pockets his hands and crosses the room to stand before us. The flickering light catches the side of his face, his curls, the collar of his shirt, yet not a bit of it reflects in his eyes. "Please don't make me shoot you again. But yes, that's what we're here to do, and no, I don't know what's in it and I honestly don't care."

I force my voice to cooperate. "You should. Your name was mentioned. Quite a lot, I might add."

That's a bit of a stretch. I only saw his name once, but I don't need to be honest, I just need him to believe me. His gaze swivels slowly to me.

"Is that right?"

"Nathaniel J. Crane. That's you, isn't it? Your likeness was drawn in the pages of one of the notebooks we found."

"Shut your mouth, boy. Nobody here gives a shit about some notebooks," Hugo protests hotly.

Sid moves up alongside Crane. "Maybe not, but I'm awfully curious about that skull."

Crane's eyes don't leave me. "What skull?"

"I thought you would have the answer to that," I say. "But the spirit of the woman it belonged to wants it laid to rest. I suspect whoever is in possession of that box will get no peace until that happens."

Hugo's hand clamps the back of my neck, fingers digging in until I wince and reflexively try to squirm away. "I *said* shut your mouth!"

Preston moves like lightning, slamming the full weight of his body into Hugo's to knock him away from me. The force of impact sends Hugo staggering back and Preston uses that momentum to heave him against the door, an arm shoved against his throat and a snarl upon his mouth.

"And *I* thought I warned you about putting your fucking hands on him."

I brace myself for things to escalate into an all-out brawl and I start forward, intending to try to drag Preston away. A gloved hand comes to rest upon my shoulder and Crane says, in a voice not particularly loud yet commanding the attention of everyone in the room, "*That's enough.*"

Hugo and Preston still, glowering at one another. Preston takes a slow step back, close enough that I can reach for his arm to draw him to my side. Crane moves around me, placing himself between us and Hugo. "Sit down."

"We should be killing them," Hugo seethes. "Not entertaining whatever stupid-ass idea they got brewing."

Crane takes another step forward, until the pair of them are almost nose to nose. "I'm sorry, did I stutter? I said *sit down.*"

Hugo does not cower, but he tenses and scoots around Crane, around us, to slink away like a reprimanded hound wary of being struck. He has a seat at the table, but I can still feel his fiery stare from here.

With a deep breath, Crane turns back to us. "What is your angle with all of this? What do you want? I have no interest in taking lives needlessly, so if the box is out of your hands, I really couldn't care less what the pair of you do so long as you aren't in my way."

"You need the box to take back to your master," Preston says.

Crane purses his lips at the word *master*, but lets it slide. "I don't need you for that."

"No, but you've got to be interested in what those notebooks have to say about you, right?" Preston smiles thinly and without humour. "I'm curious as hell and they aren't even about me."

"We know how to open the box," I add. "And we'll do it. You take the notebooks; we take the skull."

He folds his arms. "What interest is some dead person's head to you?"

"Like I said, that woman's spirit needs to be put to rest. I think we can do that if we have that skull."

"So, you're willing to work with the people who chased you across the continent, kidnapped you, and shot your friend here, just to…what, to bury some bones?" He arches an eyebrow, looking from me to Preston, who laughs.

"You're talking to the man who spent three days hunting for a family of stray cats around his home because he was worried that they'd freeze in the snow. He made himself sick doing it."

My cheeks warm. I could not begin to explain to either

of them how important this is to me. If they had felt what I felt, maybe they would understand. But perhaps our idea isn't so mad because Crane seems to be considering it. His impossibly dark eyes dart past us, to Sid, I think. The room hangs heavy with tension and anticipation until finally—

"We go together to retrieve the chest. We take the notebooks, you take the skull, we go our separate ways." He holds up a hand as Hugo opens his mouth to protest. "Good?"

I start to say yes and pause. "One more condition. No one dies. Not us, not anyone who may stand in our way to obtaining the chest."

Crane's eyebrows lift. "What if they have guards? With weapons?"

"Then we find another method to get around them. No one dies, or the deal is off. I'll not have more restless spirits created in my attempt to save another."

Crane folds his arms, studying me with a look somewhere between annoyance and amusement.

"Fine," he says. "You have yourself a deal."

15
PRESTON

"THEY'RE GOING TO betray us," I whisper.

Benji nods. He knows this as well as I do. Though I suspect somewhere in that optimistic head of his he's hoping he's wrong and Crane will keep his word. I don't trust the lot of them as far as I can throw them.

Especially seeing as, despite that we're supposed to be working together, Crane immediately had us escorted to and locked inside one of the back rooms of the building. A lone window sits at just about eye level but it's heavily boarded and I'm not sure I could pry it loose without making significant noise. Instead we sit with our backs to the wall, hip to hip, voices low so no one outside will hear us.

Benji says, "It's a possibility, but all we need to do is get the skull and make a run for it. They'll have the books and perhaps that's all they really care about."

Silence.

"Back in the hotel, when you first mentioned the skull, did you see the look on Hugo's face?" I ask.

Benji glances at me, curious. "What look?"

"Like he'd...well, like he'd seen a ghost, honestly. Face white as milk."

"You think he knows something?"

I shrug. "Might. Not that I think he'd share with us if he did. But you must admit, he was awful adamant about not opening the box. Maybe he already knew what was in there."

Benji returns his gaze straight ahead, mulling that over. He's still doing so when the door unlocks and Sid steps in with a paper sack in hand, which she strolls over and offers out to us.

"Lunch. Eat up."

Unlike the last time I found myself in such a position, I take the bag without question. It's still warm and smells of freshly baked goods. I flash her a thin smile. "You're too kind."

She rolls her eyes and turns to leave.

Benji gets to his feet. "Sid, wait—may I call you Sid? I wanted to ask you something."

She pauses, looking over her shoulder. Waiting.

Benji wrings his hands together. "Can you see spirits? Can any of you?"

To this, her lips press into a tight line, guarded. "What's it matter?"

"I'm just curious, is all. You have a wayward ghost that appears to be attached to your person." His eyes flick elsewhere—behind her, to the side of her, I'm not sure. I can't see the thing on my own, after all. "Are you or your companions aware of it?"

A perplexed scowl overtakes Sid's face. She turns back around, hands on her hips. "I don't see ghosts. Never used to believe in 'em, even when I was little."

"But now?"

"Now… Hell if I know. I've seen some strange things, so I won't rule it out." She inclines her chin. "Go on then, boy. Tell me 'bout this ghost you see."

"It's more like an extension of your shadow. Sometimes I can make out a face. A man's face. Deep-set eyes, shaved head. The details aren't terribly clear." A pause. "He frightened me at first, but now that I've seen him a few times, I don't get any sort of malicious intent from him at all. More like he's…looking over you."

She's trying valiantly to keep her expression schooled. Even I can see the cracks in the edges of that mask, some sort of emotion trying to break through. Sid steps forward, hands falling to her sides, voice clipped. "Can you talk to him?"

"Ghosts are notoriously shit at communicating," I say. "This isn't exactly our expertise, either."

The smile Benji offers is apologetic. "He's right, I'm afraid. I've never heard him utter a word."

For whatever reason, that single phrase brings the rest of her façade crumbling down. Her mouth falls open and her eyes go glassy with the sheen of tears. She says nothing, only turns and briskly exits the room, slamming the door behind her. The sound makes Benji flinch. He sinks back down beside me.

"I don't know what I expected her reaction to be," he mumbles.

I open the paper bag to root through it. Something smells delightfully of cranberries. "It could be someone important to her who passed."

"Could be."

More silence.

Silence that I eventually break with, "You know, you really amazed me today with how you handled everything. I woke to that pistol in my face and couldn't think to get a word in edgewise."

Benji's mouth curves up. "I was worried for a moment there that you were going to try to punch your way out of that situation."

"Usually works."

"Usually we aren't faced with weapons."

"Fair enough." I offer him a scone. "Still, your quick thinking got us here."

He laughs. "Is that a good thing? Locked in a room, captured again."

I shrug. "Captured but alive. Look on the bright side."

He flashes me a smile. The subject is dropped for now and we share the meal together. What I wouldn't give for some ham or bacon or even a few eggs, something heartier than bread, but it silences my belly so I won't complain. After we're done, Benji slouches against me and closes his eyes. We doze off and on for lack of anything else to do for the next few hours.

Hugo brings us dinner, though it's two meat pies and they're on the cold side and I'm surprised he doesn't throw them in our faces. Benji picks at his, turned off by the meat within. I wonder if Sid chose not to bring us our meals tonight, or if it simply happened that way.

We're given blankets to sleep with, though no pillows. The room is dark and damp and smells of seawater, so I wrap us up in blankets and curl around Benji, pressing my face into his hair. It may be uncomfortable as sin, but the day has been unbearably draining, so it won't take long before sleep claims me.

Yet it also feels like I've not slept much at all before something is jostling me awake.

Someone is in the room with us.

No, not just in the room with us—but close by.

I tip my head back, peering blearily through the darkness. The bulky figure I can only presume is Hugo is hunched over in the corner. And the damned bastard is going through our belongings. I lurch to my feet with a snarl.

"What do you think you're doing?!"

By the time I reach him and catch hold of his shoulder, Hugo is twisting around with Esher's notebook in hand. I've caught him off-guard enough to knock it from his grasp, clumsily shoving the both of us to the floor. But for all my strength, he's still bigger and stronger. He flings me off him with little effort, rolls to his side, and slams his hand back onto the book.

"Give it back!" I hiss, scrambling back upright.

Hugo holds it up, almost daring me to come and get it. "Is this it? Is this one of them books from the chest?"

"It's not!"

"You had some of the notes. You showed 'em to Sid."

"And those aren't it, you imbecile! Give it back or—"

He laughs bitterly. "Or *what*? You won't help us? That hurts."

A dull, metallic *throng* fills the room as something metal connects with the side of Hugo's head. He grunts, stumbles sideways. Benji, armed with the tray from our dinner, stands ready to strike him again.

Hugo doesn't drop the book, but he's disoriented and gripping his head in pain. "You little shit…"

I'm about to rush him once more when the door flies open. Flickering lamplight chases some of the darkness from the room and yet again, we find ourselves at the business end of a revolver in Sid's hands. Crane is beside her, brows twisted together, but he appears unarmed. Only just barely do I make out the other two standing behind them, as well.

"The hell is going on?" Sid asks, voice thick with sleep.

"Your thug was going through our things." I point at Hugo. "Get your dog under control, Crane, or our deal is off."

Hugo slaps my hand away. "Point at me again and I'll break your fool arm."

"Good God in Heaven, *shut up*," Crane snaps. "If I wanted to look after children, I'd visit a fucking orphanage. Hugo, *get out*."

Hugo pauses, holds up the notebook. "They got one of the books from the chest right here! I'm tellin' you, they're playing us. They already took everything we're after."

He stomps across the room and thrusts the ledger into Crane's hands while Sid lowers her gun and lifts the lamp to cast light upon its pages. Crane's head remains bowed for a moment. When he lifts it again, he looks even less amused.

"This appears to be a compilation of notes about spirit hunting."

Hugo opens his mouth, hesitates. "Huh?"

"The books in that chest belong to The Order. This? This is the scribblings of a novice. This is useless." Crane chucks the book to the floor with enough force that it slides halfway across the room. Benji scurries forward to retrieve it.

The Order, he said. Like James mentioned during my stay at Aunt Eleanor's. I bite back the urge to question him because I don't believe he's in the answering sort of mood. If Crane and his lackeys are associated with The Order after all, then this pack of wolves has just become a lot more dangerous.

Damn it all. We should have got out of San Francisco while we had the chance.

Hugo's face has gone an amusing shade of red. "All right, fine. I was wrong about that. But so help me, Crane, when the boss hears about you havin' any interest in what's in that box, he ain't gonna be happy."

"He *did* say he wanted the contents brought undisturbed," Sid says, so quietly I nearly miss it.

Crane folds his arms, unperturbed that he's got a giant of a man looming over him. "That's assuming we *tell* him that the box has been opened. *I'm* certainly not going to say anything. Sid?"

She doesn't hesitate. "No."

"Phil, Lou?"

Still lingering in the doorway, Philip and Louisa exchange looks. They mumble their agreement, not as confidently as Sid, but I suspect their curiosity has been piqued.

"Fantastic." He tips his head, peering up at Hugo. "Are *you?*"

Hugo pauses. A few seconds of silence drip through the room before he says, "I know where my loyalty lays, Crane. Solomon may have put you in charge of this job, but I ain't scared of you."

To that, Crane smiles, but there is nothing pleasant nor kind in it. Not an ounce of it reaches his eyes. "You should be."

Hugo's hands ball into fists. "Was that a threat?"

"May well have been."

"Do it again and I'll snap you over my knee like a goddamned twig." Hugo steps forward, slamming his shoulder into Crane to push past him.

Crane has a hand round his throat before I have time to blink.

I would anticipate a lot of things in this moment. I would expect Hugo to grab that offending hand and break it. I would expect guns to be drawn, an all-out brawl to ensue. Instead, Hugo opens his mouth to scream.

Not a sound comes out.

Every hair on my arms stands on-end. Benji grabs my hand. His skin is cold as death—not unlike the rest of the room has become. I exhale. The air frosts in front of my face.

Time seems to have slowed to a crawl.

Every corner of the room roils with movement, teeming shadows scaling the walls, the ceiling. Empty eyes and open mouths. A thousand whispers from beyond the grave fill every inch of space in my ears and my head.

Hugo's legs buckle and he drops to his knees, mouth still agape, Crane's fingers digging into the flesh of his throat. Crane's eyes have gone white, taking on the glassy sheen of a dead man's. I think I should stop him. I should speak up. Yet my voice has left me, a paralysing fear rooting my feet to the spot.

Sid speaks. It's muffled and far away. I can see the ghost attached to her now, its arms wrapped around her like its embrace might protect her somehow.

She clamps a hand onto Crane's arm.

"*NATE!*"

The death clears from his eyes.

Nathaniel Crane drags in a shattered breath and his grip goes slack. Hugo collapses onto all fours, wheezing, shaking. Crane himself stumbles back, Sid keeping tight hold of his arm to steady him. There's not an ounce of colour to his face, and even his voice comes out shaky when he speaks.

"Reflect on that when you begin to question who's in charge here. Next time, I'll spare us both and put a bullet in your fucking head." He glances to Philip and Louisa. "Get him out of here."

Looking just as shaken as I feel, the pair hurry into the room, giving Crane a wide berth. They heft Hugo to his feet. It takes them both to see him out. Only when they've left does Crane's façade begin to slip. His shoulders slump, his eyelids drop. He braces a hand against Sid's shoulder.

"You're a damn fool," she mutters, attempting to steer him for the door.

I cannot possibly let them walk out of here without answers for whatever the hell that was. "What did we just see, Crane?"

"He was prying Hugo's soul from his body," Benji murmurs.

Crane stops.

I look to Benji, only just now taking in the mixture of fascination and fear flickering across his face. He releases my hand and takes a slow step forward, staring at Crane as though trying to figure him out. "I don't understand how...but that's what you were doing, wasn't it?"

Crane stares down at Benjamin coolly, calculating. Reappraising. "Keep talking and you'll find out."

They leave and I think nothing we say will stop them this time. The sound of a lock sliding into place assures me they're not taking any chances that we run for it now.

I know what I saw, so I can only imagine what it was like through Benji's eyes. "What happened?"

"I…" He turns to me, at a loss. "I don't know how to describe it. I couldn't just see it. I could *feel* it, Preston. He touched Hugo and just like that, Hugo's life was being dragged right out of him."

He sounds so haunted that it makes me shudder. "How is that even possible?"

"How is any of this possible, really? Miss Bennett summons spirits inside of herself to let them communicate with their loved ones. Spencer and Esher dealt with a man who could implant the spirits of the dead into a living human body. Crane can *remove* spirits with a touch."

"Not sure which one of those abilities is the most terrifying."

Benji shivers, hugging himself and rubbing his arms. "I've never seen anything that frightened me like that."

We sink back to the floor, wide awake. There's little chance we'll fall back asleep after all that. I haven't the foggiest what time it is. We huddle together beneath the thin blankets, silent, taking in this new information and what it might mean for us. Namely, that we've promised to work alongside a man we ought to be getting far, far away from.

It feels a bit like we've sold our souls to the devil.

16

BENJAMIN

BY NOON THE next day, we depart for San Mateo—where we had the telegram sent to Mr. Carlton—in the same carriage we arrived in with the same black mare hitched to the front. Sid and Philip sit across from us, but Crane has a seat directly beside me. The proximity makes my skin crawl. I push closer to Preston until our hips and shoulders are shoved together almost uncomfortably close. Thankfully, Hugo is forced to ride on the driver's bench with Louisa. Small blessings. I'm not certain he'd fit in here with the rest of us, anyway.

During the ride, Crane doesn't speak, only gazes out the small window. Philip and Sid busy themselves with a game of cards. Their backs are pressed to the sides of the carriage in order to use the middle of the bench as their table. They're playing an odd game I haven't heard of, but the rules resemble draw poker, so at least I can entertain myself by following along.

Sid catches me watching and grins. "Want in?"

Beside me, I can practically feel the heat of Preston glaring in her direction. I'm half-tempted to say yes, just to see if she's being serious, but... "Quite all right, thank you."

I find I learn the most about these people by watching them interact with one another. The relationships they hold with each other. The tensions, the friendships, the uneasy alliances.

The obvious bits of information are that Nathaniel Crane is the head of this operation, although not the man they all answer to all the time. They're working for someone who has only their tentative loyalty; perhaps he's paying them, perhaps he's blackmailing them. Hugo mentioned someone named Solomon last night. I've filed that name away for safekeeping.

Sid and Crane appear to be friendly. Their posture around one another is easy but not overly familiar. A sign of people who have known each other a while. There might be some level of trust there, even. Certainly more than between any of the others.

Louisa and Philip are followers in every sense of the word. Philip is dark-haired with a thin mustachio that he tugs nervously at often, and he looks constantly worried. Louisa is a woman close in age to Preston's Aunt Eleanor. She has a sharp eye and a mean stare, but she falls obediently in line when given direction and seems to prefer to avoid confrontations. I also noted the sour look she cast in Hugo's direction when she discovered she'd be riding with him at her side on this little outing.

Ah, Hugo. Most definitely the outlier in this group. After his encounter with Crane, he's been cowed, but I wonder for how long. A beaten dog only behaves until it thinks it can get away with biting someone it does not like or trust. Should that happen, I fear Crane won't hesitate to retaliate. Fatally.

They play a few more rounds of their game before Philip grows tired of losing and calls it quits. Sid then busies herself playing a game of solitaire, though I cannot for the life of me figure out what rules she's following. Her ghost hangs in the darkest recesses of the shadows, never far, watching all of us. A chill settles over me and I huddle closer to Preston.

Over the next few hours, the city vanishes behind us, giving way to dusty roads and towering oaks and maples and stretches of vineyards.

Dark is almost upon us by the time Sid says, "This is the road. I think we're almost there."

Crane knocks on the roof of the cab. Louisa leads the horse off to the right, allowing the trees to swallow us from view of the road. We climb out. The woods around us are black and cold, a heavy layer of fog rolling in to make its home for the night. The carriage lanterns offer just enough light that I can make out the faces of my companions. Preston's hand comes to rest against the small of my back as Hugo hops down from the driver's bench, landing solidly only a foot or so from us.

The others begin to assemble themselves, pulling on their dark coats. To my horror, Crane leans back into the cab to retrieve his revolver from beneath the seat along with a few firearms, which he begins to hand out to the others.

I grab hold of his arm. "We had a deal. I said no killing."

Nathaniel Crane's stare is as cool as the night air around us. He closes his gloved fingers around my wrist and squeezes until the pressure makes me wince and release him. "Our host is not going to allow us to simply walk in and take what we want because we ask nicely."

I pull my hand from his grasp. "If anyone dies, I'm not opening the chest for you."

Hugo laughs. "Go ahead. Give us an excuse to shoot you too."

Crane stills him with a stare before he turns and shoves one of the revolvers into Preston's hands. Preston startles, staring down at it as though he hasn't the foggiest idea what to do with it.

"It ain't loaded," Sid assures him. "But wave it around like it is and it'll make your night a helluva lot easier."

Preston's mouth tugs down disapprovingly, but he tucks the barrel of the gun into his belt like he's seen the others do. Crane turns to offer another of the guns out to me. He looks utterly unimpressed—and unsurprised—when I only stare back at him, defiant. He sighs and puts it away.

"As it pleases his highness. All right, ladies and gents; here's the plan. Neighbours are spread out enough that we ought not have too much of a problem being stealthy. Do the pair of you happen to know if any servants are present?"

Preston shakes his head. "He met us at the hotel. There were two men with him at the time, but they didn't look like servants."

"Probably hired muscle, is all. In a house the size of his, I suspect Carlton doesn't have anyone who lives on-site, but you never know. Let's proceed based on the assumption he has four on his staff and at least some of them might be there. I'd rather over-estimate." Crane looks askance, peering through the trees where the moonlight illuminates Carlton's house across a stretch of trees and grass. "Sid, Your Highness, you're with me. Hugo, Louisa, Philip, you three take the guard dog here and go in through the back. Ensure anyone you find doesn't sneak out to alert a neighbour."

I scowl at his use of insulting nicknames and bite back the urge to comment. The sooner we go in, the sooner we can get what we came for and be on our way.

We approach the building on foot, keeping to trees and shrubbery as we step onto the property. Everything appears still quiet, only a single faint flicker of light coming from an upper storey window. With any luck, Mr. Carlton will be the only one home and we needn't frighten his poor house staff.

Crane gestures as we approach. Philip nudges Preston, who casts a forlorn, uncertain look in my direction. I nod and he reluctantly follows his partners. I'm left to approach the front door between Sid and Nathaniel Crane.

A wolf howls.

The sound sends a shudder straight down my spine and almost makes me gasp. Crane pauses, hand upon the doorknob. "What is it?"

"You didn't hear it?" I whisper.

Crane frowns. "Hear what?"

I wonder if Preston can hear it from where he is. I shiver again, rubbing the gooseflesh from my arms and shaking my head. "Nothing. Nevermind."

Crane tries the door, unsurprised to discover it locked. He steps aside and Sid drops to a crouch, pulling a roll of lockpicks from her coat. It takes her nary a minute before the door lets out a definitive *click* and she pushes it open.

All the lights have been put out for the night, making what seems to be a neatly decorated space look haunted and abandoned. Still, I hear the howling and this time it rattles off every wall, and when Crane says something to me, I cannot hear it for the haunting sound ringing in my ears. The howls are like a warning as much as a summons.

Sid gives my shoulder a nudge. "*Hey.* Get a move on."

I force myself to breathe in deep, trying to block out the noise in the same way I have learned to block out spirits in general all my life. It works, vaguely. "The skull is upstairs."

Crane and Sid exchange looks and we head for the stairs. Every breath, every creak of wood beneath our feet makes me cringe, convinced someone will jump out from the shadows to ambush us. At the top of the steps, Crane gestures, expecting me to lead the way since my sixth sense has a lock on the location of the box. That means I'm left to move ahead of the group, unarmed, into the darkness.

I lead them toward the sound of howling to a closed door. It's unlocked and swings open soundlessly, letting us into a wide study awash in moonlight.

The chorus of wolves stops. The ensuing silence is almost as deafening.

Sid steps around me, gaze sweeping the room. "So, where's it at?"

"I don't know. In here…somewhere. The cabinets? Drawers?"

"Find it," Crane orders. He leaves the room, moving soundlessly down the hall. Sid and I begin to look about the study, searching shelves and drawers and cupboards, to no avail. It's in here somewhere. I *know* it is.

Commotion from elsewhere in the house draws us both to standing upright and Sid pulls her gun from its holster. The door slams open and in stumbles Mr. Carlton, hands above his head, dishevelled and disoriented in his pyjamas and mussed hair and drooping moustache. Behind him comes Crane, the barrel of his revolver jammed between Carlton's shoulder-blades and his free hand fisted into the man's shirt. He shoves Carlton into the centre of the room, and Carlton's eyes land on me and grow wide.

"You—"

"Where's the box?" Sid demands. She's lowered her gun but has not put it away.

"Who in the hell are you?" Carlton demands hotly. He braves turning around then, and it must be the first time he's got a look at who dragged him from his bed, because all the colour drains from his face. "Crane...?"

Crane doesn't bat an eye. "Good to see you, Michael. Where's the fucking box?"

Carlton wets his lips, eyes flicking from Crane to Sid to me and back again, as though uncertain who here poses the largest threat. Or perhaps who stands to be his greatest chance at getting out of this unscathed. He seems to decide that person is me, because he swivels back in my direction. "Mr. Esher, please, remember what I told you..."

Sid lets out a sharp laugh. "That ain't William Esher, just like that other boy ain't James Spencer. Just some buddies of theirs they got to do their little delivery for them."

Carlton falters but does not relent. "I don't care who he is. He knows that box belongs to me."

"I don't," I admit quietly. "I thought that I did, but those notebooks... You didn't write them, did you, Mr. Carlton?"

A pause. "I..."

"And the woman's skull. Who did that belong to?" I advance a step, and he retreats two. "I've seen her, or whatever is left of who she used to be. And she is not happy."

His expression drops. "What skull?"

"He ain't opened the box yet," Sid says.

"Of course I haven't opened the damned box. I don't know the combination to get into it!" Not once do his eyes leave me. "How do *you* know what's in there?"

Crane makes an amused noise. "He's a smart lad. Figured it all out himself."

"I did not. The spirit whose skull resides in there showed me." I incline my chin as Carlton stares me down, unwilling to be intimidated. "I have no interest in the notebooks. You lot can fight for them all you want. All I want is that skull so I might grant the woman it belonged to some peace."

Carlton runs a hand over his face, tugging at his moustache. "I don't understand. It was just supposed to be the books, so why…" He stops, turns, gapes at Crane in horror. "Nathaniel, what's become of Ellie?"

Crane returns that stare with a blank one of his own, brows furrowed, suggesting he doesn't have an answer to that. "I don't keep tabs on your wife for you."

I've the worst sinking feeling in my stomach. "She has long, dark hair. Dark eyes. She sometimes speaks a language I do not know. She was beautiful."

In a flash, Carlton rushes to his desk near the window, snatching a frame from its surface. He shoves it out to me—an old tin portrait of himself standing beside a lovely, dark-haired woman. He is smiling. She is not.

There is something deeply unsettling about seeing a photograph of a person in life when all I have seen of them is their tormented spirit, but there is no doubt. "Yes. Yes… That's her."

Carlton's face falls, fingers curling around the edges of the wooden frame so tightly it might splinter in his grasp. Slowly, his eyes move past me to lock onto Nathaniel Crane.

"Was it you, Crane? Did you kill her?"

"I don't make a habit of killing people who don't deserve it. Ellie was a nice woman." Crane shrugs. "The last I had heard, you'd taken your chance to get out from under the boss and you took it. You left your wife behind. I'm willing to bet Solomon had no more need of her. If that's the case, I might go so far as to say *you're* just as responsible for her death as anyone else."

Carlton's face flushes crimson in shame and fury. He drops the frame to the desk and lunges for Crane, grabbing fistfuls of his coat and shirt and shoving him back against the fireplace mantel. Crane only lets out a bitter laugh, unconcerned.

"Go on then. Take your anger out on me if it pleases you, but *I* did not kill your wife."

They stare daggers at one another while I'm struggling to keep up, to grasp the situation. If I had to wager a guess... "Solomon is your employer. Is he the one who runs The Order?"

Stillness falls over the room. Carlton, Sid, and Crane all look to me as though they forgot I was even there. Carlton laughs, shrill and amused. "You really don't know anything about what you've gotten yourself into, do you, boy?"

"I know that woman's spirit wants what's left of her bones laid to rest. I know you did not seem to like the way things were being run under your employer, so you had some of his work stolen. Either to get back at him, or perhaps as blackmail."

"Smart lad. Not that any of that matters right now." Crane lifts the revolver, jamming it into Carlton's stomach to force him back several steps. "The box. Now. Unless you'd rather I put a few rounds into your face and then tear this place apart until I find it. Your choice."

My eyes widen. "We had a deal, Crane. No one dies!"

"Boy, shut your goddamned mouth," Sid snaps.

He could be bluffing, but with that glint in his dark eyes, I do not think he is. I push past Sid, putting myself between Crane and Carlton, my heart racing so quickly I can scarcely breathe around it. Behind me, I can hear Crane letting out a low, impatient growl, but my focus needs to be on *this* man—the one we need something from.

"Mr. Carlton, I implore you. Just tell us where the chest is. Mr. Crane will take back the notebooks to the person who wrote them, and all I want is that skull. If she was your wife, then surely you loved her and you want her laid to rest, don't you?"

"Coward left her at the mercy of wolves. Do you think he really cares?" Sid scoffs.

Carlton's lips pull back into a sneer. But perhaps he knows he won't win this standoff, because he steps forward, gesturing for Crane to move aside. He removes the painting hung above the fireplace mantel, revealing a cabinet door behind it. Not locked but hidden well enough that it might have taken us hours to find it.

From inside, he removes the box, still firmly sealed. He places it atop his desk and steps back as though a part of him also senses there's something amiss about it and contact feels wrong. I can still feel the woman—Ellie, if that is her name— lingering there, her presence in every shadow in the room.

"Open it," Sid demands. "So we can make sure everything's still inside."

A wise idea, at least in theory, but— "I'm not going to do that."

Sid groans, frustrated. "Why the hell not?"

I turn to face her, shoulders squared. "Because if I open it now, what use will you have for me then? You'd have no reason not to kill Mr. Carlton, myself, or my companion."

"Our word ain't good enough?"

I almost laugh. "We have been kidnapped, beaten, and chased through the streets by the lot of you. So, no, your word doesn't mean much."

"It's fine. Just grab the box and let's go." Crane turns for the door. Minutes ago I'd have jumped at the chance to hurry out of here, but now I cannot help the inane urge to press, to find out more. There are so many pieces to this puzzle that aren't lining up. So much of the picture is missing.

I step over to Carlton, meeting his dark, sullen gaze. I keep my voice low, barely above a whisper. "Please, tell me… Who was it you worked for? This Solomon. He's a part of The Order?"

Carlton's eyes narrow. "You want the God's honest truth?"

"I do."

"Boy," Sid snaps from near the door. "Come on. No questions."

I hesitate. "*Please*, something. Anything."

Carlton wets his lips, gaze flicking to the other two even as Crane is briskly crossing the room, removing his gloves. I need him to get anything out, just a few words.

"You should go home before Solomon finds out you're underfoot," Carlton says. "If you encounter him, don't trust him. Don't trust *any* of them, do you understand? They're all—"

Crane's hand shoots out, fingers closing around Carlton's throat. Silencing him.

Just like the night before, the room plummets into darkness all around us. Nathaniel Crane's eyes glass over into the vacant eyes of a corpse. Carlton chokes on a scream that does not make it past his lips, but every drop of colour has drained from his face, leaving behind an ashy grey pallor.

Crane is killing him. I can't see it so much as I can *sense* it; a soul being wrenched apart from its body to…what, to go where? To simply be tossed into the void?

Sid makes no move to stop her companion, and I…

I cannot watch a man die like this.

I latch my fingers around Crane's wrist and forearm, intending to pry his grip from Carlton's throat.

Instead, every muscle in my body locks, frozen in jolts of pain and fear.

Shadows swallow every wall, every crevice, smothered by a thousand garbled whispers of dead men and women and things far more sinister. The weight of it is crushing. Crane may as well have his grip on my neck, strangling the life from me.

Except I am staring into his eyes, which have gone wide in horrified confusion and I realise he no longer has control of this, either.

Neither of us knows what we have done, and neither of us knows how to stop it.

It's so much. Too much. I cannot breathe around it.

Darkness. Cold. *Howling.*

Then nothing at all.

17
PRESTON

THE MAID CAN'T be much older than seventeen, but she's given us a run for our money. Two attempts to sneak out the back door when we arrived, then again out the kitchen window when we tried to confine her there. Now she's tied to a chair, looking sullen and sour as she occasionally swings her legs to scuff her heels against the ground.

From here, Philip and I have a clear view across the ground floor to where Louisa is poised at the front door and Hugo is lounging in a chair not far from her, boots kicked up onto a nearby table. Other than this lone girl, we found no other staff on the property, and judging by the single small room off the kitchens, it's safe to say that anyone else who works here likely doesn't live here.

"What's taking them so damn long?" Philip mumbles, casting a glance towards the stairs.

A good question. Now and again I pick up the sound of footsteps crossing an upstairs floor, the creak of floorboards. Sometimes muffled voices.

My heart picks up speed seemingly out of nowhere. A heavy, swift drumming as though I've just run a lap around the property. When Philip next exhales one of his restless sighs, the air in front of his face frosts. I puff out a breath. I can see it. It was *not* this cold when we arrived.

A heavy thud comes from overhead, something bodily crashing to the floor. From the corners of the room, darkness ripples like curtains in the breeze. Whispers of voices long since dead caress my ears.

I bolt for the stairs with dread coursing through my veins. The others are at my heels, but I scarcely notice them as I dart down the hall, searching for Benjamin. When we come to an open door, the first thing I see is Crane prone in front of the fireplace with Sid crouched beside him, hand upon his arm. Carlton, white-faced and shaking, is on his knees nearby. I see the figures looming in every shadow imaginable, gaping mouths and dead eyes, teeming like rats.

Then I see Benjamin, motionless on the floor.

A strangled sound catches in my throat as I rush to his side and gather him up. His skin is like ice, his lips tinged blue. But his pulse, although thready, is still present. I can see the rise and fall of his chest. Thank God, he's alive.

"Christ Almighty," Louisa says, surveying the scene. "What the hell happened?"

"H-he tried to kill me," Carlton stammers as he points at Crane, white-faced and shaking. "He touched me and…"

Sid cuts him off. "We need to get out of here. We got the box, that's all we came for. Phil, help me with him. Lou, the box is on the desk there." She hoists one of Crane's arms around her shoulders while Philip goes to the other side to do the same. Crane is tall and lean; between the two of them, they manage to get him off the floor with minimal effort. Every shadow shies away from Sid when she passes them by, frightened by the spirit attached to her.

Carlton looks to me this time, disoriented. "He tried to kill me. Don't leave me with these things. Please, don't go." He crawls to me, grabbing hold of my arm. His skin is just as cold as Benji's, his grip like cold fire. "They'll kill you, too, if you go," he whispers. "The Order destroys everything, one way or another. Solomon's promises will never be fulfilled. He—"

Hugo steps around me, gun drawn, and fires a shot against the man's temple. Carlton's mouth continues moving for a split second before he crumples sideways to the floor.

"God fuckin' *damn it*, Hugo!" Sid snarls. "Have you lost your damn mind?"

She sounds far away. My ears are ringing. There is blood on the floor, on the fireplace mantel, on my shirt. I choke back a sound, shaking, fury and fear mixing into one invariable storm inside me.

"Get up," Hugo growls. "Before I shoot you, too."

I obey out of pure reflex. I gather Benji into my arms and push to my feet. He's small but he's still dead weight, and I must steady myself to keep from dropping him. My legs feel like pudding, too weak to hold me, let alone us both. Yet, somehow, I manage to follow them briskly out of the room. The shadows have descended into the rest of the house, as though someone has thrown open a door to some other realm.

A desperate cry from the kitchen has me halting in my steps. *The maid.* Hugo slows, gun at the ready, until Louisa slams a hand into his arm and says, "*Go.*"

"We can't just leave her!" I turn to look where she's still fastened to her chair. Her eyes meet mine, impossibly wide and terrified as the dead shuffle around her, flickering in and out of view. Benjamin would never forgive me if he learned I left this poor girl here, and yet…

I do not trust them to take Benjamin on ahead. I do not trust the ghosts to lay him down while I untie the maid. Benji's safety is more important than anything else.

"Lord, forgive me," I whisper, hurrying after the others.

We half-run across the dark property, tall grass whipping at my legs, low branches and brush snagging my clothes. The voices finally begin to fade, the heavy chill steadily lifting the more distance we put between us and that house. I hug Benji to my chest, never permitting my eyes to stray, always remaining locked upon the group ahead of me. The lonely glow of our carriage lanterns guides us through the trees. Hugo and Louisa haul themselves into the driver's seat while Philip and Sid make careful work of loading Crane into the cab. Philip then leans back out. "Come on!"

I don't move. Why should I? They have what they wanted. I could take Benji right now and get the hell out of here, run as far as I possibly could. I do not have our belongings or anything else, but does it matter? I'll find another way for us to get home. I *need* to get him safe.

Hugo starts to climb back down, sneering hideously, gun still in hand. "Get in the damn cab, boy."

I meet his eyes. There isn't a doubt in my mind he would gladly grasp for any excuse to shoot me now.

So, in I go.

No one speaks a word the entire drive back. Crane doesn't stir and Benji only does so towards the end of the trip. He turns, pressing his face into my chest. My legs have long since gone a bit numb from cradling him in my lap, but I refuse to relinquish my hold on him.

"Benji?"

"Mm." His long lashes flutter, revealing dark, tired eyes. "What's happened…?"

I could cry out in relief. Instead I hug him to me, squeezing my eyes shut. "I should be asking you that."

He appears to be coming to his senses swiftly as he twists in my arms to look across at the others, takes in the sight of Crane, still motionless. He begins to push himself up to sitting, all awkward limbs.

"Is he—"

"He'll be fine," Sid says in a tone as chilly as her stare. "Dunno what you did when you grabbed him, but clearly it didn't work out well for anyone."

Benji bites his lip. "The ghosts…"

"They were everywhere," I murmur, stroking his hair back. "I saw them."

"Think we all did." Philip is staring at Benjamin as though he's grown a second head. "What *did* you do back there? What the hell was all that?"

"I don't know. I realized he was going to kill Mr. Carlton so I grabbed him to stop him and everything just…" He stills, swallows hard. "I've never seen anything like that. I don't know what we did, but—Good Lord, what about Mr. Carlton? Is he all right?"

Sid opens her mouth to respond and I cut her off. "He's fine." I pin our companions with a stare, daring them to contest me. "Everyone's fine, Benji."

I do not *want* to lie to him, but I can't stomach the idea of seeing his face when he hears that someone died because of us. Not to mention if he learned about the girl we left behind to some possibly horrible fate… It would wreck him. He'd never forgive me nor himself.

I'll carry that burden for the both of us.

Sure enough, Benjamin relaxes, going boneless in my arms and dropping his tired head to my shoulder. "Oh. Good," he says. Within mere moments, he's asleep.

Sid holds my gaze when I look at her again, her mouth downturned and displeased. "Smart idea. He'll find out."

"Only if one of you lot opens your mouth. And I'll caution you not to do that."

She purses her lips but doesn't call me on my obvious threat. "Benji. That's his name?"

Damn. I'd forgotten we never had told them our names. "Not really any of your business."

"Just curious, is all. Don't see much point in secrecy now." She shrugs, turning her attention out the window to the darkness rolling by.

She has a point, to be sure. What would they be able to do with our first names? But I prefer to err on the side of caution where they're concerned. All I want to do is to get back to San Francisco, open that bloody box, and get the hell out of here.

It's nearly three in the morning by the time we roll to a stop outside the old building. Benji rouses reluctantly. I keep an arm round his middle as I help him from the carriage, not bothering to see if the others need assistance with Crane. Not my problem. I get Benji inside, laying him down on our little palette of blankets, removing his shoes, and covering him up. I slide out of my coat to fold it and tuck it under his head.

That done, I push up my sleeves and return to the main room. There, Philip, Sid, and Louisa have got Crane on a bedroll in the corner. Funny how small and vulnerable the man looks like this, with his people rallied around him like wolves protecting one of their own. Only Hugo seems on the outskirts, alienated, watching the lot of them as though he has half a mind to take out that revolver and start shooting again.

The sound of gunfire still echoes in my head. When I close my eyes, I see the side of Carlton's skull exploding in bits of bone and brain. I shudder, biting back the nausea. Small blessing that Benjamin was out cold for it. He'd have nightmares the rest of his life. I'm not so certain that I won't.

From the moment I step into the room, Hugo's eyes are on me. "What are you doing out here?"

I'm in no mood for him. "Oh, am I still a prisoner? Make no mistake, the moment my friend wakes, we'll be leaving. I suggest you do not try to stop us."

Hugo straightens up to his full height. "Or what?"

I shouldn't be picking fights. I already know I can't win against Hugo. Certainly, not against all of them. Yet all I can think about is Benji lying on the floor in that house, the panic that had surged through every nerve in my body. I don't think I've ever been so frightened—and it's because of this lot.

"Or it would do you well to watch your back at all times lest I get a hold of that gun and shove it down your throat," I snap. "We'll keep up our end of the bargain. You had better keep yours."

I don't wait for him to respond before whirling on my heel and marching back to the room. I do not fancy us being locked in again tonight, so I take a seat near the door, slouched against the wall, and watch Benji sleeping across the room.

Lord, what have I got us into? Can we really expect these people to let us go after we've given them what they want? Crane might be furious with Benji's earlier intervention, and Hugo—well, he's had it out for us since the train station.

I remain awake, staring across the room, straining to hear any conversation elsewhere in the building. For a while I hear the others murmuring amongst themselves, but it doesn't last long before they've settled and, I suspect, gone to bed. It must be close to five when Benji stirs again, rolling slowly onto his side and opening his eyes, meeting my gaze through the darkness.

"Preston…?"

"I'm here," I call softly, getting to my feet to go to him. "Are you all right? How do you feel?"

He sits up. "Head's a big foggy. But…all right, I think. Where are the others?"

I crouch at his side, elbows resting on my knees. He *looks* all right. Perhaps a little tired, a little disoriented, but well enough. "Asleep. Look, I think we ought to sneak out. We may have some time. We could nick the carriage and horse and get as far out of town as possible. What do you say?"

A frown tugs at his face as he struggles to mentally catch up. "But we made a deal."

"I don't think they'll honour that deal, Benji. Do you?"

A pause. "They… They *might*."

"Is *might* worth our lives? I say we make a run for it now."

"What of the box?"

Ah, damn it all. The bloody box. "Honest opinion? We ought to leave it. They'll have what they want, and no reason to come after us, right?"

He bites at his lower lip, troubled. "But Ellie…"

I reach out, touching my fingertips beneath his chin. "Wasn't it you who recently told me that we can't fix everything? This might be one we have to let alone, sweetheart."

Benji's expression smooths out, mouth drawn taut. "I am not leaving without that skull."

I pull back and shove a hand through my hair. "*Damn it, Benjamin.*"

"Don't you dare," he says tersely. "I've asked for nothing this entire trip. I've gone along with it, every step of the way, even when I thought it was a bad idea. But *this?* This is important to me. If you're afraid, then go on without me, but I am not leaving here without at least trying to help that woman."

"Even at the risk of getting caught or killed?"

"Suffering the same fate as Mr. Carlton, you mean?" he asks.

I freeze. "What—"

He scowls. "I saw the way Sid looked at you when you said everyone was fine. I woke to blood on my shirt—and yours. Unless you have another lie squirreled away to explain that?"

Damn it all. I grit my teeth, guilty but frustrated all in the same breath. "I was only… I didn't want to upset you."

His frown deepens. "Lying to me is never a good alternative. Will you help me or do you want to go home alone?"

"I would never abandon you when you needed me," I reply softly, feeling well and thoroughly chastised. Especially since Carlton's death is hardly the only thing that I'm keeping from him. If I told him about the girl we'd left behind, he'd no doubt beg for us to return to the house. Maybe we should. Yet what good would we be able to accomplish if we tried? We have no experience in banishing ghosts, let alone hundreds of them and restraining whatever it was Crane and Benjamin accidentally unleashed. Perhaps after we left, the issue cleared up on its own. If so, us returning there while the maid is no doubt summoning the police to investigate Carlton's murder would not be wise.

Lord, my head is hurting from trying to think this through. What is the right answer? What would James say? Aunt Eleanor?

They'd never have left the damned house to begin with, something tells me. I grit my teeth, staving off the overwhelming guilt.

One thing at a time, I decide. "Let's open the chest. Take the skull, leave the rest, and then get out of here. We'll have kept our end of the deal and won't give them cause to follow— aside from stealing their horse, I guess."

Benjamin's features begin to relax into an easy smile. "Thank you."

I pat his leg and rise to my feet, offering a hand to help him up. "Best not to thank me 'til we're out of here alive."

We make quick work of gathering our things, ensuring all travel documents and our money is where it ought to be. Easing into the hall, I stop to listen for sounds from the main room. If any of them are awake and keeping watch, this entire plan will have been for nothing.

Silence. The lamps have been put out. Good.

At the entrance to the main room, I stop to count out the various lumps asleep in their respective bedrolls. Crane still lies unmoving in the corner, with Sid a foot or so away. That must be Louisa against the far wall, hidden almost entirely under a blanket, and Philip beside her.

Hugo, however, is slouched against the wall to my left. He does not turn or lift his head, so he must be asleep. I allow a few seconds to pass by before I dare to step out into the room. Benjamin is at my back, a hand fisted in my shirt sleeve.

In the centre of the room, we come to a halt, surveying the area. Benjamin releases me and begins to pick his way toward Nathaniel Crane and Sid. I grimace, but admittedly, he's smaller and much better at moving quietly than I am.

The box is tucked up against some of their other belongings, right between where Sid and Crane's heads are resting. Beneath his feet, the floor gives an ominous creak.

Benji stills. I hold my breath.

Sid sighs, shifting in her sleep, but does not wake. Crane is as still as the dead.

Benji steals a relieved look over his shoulder at me before bending to retrieve the box. As soon as he's returned to my side, I begin to usher him for the door. I don't feel I can truly breathe again until we're outside in the early morning chill. I feel bad for their poor horse; being hitched to a cart all night could not have been comfortable, but I suppose there wasn't a place open in the dead of night to house her when we got back from Carlton's.

We move around the edge of the building so we're out of sight of the front door. I take the box, holding it while Benji spins the dials and presses them in. I wait for the click of it unlocking…but nothing happens.

"What's wrong with it?" I ask.

Benji's brows furrow. He adjusts the dials and tries again. Still nothing. "I… I don't know. The combination we used last time isn't working now. Perhaps it's been changed?"

"They didn't know how to open the damned thing; how could it have changed?"

"Maybe it's random." He lifts his gaze to me. "What do we do?"

We ought to leave the box and get the hell out of here, is what we ought to do. And yet we've been over that; Benji wouldn't be satisfied with that answer.

Not that we're given much choice. From around the corner of the building, the front door groans open. I hear a snuffle and a grunt. Philip steps into view, his back to us as he approaches the horse and gives her a pat on the neck. I shrink against the wall, nudging Benjamin back behind me. The other entrance to the alleyway is blocked; if we're spotted, we'll have to make a run for it.

But Philip mumbles absently to the horse—"There's a good girl, Rogue."—takes a look around, and finally retreats back inside, never once looking our way. The door clicks shut and I let out a rush of breath.

"If he notices the box is missing, or us, for that matter," Benji whispers.

Yes. We're running out of time to plan. I shove the box back into his hands and hurry forward to begin unhitching the horse. Benji follows and stops me with a hand to my arm.

"Wait. Let's take the carriage, too."

"What? Why? We can travel faster without it."

"Because with the carriage, they need only replace the horse to give chase. Five of them won't be following with a single horse. We can abandon the carriage outside of the city, if necessary."

I pause, glancing back at the building. Fine. We don't have time to debate. Benji begins to climb up onto the bench while I stow our things in the carriage. He hands over the reins as I join him, and I think about how this is going to be a bit different than our wagon back home.

Different, but not impossible. A well-trained horse will know what to do. I give the reins a flick and click my tongue, and Rogue starts at a leisurely walk down the street. At the next intersection, I give the reins another flick and she picks up her pace, just quick enough that the cab rattles precariously beneath us as its wheels roll across the cobblestone.

I'm unfamiliar with this city and we have no map to go by. For now, I focus on getting as far from the empty building as possible, turning only when necessary. The streets are dark and as foggy as a London morning, thick swaths of mist pushed in from the bay. Even as the sun begins to rise, it does little to chase it away.

We stop only when we spot a general store opening. I remain with the cart while Benji goes inside for directions. He returns with a satchel of food and, better than just directions, a map. He re-joins me on the driver's bench, studying it a moment before he says, "Straight up ahead. Make a left on Main."

Having a direction to go is a relief. I coax the horse back into motion. "Where are we headed?"

He purses his lips, eyes still locked upon the map. "There's a city just a bit north-east of San Francisco. I figured we'd head there, try to find somewhere quiet and see about communicating with the woman's spirit again for guidance."

Good enough for me. We could be headed back to Boston on horseback for all I care.

So long as it puts us at a safe distance from Nathaniel Crane.

18
BENJAMIN

ℋ EADING NORTH FROM San Francisco would require a ferry ride across the bay. Preston does not know that, and I have no intention of enlightening him just yet. If he notices we're headed South toward San Mateo, he doesn't comment. I ought to feel guilty about deceiving him—and I do, after a fashion— but were I to tell him where I intend to go, his ensuing arguments would waste precious time we cannot spare.

Now and again, I see the ghost of Ellie on the sides of the street, her drawn face and dead eyes watching us every step of the way.

I knew something was amiss the moment I woke. It was not just the specks of blood on my shirt, or the look Sid had given me in the carriage on the way back from Carlton's. It was Ellie herself, for once present and silent. She has not spoken a word, but I know she wants me to follow her...and the further we go, the more I realise she's leading us back to Mr. Carlton's home.

Besides all of that, Preston is not a good liar.

When I grabbed hold of Nathaniel Crane last night to stop him from killing Mr. Carlton, I'm positive we did something terribly wrong. Something had clicked in the alcoves of my mind, a door swung open, a darkness pouring out of Crane that I could not control. Preston has dodged any of my questions regarding it and so I can only assume Crane and I left some sort of chaos behind us when we were taken from that place.

An hour or so away, Preston begins to glimpse around, frowning. Everything looks different in the daylight, but surely he's begun to notice this place feels familiar. It isn't until I instruct him to pull over, however, that it dawns on him what I've done. He draws the cab off to the side of the road and then to an immediate halt, twisting in his seat to take in the surrounding area. "Benji…"

I climb down from the bench, wordless.

"What in the hell?" Preston drops down on the other side, circling round as I'm opening the carriage door to dig for Esher's notebook inside my bag. "Are we where I think we are?"

What I wouldn't give for some holy water. But as I rummage around, I come across a glint of silver and close my fingers around it. The necklace little Alice gave me, the one she got from Miss Bennett. I slide my thumb over the crucifix, straighten up, and slip the chain about my neck. It's as good a form of protection as we've got. Only then do I work up the nerve to look at Preston, prepared for a fight even if my stomach hurts at the thought.

"Something happened here last night, didn't it?"

Preston pauses, opens his mouth, hesitates. "Nothing that we're capable of fixing."

"You don't know that."

"I *do* know that! Benji, if you had seen what I saw…"

I cut him off. "Were there other people in the house?"

He stills. "I… What?"

"You and the others were looking for staff in the rest of Carlton's house. Did you find anyone?" The look of shame that passes over his face is answer enough. I frown. "And you just left them there."

Preston's jaw clenches. He lifts his hands, shoving them through his hair. "What was I to do, hm? Drop you on the floor to evacuate the house? Tell the ghosts to hold a moment so I could tend to other matters? Would you have rather I left you at the mercy of Hugo and the others while I went back inside alone?"

No. None of those things would have been an option; I can hardly fault him for any of that, can I? "But you thought it appropriate to lie to me about it after the fact."

Preston's shoulders slump as his gaze darts away. "I was in shock from the whole thing. I didn't know if you were dying or injured or... All I could think about was getting you out of there. The ghosts were everywhere! It wasn't that I wanted to lie to you, I just wanted to protect you from the truth. You'd have only blamed yourself."

Some of my anger ebbs just a bit, edged out by a feeling of guilt. Can I fault him entirely, I wonder, when I have my share of secrets that I've kept because I felt I was protecting *him* by doing so? I think of the bruises that have almost entirely healed upon my arm. I think of Edwin Davies, of the ghost of Oscar Frances, and the weight of that secret I shouldered for the remainder of my time at Whisperwood and beyond. All because I knew that Preston—Spencer, too—would only be hurt by such a revelation with no balm to soothe it.

"I cannot say I wouldn't have done something similar in your shoes." I touch a hand to his arm. "Preston, you are the one person in my life I trust to always be honest with me. If I can't rely on you, then who's left?"

His mouth drops open, but anything he might think to say does not form on his lips. I let my hand fall away as I turn to head down the road for Carlton's.

It takes a moment, but Preston follows on my heels. He doesn't speak, and perhaps that's better. Any apology he might make right now would be insincere. Guilt he may feel, but he also certainly believes he did the right thing in trying to protect me. I won't concern myself with our issues right now. I want to get into Carlton's house and find out what happened.

"Who was left behind?" I ask.

Preston says, "A maid. Dark hair, freckles. Feisty thing. Philip had her tied up in the kitchen."

Tied up… Lord almighty. I pray she managed to free herself and flee the house.

"Were you able to find out if he has any other members of staff that might be on the premises?"

"She said a gardener comes every Friday and Wednesday, and a cook who comes around six in the morning."

One dead man, one maid, and possibly one cook. Assuming one of the latter two has not already summoned the police to the premises.

It's for that reason I tread carefully as we near Mr. Carlton's property. Yet standing there on the side of the road, looking across the grass and driveway leading to his home, I see nothing out of the ordinary. No police wagons, no men milling about, no nothing. It looks as still and quiet as it did last night. I'm uncertain as to whether that is a good thing or a bad thing. The presence of others would at least suggest the ghostly force we unleashed last night had dissipated on its own.

But I sense it, even if I cannot immediately see or hear it.

A weight bears down on my chest as we begin our trek up the gravel driveway. In an upper-storey window, a figure passes by the glass, curtains fluttering in its wake. A second figure passes in another window, just as shadowy as the first.

My heart lurches into my throat. I stop and clutch at my chest, the heaviness in the air stifling. It's so cold my lungs burn. Even Preston seems to feel the wrongness of it, because he touches the door and jerks his hand back as though burned. He rubs the pads of his fingers together and looks askance at me. "All right?" he asks.

That is a very good question. "Stay close to me."

"That ought to be my line." He cuts a thin smile, grasps the doorknob, and pushes the door open to step inside.

The sun is up and yet the moment we enter Mr. Carlton's home, it may as well be midnight. Every inch of light seems to be swallowed whole. And the shadows...

Oh, the shadows.

I recall an afternoon that feels a lifetime ago, seated before Miss Bennett for the first time, her hands clasping mine and Preston's. The swarm of darkness that had blanketed my vision as she showed us what she sees every day. I had never seen so many ghosts in one place...until now.

They flicker in and out of view in my periphery. Some are faceless blots of ink, scarcely human-shaped. Some move like smoke. Some look more solid and humanoid. Or, well, like corpses that once were human, sometimes with limbs that look too thin or too long, curved, gnarled fingers and gaunt, hollowed-out faces and dark pits where their eyes used to be. A woman, skeletal and naked, crawls across the ceiling. A man stands facing the wall at the base of the stairs, head bowed. He whispers to himself, hurried and desperate, edging on angry.

My hands are clammy and shaky, but I dare not release my hold on Preston. He squeezes my fingers tighter.

We head for the kitchens, stopping in the doorway. I spy the chair the maid must have been tied to, with the rope cut and coiled on the floor. No living person in sight. Perhaps she freed herself and fled. Perhaps someone else showed up and set her loose. Whatever the case may be, I pray they made it out safely.

Bang.

We whirl toward the sound, heads lifted.

It came from upstairs, I think.

Bang.

Again. Nothing more than a sharp thud.

Bang, bang, bang.

My heart is three seconds away from leaping from my chest. Preston does not try to stop me as I lead him for the stairs. We skirt around the angry dead man muttering, watching him cautiously, just in case he diverts his attention to us. A woman shambles down the stairs as we ascend, her dress as torn as her throat. She pays us no mind, but her arm brushes mine and I cannot help but gasp at how the cold burns through my coat.

Upstairs looks no different. Dark. Even through the open doors, very little light shines through. The gas lamps upon the walls are lit, but even their flicker seems to have trouble penetrating the shadows.

Preston stops me. I'm uncertain if it's fear I hear in his voice, but it's certainly nerves. "Benji. Are you sure? The girl isn't here…"

"We don't know that yet," I insist. "A bit further. Please."

He relents. Nods. Begins to walk away, insisting on taking the lead with me just behind him.

Lord, please do not let me regret this decision.

My own nerves notch up and up as we approach the door leading into Carlton's study. I was unconscious during his death; I don't even know how he died, though I can make an educated guess—a guess whose name is Hugo. Some part of me wishes to avert my eyes and not look at what remains of him, and yet, it would be selfish. Unfair. His fate is partly my own fault. I deserve to see the consequences of my choices and actions.

Bang.

Preston and I stop just outside the ajar door. Is it coming from here? He lifts his free hand, hesitates, peers through the crack, and then pushes his way inside.

He swears. I budge in beside him to see what he sees.

Or rather, what he *doesn't* see.

Mr. Carlton's body is not there. Only a dark stain upon the rug remains with the scent of blood and death permeating the air.

"*Oh,*" I gasp. "That's not good."

"Bit not good," Preston agrees. He tries to laugh, but the sound comes out high and uncertain.

Bang.

It hasn't stopped. It isn't coming from the study, but further down the hall.

I almost tell Preston to nevermind, that we ought to leave. I open my mouth to do just that as we exit, but I cut myself off when I see the ghost of Ellie in the hallway, lingering outside another door at the end. She watches us, one skinny arm lifting and pointing.

For half a second, I'm standing outside of Whisperwood, watching William Esher shamble his way toward the cemetery, pointing at the cemetery. As unresponsive as a ghost himself.

I shake off the memory and drag in a breath. Steady on.

Ellie vanishes into the shadows as we approach.

Bang.

The door stands wide open, giving us an easy view inside the bedroom. Everything is a mess. It appears to be Mr. Carlton's room—likely the bed Crane dragged him from in the dead of night.

Bang.

And, standing before a towering wardrobe, is Carlton himself.

He's still in his dressing gown, one shoulder and sleeve darkened with blood. He's slumped forward against the armoire doors, slamming the heel of his hand against the door.

Bang.

I cannot breathe.

What did Esher's book say about this? About dealing with a dead man. No—he and Spencer dealt with the living possessed by spirits. Not reanimated corpses, right?

Preston doesn't give me a chance to think of what to do, and for once, I am grateful because my mind has blanked. He steps back, drawing me with him, slow and easy.

Then a floorboard beneath our feet creaks. Carlton stills. We freeze, breaths held in silent prayer. The dead man turns. His eyes are milky white, his jaw slack. He surveys us for no more than a second—nowhere near enough time for us to decide on whether we ought to run or remain still and quiet.

The dead man lets out an ear-piercing, unholy shriek. He lunges across the room, closing the distance between us before I can process what's happening. Preston's reflexes are better; he shoves me back, putting himself between the corpse and me. My back slams into the door frame while Preston grabs for Carlton's outstretched arms. They hit the ground in a tangle of limbs. It doesn't matter that Carlton is half Preston's size. Preston is having difficulty keeping him at bay; Carlton is all gnashing teeth and grasping, twisted fingers.

I cannot think.

What do I do?

What would Spencer do? Esher?

Miss Bennett?

Preston.

I promised his sisters I would keep him safe.

Alice...

My hand flies to the crucifix around my neck. I yank it from around my head and throw myself at Carlton's side, shoving the metal to his cheek. There's a rite of exorcism I ought to be reciting, but I wouldn't begin to know the words. In my panic, I fumble helplessly for any prayer that comes to mind, something I can hear in Mother's voice.

"O, my Lord and Saviour, in your arms I am safe. Keep me and I have nothing to fear. Give me up and I have nothing to hope for. I do not know what will come upon me before I die. I know nothing about the future, but I rely upon you—"

From the moment the cross touches his skin and I begin to speak, Carlton jerks his head to the side, trying to distance himself from me. He slams Preston to the ground and then scrambles off him. Concern overtakes me and I make the mistake of halting my prayer. Carlton swipes out in that moment, knocking the crucifix from my grasp. It clatters to the floor several feet away, lost to the darkness beneath the bed.

He's on me a second later, a bony hand locked around my throat. I choke in as deep a breath as I can before his grip tightens and blocks my airways. Preston is on him, trying to drag him off me. I grab at his wrist, attempting to pry his fingers loose. I may as well be trying to bend iron.

I try to cry out. The sound does not make it past my lips. Instead, I squeeze my eyes shut.

Even behind my closed eyelids, I cannot seem to escape the dead. Instead of Carlton looming over me, I see the ravaged face of a spirit, angry and...frightened?

Are you afraid? I want to ask.

The emotions are all-encompassing, difficult to place into words. It is nothing and yet everything at once. Fluctuating emotions from one second to the next. The only word that comes to mind is *wrong*. It's all so very, very wrong.

Whatever is inside of Carlton, it does not belong there. *It needs to leave.*

The fingers around my neck twitch and then slacken just a bit. Just enough that I can gasp in a lungful of air. My eyes snap open. Carlton has gone still, face twisted into fury and frustration. Preston meets my gaze from over Carlton's shoulder and seems to sense what I mean with only a look: *wait.* He releases Carlton slowly, but does not venture far.

I uncurl my fingers from Carlton's wrist, lift a hand, and touch his face. My voice comes out hoarse. "You don't have to be afraid, but you can't stay here. It's time to go."

The dead man's eyes roll into his head. He rocks back, releasing me completely, and his mouth drops open. A shadow slides across him, away from him, with a sound not unlike a sigh.

Then his corpse slumps gracelessly to the floor and stills.

I cough, dragging in a few deep breaths. Did I do it? Did I truly drive the spirit away?

Preston stares at Carlton's body, his mouth agape in uncertainty. "What… What was that? What did you *do*?"

I push myself up to sitting. I'm shaking like a leaf. Am I afraid? Oddly enough, I'm not certain. I ought to be, but it's…something else I cannot pinpoint. Maybe it's shock. "I don't know. I just… I told whatever was inside of him that it needed to go and…and it *did*. It listened to me."

Miss Bennett had told me once: *You have a gift, if you would learn to harness it.* Was this what she meant? At the time, all I had wanted was for her to close whatever door existed in my head to make me normal. The idea of anything else had been too frightening. She had only given me a gentle, sympathetic smile and apologised, saying that it was not something she could do.

Preston opens his mouth to speak, but another voice intervenes. Small, quiet: "Someone out there?"

The wardrobe!

We pick ourselves up, shaky on our feet. Preston steps to the armoire and opens the door.

He promptly lets out a loud squawk as he's met with a broom to his face. "Hey——!"

The maid steps out from the closet, followed by a short, portly woman who looks just as shaken as I feel. Recognition dawns on the maid's face as she stares at Preston, and her expression darkens.

"It's you! You filthy, sonnuva—"

I step back. Maybe Preston deserves to get swatted in the face a few times. I wouldn't object if she turned that broom on me, either; we *did* abandon her here.

After she's got in a few good smacks and Preston has skittered back, swearing loudly in protest, I step forward to ask, "Are you all right?"

Both the maid and the cook turn their attention to me.

"Fine," the maid says, still brandishing her weapon. "No thanks to all of you."

The cook wavers. "Was it you who killed Mr. Carlton?" she asks, eyes darting nervously to the body on the floor like she expects it to get back up again.

The answer to that is complicated. No, yes, not really but some of the blame is ours? I'm not certain.

"We didn't kill him," Preston insists, rubbing at his face and glowering at the broom. "Those people were our captors too. We escaped and came back here to make sure you were safe."

The two women cast furtive glances about the room. I don't think they can see the ghosts like we can, but it's apparent by their wide eyes and the cook's trembling that they can feel the wrongness of it all.

"Let us see you both outside," I say.

They don't argue this; in fact, they appear more than happy to scurry out into the hall, putting whatever distance they can between us and Carlton's corpse. I retrieve the crucifix from where it landed on the floor, and then we escort the women to the front door. They step into the sunlight, blinking and squinting, no doubt confused by the sudden onslaught of brightness where the house was still swathed in darkness.

The maid turns back to us. "Wait, you're going back in there? What are you two going to do?"

"We're going to see if we can't fix the house." I pause, unsure how else to word that. "So that what happened with Mr. Carlton doesn't happen again. Will you wait for us out here, just for a bit?"

The pair glance at each other. Although the cook looks ready to turn and run the first chance she gets, the younger girl shrugs. "For a bit."

Preston and I head back inside. It's possible they could leave, run off to a neighbour's down the road. But even if they chose to, it would take them time, and likely we'll be well and gone before any law enforcement can arrive.

Preston lingers close to me. "What do we do now?"

I look up at him. "None of these spirits belong here. If I was able to dismiss one of them, do you think I can do the same with the rest?"

He cracks a slight grin that I think is meant to be encouraging. "Don't see why not. If you think it's safe."

I don't know how safe it is, but that honestly isn't the foremost thought in my mind. The spirit inside of Carlton had been so pained, so *tortured*, that I cannot stand the thought of simply leaving them all here like this. Besides, who else will they hurt when others come into the house? It's only a matter of time. And yet, the house is so full of the dead right now that I don't even begin to know where to start, either.

Preston takes my hand and squeezes, watching me. Waiting.

After a spell, I bolster my courage and venture further into the room. The shadows roil around us, restless, anxious. I look up at the woman on the ceiling, crucifix clutched tight, and I tell her this is not where she belongs and it's time for her to go. I repeat it three, four times, and each time she recoils and hisses, but then she melds with the darkness and her eyes close, and I think I see a sense of…even if not peace, perhaps reluctant resignation pass over her features before she vanishes from view.

I move to the next.

I could not possibly address every spirit individually, but I look in the eyes of any who will—or can—look into mine and I tell them this isn't where they belong. That they've moved past this realm, or this world, or whatever separates the living from the dead, and they'll find no happiness here amongst us.

Each and every ghost slips away like a sigh, some easier than others. The angry man near the stairs charges us when we address him, all rage and bared, blackened teeth and fiery red eyes, but I clutch the crucifix tight and repeat the words louder while Preston begins to pray aloud, and the creature is finally reduced to nothing more than a whimper as he shrinks into the dark.

By the time we advance upstairs, my chest is pinched tight and my vision has begun to blur. I press on, unwilling to leave this job half finished. Just a little further. Surely, the worst of it is behind us now. I will fix whatever it is Nathaniel Crane and I broke. It's the only way I can make amends.

The room where Carlton died feels the heaviest. Despite the broad windows behind his desk, everything is bathed in black, the air a murky, dusty grime so thick that it feels as though one needs to swim through it. Here, the creatures are darker and I wonder if they're drawn by the stench of death, the blood on the floor. A pair of red eyes that remind me of Nicholas

Mordaunt flash from the shadows. I wrap my fingers round the cross until the metal feels like a part of my skin. I speak loud and clear, unwavering. Even when the room has begun to brighten, I'm not so sure if I've truly cleansed it or if I've simply sent some of them away and others scurrying into hiding…for now. But without Miss Bennett, without Esher and Spencer's guidance, this is all I know to do.

We save the bedroom for last. The corpse is still on the floor. What a relief. Standing over him is the visage of Ellie, her chin tipped down, murky eyes watching him. She's given us a fright more than once now, yet I feel nothing but sympathy for her. I release Preston's hand and step around the body to stand before her, though she doesn't so much as lift her head to regard me.

"Was he truly your husband?" I try to read the lines of her face. Is she sad? Is she relieved? What sort of relationship did the two of them have? The way he spoke of her was not the way I would have thought a loving husband would speak of his wife. What had Crane meant, when he said Carlton left her behind? I recall how I felt when she grabbed me in the alley way, the sensation of trying to escape…

Every time we get more answers, more questions reveal themselves.

"Should you send her away, too?" Preston asks. I hesitate and look over at him. Without even answering, he gives a faint smile. "Hm. This isn't where she wanted to go, is it?"

"She wants to be near the sea. Ellie, please, we want to help you, but you're going to have to help us." A pause. "And you'll need to show us how to open the box again."

This time, Ellie's dead eyes slowly roll up to look at me. She does not speak, but she turns and walks out of the room, all disjointed, stiff movements. By the time we step out after her, she is nowhere to be found.

The house feels…perhaps not as it was, but better by leaps and bounds. I feel half a ghost myself as we return downstairs. My limbs are heavy and the room spins a bit, but I stave it off as best as I can.

Outside, the cook has taken a seat on the front steps and the maid is pacing the walkway before her. She stops, head snapping up, while the cook twists around to look at us.

"The house ought to be safe now," Preston announces. "Don't suppose you'd give us an hour or two before summoning the police?"

The maid scowls. "You murdered my employer and you want me to help cover for you while you make a run for it?"

"I told you, *we* didn't kill him. We chose to come back to help," Preston insists.

She sighs. "Fine. An hour, is all. Poor man deserves to be treated with dignity. Not that I've got any idea what to tell the police when they get here. No one's going to believe a dead man chased us through the house."

I offer her a smile. "You're smart. I'm sure you'll think of something. But before we go… How long have you worked for Mr. Carlton, Miss…?"

"Mildred." She sniffs and gestures to the cook. "This is Tabby. We both been working here for about two years now."

"Miss Mildred," I nod. "Then, did you ever perchance meet Carlton's wife, Ellie?"

For the first time since I've laid eyes on her, Mildred's expression twitches into something other than annoyance. Her mouth downturns and her eyes soften. "Course we knew her. She was a nice lady. Very quiet."

"And their marriage, was it happy?"

"Scarcely woulda called it a marriage myself," Mildred says. "Ellie lived up north a ways, in a little town on the coast. Mr. Carlton rode through, took a shine to her, and after he'd put a child in her belly, she didn't have much choice but to come live with him. That's all I really know."

Preston frowns. "They have a child?"

"*Had.* A little girl. She passed about six months after she was born," Tabby says regretfully. "Mrs. Carlton was beside herself. Never was the same after that."

No, I imagine she wouldn't be. How horrible. "After that, what happened?"

Mildred shrugs. "The pair of them packed up for a trip out your way. You know, England." She gestures vaguely at us. "Not sure where or why, other than Mr. Carlton said he knew of a man who might be able to 'help.' That was all he said on it. When he returned, he returned alone."

That was what Crane had meant, then. Carlton left her behind, somewhere in England, for reasons unknown to us. I want to inquire more, yet my mind has begun to slow to a crawl and the fatigue is rapidly catching up with me. I want to sit down. I close my eyes, willing the dizziness away. Preston's hand comes to rest against my elbow, steadying me. His voice, addressing the women, comes across tinny and far away.

"You mentioned somewhere up north. Any idea where?"

"*Punta de los Reyes*, she called it," Tabby says. "'Bout a day or two straight up the coast, I believe."

Up the coast. Near the ocean. *Yes.* We finally have a destination to aim for.

Preston gives my arm a gentle squeeze. "Thank you for your help. We'll be on our way. You two will be all right on your own?"

"Well enough," Mildred says, though there's a sour note to her tone. "Though suppose we're both technically unemployed now, thanks to those acquaintances of yours. Go on, off with you, so Mr. Carlton doesn't have to lie up there any longer than necessary."

We bid them farewell and start off across the property, skipping the driveway in favour of crossing the fields instead. Every step is an exercise in willpower for me now. If I can just make it to the carriage, I might lie down for a spell and sort myself out.

Halfway there, the vertigo becomes too great. One moment I'm walking and the next my feet are tangling with each other, and the ground is swiftly rising to meet my face.

19
PRESTON

ENJI'S WORDS BEGAN to sound off the moment we exit the house. Slightly slurred, halting, as though he can't quite get them to fit together properly. He pinches the bridge of his nose, closes his eyes, and I see the exhaustion stretch across his face.

The way his steps slow as we walk across the property clues me into the fact that he may not make it far. So when he stumbles and falls, I'm prepared, catching him in my arms and easing him to the ground.

"Benji?"

"I'm all right." He presses his hands flat across his eyes. All the colour has fled his face and his fingers tremble. "I'm sorry, I'm just...a bit tired, is all."

"Can't imagine why." I try to keep my tone light, belying my concern. "We've got a bit. Let's rest here a moment until you feel like walking again."

"Thank you."

I settle upon the grass with Benji's head in my lap. His eyes remain shut and I keep quiet, wanting to grant him some silence to settle himself. I think to offer to carry him, but he'd no doubt wave me off, possibly even force himself to walk again before he's ready. Patience, right? I ought to learn a bit more of that.

After a few moments tick by, once Benji has opened his eyes again and the pallor has left his face, I look down at him and say, "I'm sorry."

He blinks once. "For what?"

"For lying about Carlton. It wasn't fair of me, but honestly, I'm not sure I can promise I wouldn't do it again. There's little I wouldn't do to keep you safe, Benji."

A small smile tugs at his mouth. "I know." He reaches for my hand, lacing our fingers together. There's a pause at the end of his words, a breath, as though he wants to add onto it, to say something, but his gaze diverts and whatever it is remains unspoken.

We remain like that for another fifteen minutes, until the worst of Benji's vertigo has subsided and he can get to his feet. By the time we reach the carriage, he seems to be feeling a little more like himself, albeit still tired. I convince him to stay inside the carriage to lie down and rest while I drive us to the nearby town of San Mateo. Significantly smaller than San Francisco, but no less dizzying to navigate.

There, we locate a general store to ask for advice on how to get to Punta de Los Reyes. The clerk procures a map, pointing to a spot directly north of San Francisco, a sprawling peninsula with a tiny town labelled *Point Reyes Station*.

"Not much up there but a few dairy farms," he says with a shrug. "You'll wanna head up through San Francisco and take the ferry across the bay."

Benji grimaces, a sentiment which I share. I stare down at the map. While it's true backtracking through San Francisco would be the most effective route timewise, it would also succeed in placing us far too close to Nathaniel Crane and his people. The city is large, but he seems to have a talent for finding us.

I point to where the bay extends down to San Mateo itself. "Can we cross the bay here instead? Then head north?"

The clerk arches his eyebrows and scratches his head. "Sure, you could. Makin' the trip a lot longer than it needs to be, though. Maybe head across, then north to Berkeley, but then you'd be taking another boat across there."

Benji and I exchange looks. We thank the clerk, grab a few supplies, and head for the docks. The detour is going to add a good two days to our trip—and that's assuming any ferries capable of taking our horse and carriage across are available in a timely manner.

As it stands, the only ferry left for the day has room for a horse, but no carriage.

"We don't technically need it," Benji says to me. "We can leave it now. We'll move faster without it, anyway."

True, though it also means we're out a place to sleep if we find ourselves stuck overnight outside. And given the cold and the rain here, that isn't an ideal situation. I sigh. "When's the next ferry with room for a carriage?"

"Tomorrow afternoon, looks like. If they got space."

Too long, I think. Every hour we stay here is an hour that could put Crane closer to finding us, if he's smart enough to check back at Carlton's place then search the nearby town. "Two tickets, then, please. And transportation for the horse."

Tickets obtained, we unhook the horse from the carriage and lead her to the waiting ship. By some small miracle, we find a dock worker willing to trade the cab for a small fee and a saddle for Rogue; it's a great bargain for him, and some extra money in our pockets.

Benji cautions me against eating before we board the boat and it's a good thing, too. The boat isn't as small as some of the passenger-only ferries we see on the water, but it's significantly smaller than the steamship we took from England, which means the choppy waters of the bay toss it about like a toy in a tub, and I spend the duration slouched over the railing with Benji rubbing my back in sympathetic circles.

At least the trip isn't terribly long. We fetch Rogue and set about finding lodgings in Ocean View, a subset of Berkeley, for the night.

The small town of Ocean View is filled with saloons and shops and businesses overlooking the bay. A newsboy on the corner shouts about the coming transcontinental railroad line being constructed to link Oakland to Berkeley, and peddlers galore try to stop us as we lead Rogue down the street in search for a hotel that might also be able to house our companion.

We find an inn just off the waterfront. More expensive than I'd like, but given our last several nights, I think we could use a little pampering. The money we received for the carriage more than covers it. We have Rogue housed in their stables, stuff ourselves at their restaurant, and by the time the sun is going down, we drag ourselves up to our room and all but fall into our respective beds without so much as bothering to undress.

As I lie there in the darkness, I become aware of how badly my entire body aches. A combination of exhaustion, lack of proper sleep, stress, and physical exertion, I suppose. All that heaving on the boat likely didn't help matters. Here I always thought myself to be in peak physical health; this trip might be proving me wrong. If I'm this worn out, I can't even imagine how Benji is feeling. He's never been the physical sort.

I look through the darkness at him across the room, nostalgia from our days at Whisperwood settling in as I study his sleeping face. He looks terribly unkempt, his hair a tousled mess, clothes dirty and rumpled, one arm hanging gracelessly off the side of the bed and his lips parted. He's beautiful. Just watching him makes me smile.

I fall asleep without quite meaning to. One moment, my eyes are on Benji, and in the next I'm opening them again and staring at his empty bed. The sudden switch is jarring. I suck in a breath, disoriented, twisting my head until I spot him standing at the window.

He's got himself changed into a clean nightshirt. Or, well, as clean as any of our things presently are. He has a brush in hand and has tried to tame his soft curls, though at the moment he is still and silent as he gazes through the glass. For half a second, I worry something is wrong. He looks to me and smiles when I sit up.

"Did I wake you? I'm sorry. I was having difficulty sleeping."

"No, you didn't wake me." I wince, stretching out my arms until my shoulders pop. My bandaged one could do with new dressings about now, too. "Everything all right?"

"Yes. I think." A pause. "No… Actually, I have a confession to make, and an apology."

Oh. I rub my hands over my face and jaw, noting the stubble there, how badly I'm in need of a shave. "In the middle of the night…?"

He lowers his gaze, running a thumb over the bristles of his brush. "It can wait, if you'd rather."

I have a knot of tired dread in my belly. Now that I

know there is something to be said, I can't very well sleep now. "No, no. I'm listening."

He places the brush aside and has a seat on the edge of his bed, sighing. "Here I've been harping at you about being overprotective and keeping secrets, and yet... I've been doing the same to you. For quite a while now."

A long silence settles over the room. I wait patiently, letting him approach this at his own pace, no matter how much anxiety has begun to course through my veins. Benji stares down at his hands, shoulders slumped, a weight present there that I feel I've seen before.

Finally he says, "Remember how we wondered who it was that sold out Frances to the Headmaster?"

My heart about stops.

"...It was Edwin Davies. He found the letter Oscar wrote to Mr. Hart and gave it to Simmons."

Of all the things I expected, this was not one of them.

This is a secret that is years old. A secret related to someone we both held dear. I swallow hard but cannot seem to find the words.

Benji continues, "He thought Frances would simply be scolded and spoken to."

"And you didn't..." I flounder, somewhere between furious and confused and hurt, old grief being dredged to the surface from where I've buried it. Angry tears prick my eyes and I blink them back. "You just decided to carry it on your shoulders alone all these years and keep us in the dark. James and I deserved to know!"

"You did," he quickly agrees. "But what would you have done with the information? Either you and Spencer would have spent the rest of our time at Whisperwood biting back your rage every time you laid eyes on Davies, or else you would have done something that would have got you expelled—or worse."

He's right. He is absolutely right. I'm not sure if that makes it better or worse. Am I angry with him? I don't know that I am. My anger is directed elsewhere, at a boy who we took in as one of our own. A boy who should have had Oscar France's back, not been turning him over to our prick of a headmaster. "How did you find out?"

"I pieced it together, knowing Davies the way that I did. He had a habit of spilling secrets." He hesitates. "And I was the one who told him that I'd not permit him to have anything to do with helping us with Mordaunt. I refused to let him try to assuage his own guilt and find some sense of self-redemption. Maybe I was just being spiteful."

"I don't know that you have a spiteful bone in your body."

He laughs like he's not so sure about that. I think back to every time I saw Edwin Davies after the conclusion of our third year. I'd already been furious with him for supposedly abandoning all of us when we stayed behind to help James and Esher. The anger had dulled to apathy after a while, to where whenever I saw Davies, he scarcely registered as someone that ought to have mattered. Yet the way he'd inch to the edges of the halls to avoid coming close, sitting clear across the room in classes we shared, had grated on my nerves. He'd acted as though *I* had wronged *him*. Now I know why. He no doubt spent that last year at Whisperwood wondering if I knew his secret, waiting for the day I'd corner him about it. I wonder if Benji anticipated that reaction. I wonder if that had anything to do with his decision. Maybe he *is* a touch spiteful after all.

Benji still doesn't look at me. He tugs at the hem of his sleeve, running the fabric between thumb and forefinger, studying it as though it's the most fascinating thing in the room. "Can you forgive me?"

I was so busy thinking how badly I want to strangle Edwin Davies that I'd almost forgotten about Benji's role in this.

Am I angry with him?

No, I'm not certain that's the word. It's far more complicated than that.

I sigh. Everything feels more complicated now, doesn't it? Benji. Me. Life. "You know, I used to be under the impression that you and I had this picturesque relationship. That we knew everything about one another, that I understood you more than any other person alive. I thought nothing could surprise me with you, because we trusted each other so implicitly." A pause. "And then you were keeping things from me and I've kept things from you, and you've surprised me so much on this trip. Ever since you decided to accept that job from your father, I've had no idea where we stand with one another. Nothing has made sense."

I've kept reaching for a sense of that old normalcy, for a time where the world orbited around just Benjamin and me. Where our afternoons were spent among friends but still, truly, focused on one another more than anything else. Where the future felt uncertain, but I had been confident it would involve Benji at my side and so nothing else mattered. Back then, everything was *simple.*

Now, every day feels raw and unpredictable, and not in a way that I much like.

I wonder if this is what it means to grow up.

Benji's smile is a sad one and it suggests he agrees with me. "We've got so caught up in keeping one another safe that we've stripped each other of our autonomy to make our own choices, I think."

"And what do we do about that?" I ask.

He draws in a slow breath. "We…learn from our mistakes, I suppose. We start trusting one another. Something I've always admired about Esher and Spencer is the way they lean on one another. They have this…this unshakeable trust in the other's ability to handle the truth. At least, that's how it comes across."

I know for a fact that James and Esher's relationship is more complex than that, but I understand where Benji is coming from. I've witnessed it too. I noticed it even at Whisperwood, but even more during the weeks I spent at Aunt Eleanor's prior to taking on this job. The way James and Esher doted on one another, the way they bickered, the way they frustrated each other and made each other smile and every intricate little thing that only seemed to make them stronger together… It was fascinating to watch.

I study Benjamin, wondering if he made the comparison for a reason, my chest tight with the weight of it. "Except that you and I… We aren't what James and Esher are."

Finally, Benji lifts his head to meet my gaze, unwavering. Present is the remnant of a boy freshly shoved into the mud from what feels like a lifetime ago, but there's more than that now. I wonder when it was that Benji stopped being so afraid to make choices on his own and began to take his own confident steps forward. Where was I, and has my over-protective streak been holding him back?

He asks, "Aren't we?"

I swallow the lump in my throat, not trusting my voice. "That's up to you, Benjamin. It's always been up to you."

A soft, almost sad laugh escapes his lips. "Have you really been waiting on me to say the word all this time?"

"You had more to lose than I did," I point out. My mother and father know, after all, about my feelings for Benjamin. They have for years. It may not be something we speak much of, but they *know*, and it never stopped them from taking Benji in and treating him like a member of the family.

But Benji? Oh, he's felt out of place all his life, what with an absent father and immigrant mother, his mixed heritage, his ability to see ghosts. Never did I want to place one more thing on his shoulders that made him feel further isolated. He has followed me everywhere all the years we've known one another.

But with this? With *us*? I wanted—no, I *needed*—him to make that first step.

I wish I knew what he was thinking in this moment. I wish he would tell me. But Benji sits there, silent and still, watching me as though he's truly seeing my face for the first time and does not know what to make of it. Every insecurity and worry I've had over the years digs its claws in deep, every time I almost told him how I felt... Surely, he *knew*, but to actually speak it aloud was something else altogether. Perhaps I was wrong. Perhaps I've truly misjudged everything all this time, and Benji has just been too kind, too non-confrontational, to correct me.

When he rises to his feet, my heart about stutters to a stop. He closes the gap between us, the only sound the soft shift of his nightshirt sliding against his skin as he moves. My entire body is wound tight in anticipation, a coiled spring ready to be let loose.

He touches my cheek, fingertips finely tracing along my jaw. The pad of his thumb brushes the shape of my lower lip in a way that makes a shiver cascade down my spine. I remain still, heart in my throat, afraid that if I move or try to speak, it will scare him off.

Finally, *finally*, Benji leans down and presses his mouth to mine.

If there was ever a moment I was born for, it was this.

One of us makes a noise that sounds suspiciously like a whimper, and I think it may be me. I can't help but slip my arms around his middle, dragging him closer, unable to think of anything beyond how badly I have wanted this for so many years. Benji's hands are in my hair. His fingers curl there, nails pleasantly grazing my scalp, even as his lips are parting and he's shifting closer still, into my lap, every movement careful as though he had every inch of it planned out before he even stood up to approach me.

He draws back, breathing in deep, yet still so close that I can feel the warmth of the words against my lips when he speaks.

"We will keep each other safe," he murmurs, "but we will do so honestly. No more secrets. Promise?"

In this moment, I would promise him the moon if he asked for it. And I would move Heaven and Earth to give it to him too. "I promise."

We lie down, blankets drawn high around us, limbs tangled together and Benji's head against my chest while I slide my hands through his hair in a way I've longed to properly do for far too many years.

20
BENJAMIN

PRESTON IS WATCHING me when I wake. His eyes are heavy and his mouth pulls into a slow smile when I look at him, rogue strands of dark hair obscuring my vision. I smile back at him.

"Good morning," I whisper. Memories of last night come inching back to the forefront of my mind. Preston's large, gentle hands holding me and his mouth against mine... I do not know where my sudden burst of courage came from to do something so bold as kissing him, but it seems to have worked out well enough. I should have done it years ago instead of being so afraid of what he might say, of how alienated it might make me in a world where I already felt so different. Now I only feel a sense of peace and calm and completion I had not been aware I could possess, as though the stars have appropriately aligned themselves.

"Morning." He brushes that hair away from my face, allowing his fingertips to find their way across my temple, down my cheek. "Sleep well?"

"Quite. Better than I have in a while, I think." And I've no immediate interest in getting out of bed just yet. Instead I drift closer, nestling into the warmth of Preston's arms. I press my face into the crook of his neck and breathe deep.

For a bit, he strokes my hair and back. "We ought to be getting up if we want a meal before we leave."

"Must we…?"

He chuckles. "We'll miss our ferry otherwise."

Ah. Right. We do have a boat to catch, don't we? With the utmost reluctance, I drag myself from bed to get ready.

We do so in relative silence, but it's comfortable, easy, peaceful. I cannot recall the last time the air between us felt so relaxed, but it's been a very long while.

I don't know that I agree with Preston's sentiment that our relationship used to seem perfect. To me, there were all those unspoken things between us that kept it from being so. I was a boy who was content to allow his best friend to coddle him and shield him from the world, much like I was used to from my own mother. It wasn't fair to put that on Preston.

Now, more than ever, it's imperative that I stand on my own. That I am my own man even without Preston, so that he has a whole person to love.

I finish dressing before he does and watch him at the mirror, bent over the washbowl while scrubbing at his face. As he reaches for the shaving soap and razor, I must make some sort of a face that he spots in the reflection because he turns with his eyebrows raised.

"What's that look for?"

I bite at my lower lip. "Nothing. I was just thinking I rather fancied that look on you."

Preston grins and sets the razor aside. "Is that right?"

"It suits you," I confirm.

He crosses the small room and slides his arms around my waist, leans in, and buries his face against my throat. The gentle scratch of his unshaven jaw makes me laugh, and I shove half-heartedly at his shoulders.

"Stop that!"

"Oh, don't fancy it so much now, eh?"

"Well, it *is* itchy!" I pull back and smile up at him.

Preston's eyes dart down then. He reaches for the chain about my throat, sliding it through his fingers. "I had meant to ask where you got this. I don't really recall you wearing religious symbols before."

I smile, touching the crucifix briefly, before reaching behind my neck to unclasp the chain. "Alice, actually."

"My sister?"

"She said Miss Bennett gave it to her as a good luck charm to ward off spirits. What do you know, it worked at Mr. Carlton's place."

He chuckles, not resisting as I place the cross about his neck, admiring the flash of polished metal against his skin. "She didn't give me any good luck charms... Tsk."

"That's because she likes me better." I grin at the affronted look that passes over his face. "And I think she had hoped *I* would be your good luck charm. Sorry, I'm afraid I'm not much of one."

"Now *that* is a lie. You are the luckiest thing to ever happen to me."

When he makes to pull away, I find my fingers seeking out the front of his shirt to pull him back down to kiss me. How could I possibly let him say something so sweet and then just leave? Preston does not resist. He bows over me, dragging me to his chest. He has a way of holding me, of kissing me, so raw and deep that it steals my breath and makes my legs weak. When he finally draws away, I'm certain my face is several shades of red.

Once packed, we retrieve Rogue from the ostler and head for the docks to wait for our ferry. Preston grumbles a bit as we board. To his credit, he manages not to get sick this time. Though that doesn't stop him from spending the trip hunched over the railing like he might.

San Rafael, our city of deport, is bustling and inviting enough that I almost wish we could justify staying. But we've most of the day ahead of us and if the weather is on our side, we ought to be able to make it most of the way to Punta de los Reyes. Rain could slow us down, as could the condition of the roads. Plus, with Rogue carrying a double burden, we'll want to give her time to rest or take turns walking beside her. No one we stop to speak with is familiar enough with the area up north to know where the nearest town is, where we might find lodgings, or what roads might be the fastest.

In the end, we are making the trip half-blind, following the main road north-west and hoping for the best. *You'll know you're close when you see the trees*, one woman advises. *Trust me, you'll know 'em when you see 'em.*

We'd been baffled by that up until, some ten hours on horseback later, we find ourselves surrounded by the most massive trees I could have dreamed up. They dwarf everything around them. Preston, awestruck, stops to hop off the horse and go up to one. When he wraps his arms around it, he laughs.

"How many of me would it take, Benji?"

"Six of you, at least," I say with a wide smile. *This* is what I think Preston had hoped for when he embarked on this trip: a chance to see and explore new places, to find something unique and different. These woods most certainly fit that bill.

It's by that massive tree that we stop for an hour to have

lunch and let the horse graze. Our meal is little more than sandwiches and some dried apricots we got back in Berkeley, but it does the job of quieting my rumbling belly. Perhaps when we get to where we're going, we'll have time and the means to get ourselves a proper dinner.

Preston chews on a piece of jerky, lying on his back and gazing up into the thick canopy high, high above us. "What's it like out here for you, Benji?"

"For me?" I ask. "You mean with the spirits?"

He turns his head slightly to watch me. "Yes, that. You see them all the time in crowded places like cities, don't you? So, what's it like out here?"

I scan the area. There has never been a place where I *haven't* seen at least one ghost, even if only from the corner of my eye. Here is no different. I've seen shapes and shadows moving amongst the trees from time to time. Occasionally, a silhouette in the fog. Ellie has appeared more and more frequently the further North we go, always ahead on the road as though guiding our way.

"Nothing I've seen out here has felt malicious, so there's that. I suppose they feel…older."

"Older? How does a ghost feel older?"

"Oh, I don't know how to describe it. Like… The shape of them. The feel of them. People who belonged to this land long before those who live here now."

Preston *hmm*'s and scratches at his jaw. "Suppose we ought to show some respect and not anger any of them while we're here." He sits up, careful to pick up the remnants of our lunch and pack everything back into our bags before we're on our way.

We take our time more than we ought to, really. Distracted by the beauty, the scenery, the sound of birds, the occasional deer that crosses our path. A herd of massive elk we spot in the distance, whose cries resonate throughout the woods around us. We wind through twisting, forested hillsides and the road gets rocky, difficult to navigate here and there, and Rogue becomes more and more reluctant to press on, especially once we begin to lose our light.

I did have the foresight to bring along a lantern, which I ignite once the sun has begun to set. It's even darker in the woods, the tall red trees blocking out much of the sky. Our earlier excitement has begun to wane because what was fascinating before begins to hinder us when our visibility is decreased.

Lantern or not, the road becomes impossible to navigate. I can no longer see Ellie. We've surely got turned around at some point or taken a wrong turn. It smells like rain, and fog has begun to roll in from the coast, thick and stifling.

Do we stop, I wonder? Do we make camp and hope to keep warm through the night? We've got no supplies to make a fire, assuming we could find wood dry enough. I wouldn't know the first thing about it, though I suspect Preston would.

"We may be getting a bit lost," I say, hating the way my voice seems to get swallowed into the blackness around us.

"Just a bit further," Preston says. His tone is tight, uncertain. I decide not to argue with him about it.

It appears to be the right choice. Shy of an hour goes by when we see lights up the road. Faint, through the mist, but there. I could cry out in relief. Preston puts his heels to Rogue, coaxing her into a trot toward the source.

What I presumed was a farm is, in fact, a town. A very small town, and very dark. Only a few windows of the buildings are aglow, making them near impossible to see until we're right on them.

I see no obvious hotels or inns, but I do spot a sign hanging from a shop window that says *Rooms for rent.* I point it out to Preston and he draws Rogue off the side of the dirt street for me to dismount and approach the door. My legs and rear ache something fierce from riding on horseback all day.

I've no idea what the hour is, but the windows are still dimly lit so I hope I'm not waking whoever may be inside. I knock firmly but only twice, then try to smooth a hand down the front of my shirt, which is rumpled and dirty. After a spell, the door creaks open and a woman peers out.

"What is it?"

"I'm terribly sorry to come calling so late. My companion and I have just found our way into town and I worry we might be lost. Are we near Point Reyes Station?"

She squints. "Yep. Bit of a weird place to get lost. Not much else out here."

Oh, thank the Lord.

"Then we are, in fact, where we'd hoped to be. I saw your sign there—might you have a room available?"

The woman is a bit older, forties or fifties I'd wager. Though that's going by the lines of her face. Her hair is still a shade of pitch black, not a sign of grey to be seen. She looks me over once, almost suspiciously. Which I suppose is fair when two men show up at one's door this time of night.

"Or anything vacant, really. We'd be happy sleeping in a barn," jokes Preston, sliding off the horse.

The woman stares. "Got one of them, too, if you'd rather."

Preston laughs as though he's uncertain if she's joking. "Ah, a room would be lovely, if we could. We can pay."

"If you couldn't, you wouldn't be staying." She beckons us to follow her around to the back of the building, where she shows us to a small set of stables where we're permitted to put Rogue. Preston makes quick, practised work of removing her saddle and getting her some feed.

Inside, a fire is burning in the main room of the shop, which is lined with shelves and supplies for, I presume, trappers and hunters. It's blissfully warm, chasing the ache from my fingers as I scrub my hands together before the flames.

Our host's name is Paige and she brings us to a room upstairs that is much colder than downstairs but will still be notably warmer than sleeping outside. She leaves us to wash and dress, though thirty minutes later, she returns with a knock.

"Got food, if you're hungry."

"Bless." Preston opens the door.

Paige steps in, offering us each a bowl. It's stew, likely leftover from her own meal, and it smells strongly of meat. Venison, perhaps. But there are onions and potatoes and carrots, and I don't want to be rude by turning my nose up at her hospitality. We take a seat on our beds to eat, given the lack of anywhere else to sit. Rather than leave, Paige lingers there, watching with her arms folded.

"Where you two from?"

"England," I say between bites. "Though we've just come from San Francisco, if that's what you mean."

She shrugs. "Just makin' conversation. You're a long way from home."

"We are. And as such, do you think you could tell us about the area? Are we close to the ocean?"

"'Course. Can't you smell it? You can reach it all around the peninsula."

"And people live here, aside from this town?"

"Here and there. Couple of dairy farms, mostly. Might find a few people living illegally off patches of land."

"What about…" I pause. "What about the Natives? The ones who originally lived here?"

At that, she gives me an odd look. "Miwok. Not many of them left these days. My granddad was one. Passed when I was little, though."

I frown. "Where did they go?"

"Died, mostly. Forty, fifty years ago. Smallpox." She shrugs. "Couple families still around, but most left, trying to secure land elsewhere. Don't know beyond that."

That sounds…thoroughly depressing.

Preston appears to have completely cleaned his bowl. I've picked out the edible components of mine, so I offer him what remains and his face lights up.

"Sad," I murmur. So much for the idea of trying to find Ellie's people, if she had family in the area. "Then, where would the nearest access to the sea be?"

Paige snorts. "Ain't that a question. I'll draw up a map for you in the mornin'."

"Ah, yes, of course. Thank you kindly for supper, Miss Paige."

She bids us goodnight and leaves. Preston polishes off my food, too, then lays back on the bed with a heavy sigh. "I say, do you know what I miss?"

"Your mother's cooking?"

He laughs. "Yes. My mum's cooking. She made the best roasts... She could make a rabbit stew that was to die for."

"We shall have to ask her nicely to make it when we see her next." I smile.

Preston turns his head to watch me. "Will we be going back after this is done?"

A good question. "I had wondered that when we first embarked, but then we've had our hands full and it slipped my mind. Do you want to stay here...? Not *here*, here, but..." I gesture broadly.

"Well, there is certainly plenty to see. Although I do miss my family."

"Visiting is always an option," I say softly.

He scoots over to make room for me as I crawl in beside him, seeking out the warmth of being near. "Mm... What do you think? Honestly?"

Honestly? Oh, he's pinning me down with that word. Before, I'd have smiled and said whatever made him happy was fine by me.

"I'm afraid I don't know," I admit. "The idea of always traveling, of never having a place to call home...of being so far from family and friends. It seems sad to me. But there are worse things."

Preston raises his brows. "Like what?"

"Like being without you."

A hush falls over the room. Clearly, it was not what Preston had anticipated me to say, but it is the truth. I have no family left to speak of—my father not withstanding—and although I have Preston's family and Spencer back home, what good would any kind of stability be if I didn't have Preston in my life? His absence takes the shine out of the world.

When Preston doesn't speak, I shift uncomfortably. "What is it?"

"Nothing. That was just a bit of an admission." Preston reaches for my hand, lightly tracing his fingertips across my knuckles. "It was sweet."

I shrug, cheeks growing warm. "I was being honest."

Preston wraps his fingers around mine and gives my hand a tug, insistent, until I lean back into him and his arms come around my middle. He says nothing, but the way that he squeezes me, hugs me to him, says plenty that his silence does not. And I have no qualms with remaining right here in his arms, cheek against his chest, my eyes drifting closed.

I must be more comfortable than I thought, and far more tired. The next thing I'm aware of is waking to a dark room and finding myself lying down, Preston fast asleep beside me.

Something woke me.

Howling. The wolves.

I can hear them again. The sound makes my pulse thrum and my blood run cold.

I slide from bed and pad over to the window to peer outside. The trees and fog are so thick that even the nearly full moon does little to lend itself to visibility. I squint. I do not see Ellie. Are there wolves in these woods? Could I be hearing real wolves instead of the phantom ones that have followed us across the country? Given the crawling sensation across my skin, I sincerely doubt that's the case.

I steal a look at Preston, uncertain if I ought to wake him. We've slept so poorly lately and we did so much travelling that I'm loath to disturb him if I don't have to.

We're safe. We have to be. There is no way Crane's group would know to follow us here.

I crawl back beneath the covers, burrowing beneath them and pressing my face against Preston's shoulder. He grunts, shifts, slings an arm across my middle and nestles against my hair with a sigh. If I squeeze my eyes shut and put my hands to my ears, I can block out the worst of the howling. It picks up in intensity for several agonizing moments, to the point where I'm convinced that I'll not be able to sleep, and then it…stops.

I almost gasp in relief, my body going slack.

Peculiar.

"Benji," Preston mumbles, voice thick. "What is it…?"

"Nothing. Go back to sleep."

He yawns, and he must not be terribly awake because he doesn't argue with me. Before long, his breathing has slowed again and he's full and well asleep. It's all I can do to force myself to try to follow suit.

Somewhere in the recesses of my dreams, as I drift off again, I could swear I hear footsteps outside our door, followed by a low, threatening growl.

21
PRESTON

I 'VE SPENT SO much time on horseback at home that soreness after a day of riding is startling. But I wake with such a prevalent ache in my legs, back, and arse that I could laugh at myself. When I was a child, I could have handled it, no problem. As I've got older, spent more and more time away from home at school and such, I suppose I've gone a bit soft.

I had hoped a night in relative safety would see us both well-rested, but Benji looks like death warmed over as he drags himself out of bed this morning. He scrubs viciously at his face at the washbowl, then braces his hands against the worn wood of the table with a few deep breaths.

"Didn't sleep well?" I ask.

He shoves his damp hair back from his face and tries a smile on for size. "The wolves. I kept hearing them all night."

"Think that'll stop once we've found some peace for Ellie?"

"I certainly hope so. I can't figure out what else would be causing it."

I step over to take his shoulders and turn him around to face me. There are shadows beneath his eyes and a faint crease between his brows. Cupping his face in my palms, I smooth the pad of my thumb over that crease to smooth it out, and Benji's expression relaxes.

I murmur, "God willing, today should be the day. Then we can get the hell out of here."

He folds a hand over one of mine. "And go where?"

We never did reach a conclusion on that, did we? Though, I did fall asleep mulling it over in my head for the better part of an hour, long after Benji had drifted off in my arms. I have ideas, but I couldn't say which of them are any good.

"We'll worry about it a bit later, hm? One thing to deal with at a time." I bow down, pressing a kiss to his forehead. Benji makes a tired noise and despite his exhaustion, he accompanies me downstairs, the box in his rucksack slung over one shoulder, to greet Paige. She's puttering about her shop, dusting and stocking shelves. Already the shop door is open wide and a wooden sign hanging in the window has been flipped from *Closed* to *Open*.

She glances up at the sound of our steps. "Mornin'."

"Good morning," Benji greets, muffling a yawn against the back of his hand.

"Sleep all right?" She turns away again.

"Of course, thank you," I say, figuring it wouldn't do to rudely point out that Benji didn't sleep. It's hardly her fault.

"Left a map on the counter there for you. Drew it myself, but it ought to do the trick."

I retrieve the paper from the countertop and look it over. It's a crudely sketched drawing of the peninsula, with wiggling lines leading to what I assume are various access points to the sea. A bit difficult to follow, perhaps, but at least she's labelled a few landmarks for us to use along the way, and which roads are likely to be unsuitable for a horse and require us to travel on foot.

"We can't thank you enough, Miss Paige," Benji says. "We'll likely be staying another night or two, if it's all right."

"Ain't exactly got people kickin' down my door for them rooms. Help yourself."

We thank her and head out to the barn to fetch Rogue. She's well-rested and seems happy to see us, snuffling at Benji's hair when he comes near and nudging her nose into my shoulder. We get her saddled and head out.

The tiny town of Point Reyes Station is awake now, though still slow and quiet. We pass a bakery, whose smells wafting from inside are so tempting that I can't help but stop to let Benji run in and grab us a few treats to snack on throughout the day. Aside from Paige's store and the bakery, Point Reyes appears to have a couple of homes, a general store, and very, very little else. But the people are friendly enough, lifting their hands to wave as we pass by, and the weather—while cold and a little drizzly—isn't altogether bad. At least it isn't snowing. I wonder if they even get snow here.

We take the road Paige labelled Sir Francis Drake out of the town and into the peninsula, again surrounded by towering trees and hills with the scent of rain and ocean clinging to the air. Benji, riding behind me, breathes in deep. I can't see him without twisting around, but I can tell that he's smiling.

The further up the winding road we go, the thicker the fog rolls in until, just like last night, we're having difficulty seeing the path. I'm fairly certain we've missed a turn somewhere, or else Paige's map is *very* off.

"Can you see Ellie anywhere?" I ask with a sigh.

Benji looks around. "Haven't seen her at all today, no. Though that might be a turn, up there, perhaps?"

I think he's right. A road that veers off to the left. I study Paige's map, trying to pinpoint which trail it might be from the volley of squiggled lines. "I say, that doesn't look like 'Chimney Rock' to you, does it? Here?"

"If it is, we've gone a fair bit farther than we intended."

Likely, given that it's now well past midday, I think. Though the fog is thick enough and the sky overcast enough that pinpointing the location of the sun is not easy. By the rumbling of my belly, however, it is most certainly around or past lunchtime.

We could turn back and try for one of the trails we may have missed, or...we could continue. I loathe the idea of backtracking just yet, though I think we did pass a farm not too far back that may be able to give us directions.

Behind me, Benji shudders. His arms tighten around my waist. "Let's keep moving."

"What is it? What's wrong?"

"The wolves," he whispers. "Can't you hear them?"

I cover his hands with my own. It takes a moment, but the faint, distant howl reaches my ears, making the hair along the back of my neck stand on-end. But it's coming from behind us, not before us.

"Onward it is." I take up the reins again and give Rogue a nudge. She hesitates, craning her head around with her nostrils flaring, but then reluctantly starts forward.

The left-leaning trail is narrow and cluttered in comparison to the main road. Branches droop low. The path is worn by the passing of those before us, but it is nowhere near wide enough for a carriage. Maybe two horses to ride abreast— maybe.

It's darker here, as well. The sky has grown so thick with angry grey clouds and the canopy of trees obscures what little sunlight we might otherwise have got. Benji folds his fingers around my chilled wrist. I begin to notice the same shadows he must see: ghostly figures slipping in and out amongst the towering red and brown trunks. Never am I able to get a solid look at them. Always gone when I turn to look.

Except for one—the silhouette of a figure lying on the side of the road up ahead.

Benji gasps, and I realise what we're seeing isn't a ghost at all, but an actual *person* lying unconscious on the ground.

Swift and automatic, we slide out of the saddle. Benji remains with Rogue while I rush forward, crouching near the figure, though a feeling of dread makes itself known the moment I've begun to drop to one knee.

That mop of dark, curly hair certainly looks familiar, doesn't it?

It's the last thought that runs through my head before Nathaniel Crane rolls over and up and slams his fist into my face.

I topple back, more startled than anything. Crane is off the ground and atop me before I know what's happening. He fists a hand into the front of my shirt, the other striking me again. The punch whips my head to one side. Blood washes over my tongue. My vision blurs. Bastard hits bloody *hard*.

I hear the horse stamping her hooves and Benji trying to keep control of her. He either gives up and lets her go or manages to secure her to something, because in the next moment, I see him running for us. His approach is enough to make Crane rear back and off me, lifting a hand—his knuckles are split and bleeding where he punched me—to point at Benjamin.

"*You* stay the hell back," he snarls.

Benji drops next to me, his cold fingertips brushing my jaw. I wince and roll to my side. "Fuck…"

"That's for stealing my horse," Crane snaps. He moves around us, giving Benji a wide berth, and heads straight for Rogue. The horse has not been secured after all, but nor has she run off. Crane strokes her face and mane, looking her over as though ensuring we didn't hurt her somehow.

"You hit me because we took your *horse?*" I growl as I drag myself to my feet. "How in the hell did you even find us out here?"

Crane shoots us a dark scowl over his shoulder. "Your friends at Carlton's place said they directed you here."

Benji's eyes widen. He keeps close to me, holding onto my arm. "What? Why would they have… Did you threaten them?"

"Threaten is such an ugly word." He releases Rogue and turns to us. As he does so, he slides the revolver from its holster, thumbing back the hammer. "You also took my box. I thought we had a deal."

Benji tenses. Habit and instinct have me nudging him behind me. As much as he permits me to, anyway. "Tell me honestly, would your people have *really* let us go when you had what you wanted?"

"They're my people. They would've listened to my orders."

"Funny, because Hugo doesn't seem like he follows orders very well."

His mouth twists into a bit of a snarl, but clearly he doesn't have an argument for that because he remains furiously silent.

Benji pushes my arm aside to step forward. "Come with us."

Crane snaps his dark eyes to him. "What?"

"Come with us," Benji repeats. "We're headed for the beach now. All we want is to put Ellie to rest and then the notebooks are yours. As promised. Just me, you, and Preston, no one else."

His jaw clenches, yet he does not immediately turn down this request. "Why should I?"

"We're an even match, us two against you, aren't we?" As though to prove this point, he takes a step closer and watches as Crane takes a half-step back. Whatever it was Benji managed to do that knocked them both unconscious back at Carlton's seems to have stuck with Crane and he doesn't appear to be looking for a repeat performance.

Benji adds, "I don't trust Hugo as far as I can throw him. But I think... I think I trust *you* to keep your word."

That makes one of us. The only one who strikes me as even remotely trustworthy of the lot might be Sid.

Speaking of— "Where is the rest of your crew?" I ask warily.

"Nearby," Benji whispers. I glance at him. He doesn't dare take his gaze off Crane. "The howling. It really was Ellie trying to warn us."

Crane scowls, tongue swiping across his upper lip. "Maybe you should've listened to her, then."

Somewhere down the road, I hear hoofbeats. I grimace. Could we overpower Crane, take the gun, and escape? Would we succeed in anything beyond getting lost in this maze of trees? I reach slowly for Benji's arm, thinking it might be worth it to try, but it's too late. The shapes of horses and their riders appear in the fog the way we came. I can already pick out Hugo's hulking figure, making his horse look far too small to carry him.

Sid slides to the ground. She gives Crane's horse a fond pat and a chuckle as she passes. "Found her, huh. Told you she'd be fine."

He frowns askance at her but doesn't comment. Perhaps because Hugo is right on her heels, though still on horseback, reining up alongside Crane and sneering down at him.

"Told ya we should've put bullets in their fuckin' heads when we had the chance. Not too late for it and I'd be happy to do the honors."

"Reach for your gun and I'm putting a bullet in *your* head," Crane drawls. His gaze, I notice, hasn't left Benji and me. He runs his hand over his face, which is looking a bit more drawn and tired than the first time I laid eyes on him. Finally, he announces, "Sid and I will continue with them down to the beach. The rest of you, head back to town and wait."

Philip and Louisa, both still astride their horses and lingering back on the road, steal looks at one another. Hugo's face screws up furiously.

"*What*—"

"That's an order, not an invitation for debate." Crane turns from us to stare him down. "Unless you want to come down here and have a chat about it."

Hugo opens his mouth, then snaps his jaw shut again, positively seething. For a second, I think he's going to take Crane up on that and get off his horse, but then he's yanking his steed around and heading back the way we came. As he and the others disappear into the mist, I let out a heavy breath.

Crane turns back to us. "Two and two. Final offer, unless you want me to shoot you both in the legs and leave you here without a horse."

"Fair enough," Benji says, though his tone is tense.

Crane's horse that he rode in on is hidden in the trees. He orders me onto it and takes back Rogue for himself. He instructs Benji to ride with Sid. To separate us, no doubt, and keep us from plotting together. Lovely.

As much as I'd like to think we're evenly matched, I know that we're not. In a hand-to-hand fight, weapons aside, I still think they might have the upper hand. Benji, bless his heart, is not a fighter. Sid and Crane have proven they are.

My only hope is that Crane will keep his word. We'll get the box open, set Ellie free, hand over the notebooks, and he and his people will go on their way.

If not...well, we're going to be dead and it's not going to matter.

My stomach rolls at the thought and I bite back the panic. It'll be all right. It has to be. We still have a chance to get out of this.

The trail narrows further still, until the horses begin to struggle, and their pace slows to a crawl. Sid suggests leaving them behind, so we tie them to nearby branches to continue the trek on foot. Benji stops us before we go, a look of determination upon his face.

"The guns. Leave them, please."

"What?" Sid asks. "Why?"

"We aren't armed. Why should you be?"

Crane scowls and looks to Sid, who rolls her gaze skyward, sighs, and unholsters the revolver from her hip. After a moment of hesitation, Crane does the same, including removing the shotgun strapped to his back. They stash their guns in their horses' saddlebags and leave the shotgun propped against a nearby tree, then Crane gestures for us to lead the way up the narrow trail.

At least being on foot lets me keep next to Benji's side, although having Crane and Sid right at our backs has my nerves alight. I'm quite grateful Benji thought to have them come unarmed; I'd hate to end up with a bullet in my back.

It's only another five or ten minutes before the trees thin and the ground begins to slope down, sharply enough that we have to take a portion of the path scooting on our arses. But at the bottom of that path, I see sand and massive chunks of driftwood and—beyond all that—the rolling ocean waves. God Almighty, we've finally made it.

Our feet hit the sand and, walking side by side, we stride across the beach, coming to a halt at the water's edge. For a spell, none of us say a word. We stare at the mist rolling off the ocean's surface, the water rushing in to try to reach our feet before gliding out again. I spot a crab scuttling across the ground, and a flock of sea birds riding on the waves a way offshore.

It's striking. I lament the fact Benji and I couldn't be here to simply enjoy it.

Benji opens his bag and removes the chest from inside. He takes a few steps forward, until the water reaches his feet—no doubt soaking his shoes and socks—and sinks to a crouch with the box resting atop his knees. I hear him murmur but cannot make out the words. He slides his fingers over the mechanical dials, presses them in, and the lid pops open.

Only when he plucks out the wrapped skull from inside and removes the cloth am I able to see the flicker of a woman standing before him, also crouched, her skeletal face inches from his. I remember the night she possessed Benji and damned near threw him from the rooftop of the hotel, and my chest seizes in fear. It takes great resolve for me to stay put, to not rush forward and ensure she doesn't attempt to fling him into the surf this time.

"Ain't that somethin'," Sid breathes beside me. "Is that really her, Nate?"

"It is," Crane solemnly replies. "That's Ellie Carlton."

I steal a glance at him, though only briefly, not wanting to tear my eyes away from Benji too long. "You *knew* her?"

"Only met her once or twice, but I remember her face."

My jaw clenches. "Did you know she was dead?"

There's an indescribable look that passes over Nathaniel Crane's face, somewhere between uncertain and wary. He tips his head back, turning his eyes skyward. "No, I didn't."

"What was she like?"

He rolls his shoulders back into a shrug. "Kind. Quiet. Grieving."

Carlton's maid had said as much. Ellie Carlton had recently lost her only child, and that she and her husband had left on a trip to see someone who could 'help them.' Benji is better at piecing these things together, but I think I'm starting to catch up.

I finally say, "They went to see your employer. Didn't they?"

To that, Crane doesn't respond. Doesn't so much as twitch an eyebrow to give anything away. He's a closed book.

I sigh. "Crane… Hugo didn't seem pleased at the idea of

letting Carlton discuss it with us." I do look to him this time, studying his profile. "Would he know something about her death?"

A pause. Crane scowls, darkness shuttering over his features. "He was there in England with the lot of us at the same time she was. He might."

"That man of yours is a loose cannon. You know that, don't you?"

Not that I wait for him to respond. I doubt he's about to have a heart to heart with me about Hugo. Instead I approach Benji, who is still watching Ellie. I can hear her voice as I come to a stop behind him, her whispers nearly lost on the wind and waves. He's digging. Fingers carving grooves into the wet sand to shove it aside. I drop to my knees and begin to help, wordlessly.

Sid joins us, crouches at my side, and she also begins to dig.

Three sets of hands, scooping away sand while Ellie's whispers fill my ears. I can't understand the language she speaks, but it's beautiful, haunting. I realise now it's the language of her people, long since killed or chased away from their home. A language she still held onto. She wasn't even able to pass it onto her child, which seems like a damned, heart-breaking shame.

When the hole is deep enough and our fingers are cold and sore, Benji places the skull inside. Sid begins to shovel sand back in with her hands, which is certainly a faster process than digging it up was. When she's finished, Benji looks up at Ellie, who stares back at him through her milky white eyes, and he says, "We've brought you home. It's time for you to rest."

Ellie seems to understand this. Yet instead of vanishing immediately, she snaps her arms out, bony fingers grasping

Benji's wrist and mine. I gasp from the cold, from the iron tightness of it, and her voice comes through more in my head than it does aloud.

Beware the wrath of wolves. He's still coming.

The tide sweeps in. Ellie washes away with it, melting into foam and fog and salt.

I rock back onto my heels, rubbing at my wrist. Purpled bruises already dot my skin from her touch. Judging by the way Benji is cradling his hand against his chest, I'd wager the same is true of him. Sid watches us intently, squinting, though she doesn't ask what that was about and nothing on her face suggests she heard what Ellie said.

He's still coming.

Damned spirits and their inability to be clear about anything.

The tide is steadily rising, sweeping in further and further over our dig site. Sid and I stand and inch back, gazing out over the water a moment, before Crane calls from behind us, "Let's be on our way."

Sid trots to his side and I turn back to Benji, still hunched over the box. He hesitates a moment and I hear the lid click shut, locks snapping into place. I wonder how he expects to open it now without Ellie's guidance for the combination. When he stands, he offers it to me and I tuck it under my arm.

"Mr. Crane," Benji calls, not yet turning around. With a sigh, Crane looks back at him. Benji touches his fingertips to his own throat, gazing out over the sea. "I think Hugo killed Ellie."

Not an ounce of surprise registers upon Crane's face at this revelation, and really, I don't even question it. Still, Crane taps his boot once against the sand and patiently inquires, "What makes you say that?"

Benji turns this time to look at him. "I've long had this sensation from Ellie of running away. Trying to escape from something and then being unable to breathe. She was strangled. And just now, I'm confident what she's been warning us about wasn't the lot of you. It was *him* in particular."

Nathaniel Crane's mouth twitches, displeased. Still not surprised. "What do you expect me to do with this information?"

"I expect you to be a decent human being and hold him responsible," Benji says, not missing a beat. "She was pressured into marrying a man she did not love, lost her only child, and travelled across the globe only to be abandoned there. And when she attempted to flee, she was murdered. Her remains were mishandled, separated. She deserves justice."

They stare at one another intently, but Crane's expression is still so cold and unreadable that I can't begin to know if Benji's words have the slightest effect on him. Finally, he turns away and begins to head back up the beach. Benji's shoulders slump in defeat, but we follow after him.

We're so close. We just need to give Crane his notebooks, take one of the horses, and get out of here.

Assuming he keeps his word.

At the end of the steep uphill trail, we're all out of breath and my already sore legs are aching something fierce. Benji looks ready to crumble. Even Sid doubles over when we come to a stop, her hands upon her knees as she catches a few deep breaths.

Crane is the one who has brought us to a halt, and at first, I assume it's merely to rest. Except this is where the trail widens, which means...this ought to be where we take our mounts and go our separate ways.

Crane turns in a full circle, then looks at us. "Where the fuck are the horses?"

That is a very good question. Rogue and the other two are nowhere in sight.

I open my mouth to respond and the words catch in my throat.

Crane does not see the movement behind him, the shape of Hugo stepping out from behind the trees with an arm raised.

And I cannot get to him fast enough before the gun goes off.

22
BENJAMIN

THE WOLVES HAVE gone silent. We no longer have Ellie with us as a means of protection or forewarning. It is only my own ears and eyes that realise something is off when we crest the ridge at the top of the trail and find our horses gone, and a sinking feeling in my stomach that tells me something is about to go very, very wrong.

It's Preston's expression. His eyes gone wide, his lips parting as though to cry out. A brief look over my shoulder is all I need to see.

I throw myself into Crane beside me with all my weight. He isn't expecting it and goes over easily until we're in the mud and leaves. For half a moment I think I have succeeded, until I see the blossom of red on his right sleeve covering his bicep. Nathaniel Crane doesn't make a sound, but he shoves me off him with his left hand, rolls to his side, and cradles his injured arm to himself with a clenched jaw.

Hugo steps out onto the trail, shotgun—Crane's shotgun, I think—trained on the two of us. The crunching of leaves behind and to the side of us tell me that he is not alone. Soon, Philip and Louisa are also in view, both armed. Philip stands directly behind us. It would take no effort at all for him to pull the trigger against the back of our skulls.

It doesn't stop us from scrambling to our feet, although Crane is a bit slower than I am. He all but ignores Philip and Louisa, turning his furious, cold stare on Hugo.

"You *shot* me."

"Shoulda done it ages ago," Hugo drawls, spitting into the dirt. "Maybe if you'd have killed these two the second we found them, all of this coulda been over and done with by now and we'd all be headin' back to the boss."

"And you think killing us is gonna earn you favour with him?" Sid snaps, ignoring the way Louisa jams the barrel of her gun in between her shoulder blades. "You're off your goddamned rocker."

"Shut your mouth or I'll put a bullet in it," is Hugo's heated reply. "Had enough of bein' ordered around by the both of you. Where are the books?"

I do not miss a beat. "In the box."

Hugo's gaze swivels to me as though just now realising I'm even there. "Give it here."

Beside me, Preston tenses, but I meet his eyes and give him a nod. With the utmost reluctance, Preston takes three steps forward, places the chest upon the ground, and backs up in line with the rest of us. Hugo shifts the shotgun and glances to the chest, though only briefly, clearly not wanting to take his eyes off us. Off Crane, in particular. After what Nathaniel almost did to him the last time they got into it, I cannot say I blame him. Perhaps he learns after all.

"Is it locked?" he asks.

"Of course."

He scowls. "Open it."

I incline my chin. "Or what?"

"What? Or I'll shoot you!"

"As opposed to me opening it and *then* you shoot me?" Flippant though my words might be, there is a tremor to my voice and my blood is ice in my veins. Why, oh why, did I tell Sid and Crane to leave their weapons behind? It's my own fault they've caught us unarmed.

Hugo takes several steps forward, snags me by my arm, and hauls me toward the box. "I said *open it*."

From the corner of my gaze, I see Preston's expression screw up into a snarl and it's only with a stern look from me that he doesn't throw himself at Hugo. There are three people with guns. It would take only one to kill him.

I stumble when Hugo releases me and straighten my spine, looking up at him, unmoving, unblinking. "No."

"Are you fucking stupid?" he growls, shoving the barrel of the shotgun mere inches in front of my face. I do not flinch. I do not take my eyes off of him.

"I have spent my life with men like you thinking they could push me around," I say, calmer than I feel. "Kill me if you must. I will die knowing I never did compromise myself. Too bad you won't be able to do the same."

It comes as no surprise when Hugo brings the back of his hand across my face, so hard it makes my ears ring and nearly knocks me to the ground. I expected it. Those few seconds of him off-guard was all we needed.

Preston lurches forward, throwing his full weight into Hugo, grabbing the gun to try to wrench it away from him. Sid whirls and slams a fist into Louisa's face; Louisa lets out a howl of pain, hands flying up, blood pooling between her fingers from a broken nose.

Crane, down to one arm, need only grab Philip's wrist.

Then the shadows come.

I gasp as the chill overtakes me, the forest darkening as

though the dead of night has descended upon us. Hugo and Preston are wrestling for control of the shotgun, Sid has retrieved the revolver from Louisa, and Crane—

Crane's eyes have gone that corpse-white colour once again, and Philip's face is pale in terror. He gets out only a choked word—"No"—before his mouth drops open and his eyes roll back into his head.

I cannot bring myself to stop him as I did for Carlton. Were I to grab him, were he and I both to be rendered unconscious again, Preston and Sid would be left all on their own and with us to look after.

I do not want to sit here and watch a man die.

But that is exactly what I do.

Watching the life leave him happens slowly at first and then all at once. He convulses and shakes and then drops to the ground. I am not fully grasping what I'm seeing—but Crane's head tips back, his lips parted, and he gasps, breathing in that shadow and smoke. Breathing in whatever remains of Philip.

He did not just strip the soul from a man's body. He *took it* for himself.

Christ Almighty. What *is* he?

"Benji!"

I whip my head back around. Preston has Hugo on his back in the dirt, still fighting for control of the gun. I plant my hands against the ground and heave myself up, scrambling over to help. But rather than try to grapple for the weapon, I get my fingers on the trigger and squeeze.

The shot is aimed off at nothing. But it means the gun is useless until it's reloaded, and the sudden sound and kickback leaves Preston and Hugo both fumbling their grip.

Crane has doubled over on all fours, disoriented after…whatever it is he did. I can still hear Louisa and Sid fighting. I grab Preston's shirt and pull, shouting that we need to go, we need to run. He rolls off Hugo, scrambling for purchase on the forest floor of pine needles and leaves. He halts for half a second, doubles back, snatches the box, and hurries after me as I dart off the trail and into the woods.

I have not had a chance to tell him the box is empty. Both notebooks are safely tucked away inside the rucksack about my shoulders.

I haven't a clue which direction to go. I cannot see where the sun is in the sky through all the trees to determine north from south. So long as I can put some distance between them and us, that's all that matters. We can figure out the rest from there.

But I can hear Hugo crashing through the trees behind us. I have half a mind to tell Preston to throw the box aside, but I can't catch my breath enough to do so.

We run until I'm positive I cannot run much further. A stitch has developed in my side and my lungs are ready to burst. Preston catches my hand and half-drags me along, winded himself but still marching onward. There is no telling if Hugo has reloaded his gun, if he has another, if he's armed with anything else, or even if he was unarmed that Preston and I would be able to take him.

Ellie was right. The wolf is still coming.

I see light up ahead. There is finally a break in the trees, a ridge coasting upward. And then…

A drop-off.

We skid to a halt, peering over the ledge. The cliffs are a

straight shot down and although the fog obscures everything, the sound of waves crashing against the rocks far below can be heard.

I cannot help it. I crumple to all fours, gasping to catch my breath. Preston turns around, bracing himself, because Hugo is not far behind us. I pray to God he's as exhausted as we are.

Hugo bursts through the trees like a rampaging bull. In his hand he now has a revolver instead of the shotgun. Is that better or worse for us?

Preston stands poised in front of me, braced for a fight that I'm not convinced he can win. "You want it that bad? Take it," he calls, tossing the chest to the ground between us. "Good luck getting it open."

"I got me some friends who can saw it open, no problem," Hugo growls. "You two have been a thorn in my side from the day I started out on this God-forsaken job. You gone and made it personal. So, I'll get them books, and I'll get to see your dead faces and I'll consider it a job well done."

Preston doesn't try to argue further. He charges at Hugo, taking a swing at his face. It nearly lands, but Hugo side-steps, brings an elbow up, and drives it between Preston's shoulders with enough force that he staggers and falls to his knees. Hugo lifts the gun. He presses it to the back of Preston's skull.

No no no no no.

"The box is empty!" I shout, yanking the rucksack from around my shoulders. "I have the books!"

Hugo looks about ready to ignore my very existence...until I've opened the bag, fished out the notebooks, and thrust my arm out and over the edge of the cliffs in a silent threat to drop them. Only then does he still, lips curling furiously, eyes darting from me to the box and back again.

"Give them here."

"Get rid of the gun," I demand. "Or you can explain to your employer that your need for petty revenge lost him some of his research."

He hesitates. Preston is panting for breath, too worn out to take advantage of the situation, though I know he'll try again. I need that gun out of Hugo's hands first.

Hugo drags in a ragged breath and then plants one foot forward to approach. I tense, uncertain what I will do if he rushes at me or decides to forfeit the books in favour of shooting me instead. But he finally flings the gun aside, over the ledge of the cliffs, and it vanishes into the fog. He extends his hand for the notebooks.

He kept his end of the bargain. It is only proper and fair that I keep mine.

Slowly, I withdraw my arm from over the cliff and hold the books out to him.

It feels a bit like giving up. We've fought so hard to keep these; Esher and Spencer will need them. Crane will be furious— if he's not dead. But none of that would matter if Preston were to be hurt, if one of us doesn't walk away from this alive.

Hugo reaches for the books.

Then he clamps his massive hand around my wrist and drags me to him.

I hear Preston scream my name, but it is not in time. There's a glint of steel, and then white-hot pain embedded into my side.

It's a peculiar sort of pain; excruciating and yet my nerves seem to immediately black it out. I look down at where the knife is buried inside of me, the red blossoming and staining my shirt. I choke on a sound, too shocked to do anything.

Time slows to a crawl.

Hugo twists the blade, retracts it.

I realise in dim, stupefied horror that he's going to stab me again. I cannot do anything about it.

Preston comes out of nowhere, arms about Hugo's middle, tackling him away from me. I fall to my knees, pressing a hand to my injured side. They're so perilously close to the edge, with Preston holding onto Hugo's knife-wielding hand, trying to shove him back. He succeeds too. One of Hugo's feet slips, right off the cliffside, and gravity does the rest.

But he grabs hold of Preston in an iron grip.

They go over the edge together.

Oh, God.

I choke on a sound. I crawl for the ledge, looking over, peering into the fog.

I scream for Preston.

I scream for help.

For someone, anyone.

How far of a drop was it? How many rocks were waiting for him at the bottom?

This isn't happening. It's *not*. Preston would not, *could not* be...

I shout until my throat has gone raw, and the world has blurred through my tears. My hands are sticky with blood. When I attempt to stand, the ground tilts beneath me and sends me back to my knees.

A hand presses to my back. Someone's voice, speaking to me. I'm not sure who it is, but it is not Preston. I plead for someone to help him, to bring him back.

I do not know whether I'm begging them, or God himself.

23
PRESTON

WEIGHTLESSNESS IS A funny thing. From the very moment I recognise that I am falling, it seems to both take forever and pass by in a split second. Hugo loses his hold on me and I see him disappear into the fog well before I do. Helpless, I reach out, grasping for the cliffside passing me by.

And I hear Benji, screaming. I've never heard him shout, have I? Always so soft-spoken, never one to raise his voice. I hate hearing it now, knowing I'm the cause of it.

I hear the water before I see it. Angry, dark waves, foaming at the base of the cliffside. Only barely do I have time to suck in a breath before I hit the surface. For all the good that it does; the impact, the cold, knocks the air right out of me as the surf drags me under.

Dimly, I recall Liverpool. Standing on the docks and observing the boats. Joking with Benji that I don't know how to swim. That was not a lie, not a jest. Now, I find myself groping blindly, breaking the surface of the water and screaming as loud as I can manage before I'm pulled down again.

The current yanks me around like a rag doll until I can't even tell which direction is up to try to swim *to*. I'm slammed against the side of a rock. I try to wrap my arms around it, to hang on, which works for only a few seconds before I'm torn back away.

Lord, I'm going to drown in this place, thousands of miles from home. Benji is hurt. He could be dying too. We will die together and yet alone, away from everything we know and love, and it's all my bloody fault. I never should have dragged him along.

When fighting against the waves becomes too much, I just…stop.

Boneless, I force my eyes open beneath the water, staring into the murky depths. Oddly enough, doing so seems to orient me, carries me up, at least long enough for me to choke in a waterlogged breath.

A wave crashes over my head and I brace for it, to be swallowed up once more—except something grabs the front of my shirt. Cold air strikes my face and I gasp, disoriented, uncertain just what or who I'm seeing.

"*Kick your bloody legs!*" Nathaniel Crane shouts.

He holds onto me. I kick, clumsily, holding onto his outstretched arm—his injured one, I think.

Somehow, some way, Nathaniel Crane navigates our way through the sea, keeping me afloat every time I would otherwise go under.

Hours or minutes pass. I'm not sure which.

Then there's solid purchase beneath my feet and I could cry in relief.

We wade forward, clambering out of the water, onto an outcropping of rocks being battered by the ocean but just safe enough for us to sit on.

Exhausted, I collapse onto my side, coughing up all the water I've swallowed. Oh, everything *hurts*. Muscles I didn't even know I had in my legs and arms and back ache.

Crane has collapsed beside me, panting, nursing his injured arm to his side. I'm almost in awe. I don't know how he got us here, or what in the world happened that put him in the water with me, but I'm so grateful I could hug him.

I push myself up onto an elbow. I have to raise my voice to be heard over the sea beating itself against the cliffs. "Benji... Is he—?"

"Sid's got him," Crane replies, his voice just as hoarse as my own.

That was the only question I needed an immediate answer to. For the time being, I fall silent, too sore and tired to care about much else—like how the hell we're supposed to get off this rock.

The sky has grown darker. It must be getting into late afternoon now. I drag myself up into a sitting position, pressing my back to the limestone cliffside. Crane doesn't budge, save to sling his good arm across his eyes.

"You saved me," I finally say, when enough time has passed that my head has begun to clear. "Why?"

Crane sighs. He scrubs his arm over his face, sweeps his wet mop of curls back. "Your friend saved my life. It seemed that I owed him."

"You could have saved him, then, rather than fling yourself off a cliff. What if there'd been rocks at the bottom?"

"I heard you shouting. Figured it was a safe bet."

"Yes, but—"

"Are you going to talk me out of thinking it was a good idea to rescue you? I'll throw you back into the ocean if that's the case."

"No, I..." A pause. "Thank you."

He grunts. Sits up slowly, wincing, and moves to sit beside me, reclining against the rock face.

"Is Benji going to be all right?" I ask, quietly.

"Don't know. I suppose that depends on if he makes it long enough for Sid to get him to someone who can help."

"On foot, she—"

He interjects, "We found two of the horses. So long as she can get back to the main road and find her way to town…"

"There were farms along the way. If any of them know how to treat him, or if—"

"Christ, calm down, would you? There's no helping him so long as we're stuck here."

He has a point, even if I sort of want to punch him for it. I clench my jaw. "Right, then. How do we get off this rock? Do you suppose when the tide goes out, we can wade further up shore?"

"That's the hope, but it might be a bit of a wait. I don't know about you, but I haven't any idea when low tide is."

Neither do I. Not that I know what time it is, anyway.

Yet again, we lapse into silence. It begins to rain. Cold, fat droplets bear down on us, making us shrink back against the cliff trying to seek shelter. Unconsciously, we seem to shift closer together, seeking out warmth. Not something I am able to find, what with my clothing soaked through.

Despite that there really is nothing I can do and dwelling on it does nothing but upset me, I can't help but think about Benji. Sid had a horse. That's good. She's a tough thing. She could have hauled him onto it and ridden back for Sir Francis Drake, followed the road back. Would Paige at the shop be able to help? Surely there's a doctor in the town somewhere. No matter how small it might be, every group of people needs a physician or a surgeon.

Every time I close my eyes, the scene replays in my head. Benji offering out the books. Hugo reaching for them, in the same moment that he slid the knife from its sheath on the back of his belt. Benji's eyes growing wide. The blood instantly flowing through his fingers as he clutched at his side, stared down at it as though he could not figure out what had happened.

I shiver, pressing the heels of my hands against my eyes. My chest aches.

Despite it all, despite the rain, the uncomfortable position, the fear and concern, exhaustion gets the best of me and I drift off into a peculiar state between asleep and awake.

I dream of home. I dream of Whisperwood too. I dream of digging up a grave in a cemetery while Nicholas Mordaunt's ghost roared through the tombstones towards us. Benji shrank back into my side, and Virgil—he'd yanked the torch from Benji's grasp, climbed from the hole, and fended off the spirit who seemed too frightened to get too close to the firelight.

I recall that bone-deep ache in my arms and back from digging. It was nothing compared to this. I could almost laugh at that. Oh, how dramatic I'd been over it then. Little did I know what awaited me.

This will be a fine story to recount to James.

If I see him again.

24
BENJAMIN

I DO NOT REMEMBER getting onto the horse.

Sid must have helped me.

She hands me a balled-up piece of cloth, tells me to press it to my side as hard as I can. I try to follow her instructions, but my hands quake with the effort. I keep staring down at it.

There is so much blood.

And Preston is...

A sound not unlike a sob catches in my throat. My vision blurs.

Sid is behind me on the saddle. She must hear me, because she catches my face, leans forward, peers at me.

"Hey, hey, boy. What's your name? Benji?"

I blink at her slowly, not grasping the question at first. *My name?*

"Benjamin..."

"Sidney Rhodes. Now we officially know each other, so don't bleed out on my horse. Got it?"

She's trying to...what, make me feel better? Calm me? I do not know. I haven't the strength to converse beyond that anyway. I slump back against her, the steady plodding of hooves against the dirt road like a heartbeat in my ears. Or maybe that's my own pulse, struggling to keep up with all the blood I'm losing.

Whatever it is, the sound pulls me under while I'm mid-prayer to whatever God above that Preston is all right.

25
PRESTON

I T'S PITCH-DARK OUT when Crane nudges me awake. I blink my eyes open, startled. The fog has let up a bit, revealing a nearly full moon that glitters off the water. More importantly, it reveals that the tide has receded a great deal, exposing rocks on either side of us. We can't see how far up the shore it extends, but if the other option is simply to sit on our arses here...

It's perilous going. Every sharp piece of stone digs into my feet through my shoes. Now and again, one dislodges under our weight. I slip twice. Crane is better balanced than me, but even he struggles, going at it largely one-armed. He staggers, tries to catch himself, and lets out a strangled cry as he does so. I hurry to his side and try to help steady him. He ignores the offered hand, but I can see his face is drawn with pain as he rights himself.

I have never felt so relieved to see a beach in all my life. The cliffs finally give way to a massive stretch of sand, leading up into the trees.

We've made it. We're safe.

Well, safe from drowning, at least. Onto the next obstacle.

Namely, figuring out where we ought to go now. Crane tips his head back to squint at the sky, likely searching the stars to figure out directions. But the fog is still thick enough that little more than the moon is visible.

There appears to be a trail, however, winding away from the beach. It's overgrown and looks rarely used, but it's better than nothing. I imagine neither of us fancies spending the entire night outside, especially in wet clothes and with the temperature steadily dropping.

We walk for miles, it feels like, but I don't know if that's just the exhaustion and soreness making time slow to an agonising crawl. The entire time, I'm unnerved by the sensation that we are not alone, that something—someone—is watching us.

Crane comes to a halt before me, listening. "Do you hear that?"

I scrub my hands tiredly over my face. "Hear what?"

"That." He pauses, turns, and begins to hurry slightly off the trail, crashing none too gracefully through the undergrowth and trees. Swearing, I stumble after him, nearly ending on my face more than once attempting to keep up.

The forest spills us out onto a larger road. It could very well be Sir Francis Drake, and if it is, then thank the Lord, it will lead us straight back to town. But what got Crane's attention is a horse—*Rogue*—tied to a low branch of a nearby tree.

He hurries to her, scratching her neck, then goes for the saddlebags. He draws out his revolver from inside with a relieved sigh, sliding it into the holster on his hip.

I linger, hesitating. Surely, he has no intention of shooting me after he went through all that effort to rescue me, right? I wonder if that will change once we've made it to safety, once he has his notebooks and has no more need of us.

Still, something about this feels...off. Too convenient.

"Why is she here?" I ask of Rogue. "Who tied her up?"

"Don't know, don't care, and not sticking around to figure it out. Come on." He braces himself and then heaves himself one-armed up into the saddle. I decide I'd rather not argue and risk being left behind, so I swing up behind him, awkwardly resting my hands upon his waist.

Crane wastes no time. He flicks the reigns, shouts for Rogue to move, and she promptly begins at a gallop down the road.

My heart is racing faster than she is. Why? What is it that I'm sensing that is not right? Benji would know. He's better at these unsettling feelings than I am.

I've got a feeling that we are not alone. That something or someone is nearby.

I feel as though we're walking right into a trap.

We get no more than a quarter mile up the road, rounding a sharp bend, when a thunder-like *crack* fills the air.

My ears ring. Crane swears as Rogue rears, further and further, until the three of us are crashing to the ground. I only barely manage to avoid having a twelve-hundred-pound horse crush one of my legs, rolling away as Rogue thrashes. Crane scrambles back, but not far, and the cry he lets out is one of anger and panic. I realise Rogue wasn't spooked by the sound. She was *shot*.

The mare kicks and screams in pain. The bullet struck her in the throat, and the blood pouring out of her is coming far too fast for us to be able to do a damned thing about it. Crane kneels near her head, touching her cheek, whispering gently to her.

Never have I seen him like this. Distraught, afraid, wounded. Human.

I move to his side, wanting to help somehow, knowing by the sheer amount of blood that there is nothing I could hope to do. Perhaps if we had a doctor immediately, but…

"She's dying," Crane chokes out. He reaches for the revolver, having to use his non-dominant hand to wield it, and he hesitates, dark eyes tortured.

I've grown up alongside horses. Mum sometimes jokes I learned to ride before I learned to walk. Father also taught me early on that sometimes, the kindest thing you could do for an animal you loved was to put it out of its misery when it's suffering. But it never got easier. It never stopped hurting.

It's for that reason I gingerly take the gun from Crane.

He lets me. He holds her muzzle, speaks in hushed tones that seem to settle her fear.

I take the shot, and I make it count.

Rogue goes still. Crane presses his face to her mane, and I think I hear him crying. Or trying not to. I wish I could grant him time to grieve, but I cannot. The bullet that took her came from somewhere, and it's with a sense of dread in my belly that I turn around full circle to scan the trees around us.

Hugo has made no effort to conceal himself. He stands ahead of us on the road, looking worse for wear, half-crazed with a sneer upon his face. His shirt is stained with blood. A wide gash mars one side of his face. Perhaps he had worse luck with the rocks than we did.

When I meet his eyes, his mouth curls. "Poor beast. Ain't that a damned shame."

Crane's head snaps up at the sound. Every ounce of his distress morphs into unbridled fury. He lurches to his feet and snatches the gun from my grasp, marching forward and lifting it, not caring that Hugo, too, is still armed.

"I'm going to rip your fucking soul from your screaming corpse," he rasps.

Hugo's smile widens. "Are you now? 'Cause it seems to me that my little setup worked."

"If you wanted to play a game, then you ought not to have left my gun," Crane snarls. He lifts the revolver, aimed steady and true at Hugo's chest, and fires.

Nothing happens.

Hugo *laughs*. "That was my gift to you, Nate. Left you one bullet. You could've saved it for me, but I knew you'd use it on your stupid horse."

I have gravely underestimated Hugo. I thought him a fool, and yet he's laid out this trap for us for no reason other than to toy with us, to exact revenge. He knew exactly how Crane would react.

Swearing, Crane rams the gun back into its holster. He does not stop marching toward Hugo, even as the larger man lifts his own gun, aiming for one of Crane's legs.

Now is the perfect opportunity for me to escape. I could vanish into the woods and find my way back to town, to wherever Benjamin has been taken. With any luck, we could lay low and then flee before Hugo has a chance to find us. We've completed what we set out to do; nothing is stopping us from getting on the next ship home.

Nathaniel Crane is the reason we're in all this mess to begin with and I wonder if that does not cancel out the fact that he saved my life. There'd have been no need for it had he not hunted us down in the first place.

I wish more than anything I could bring myself to run. Yet I hear Benji's voice in my head.

Save him.

God almighty, I am going to punch Crane when this is over and done with.

Hugo fires a shot. Miraculously, Crane pitches himself to one side and narrowly avoids it, reflexes sharper than I had anticipated. Hugo curses, re-aims, and tries to take another shot. Crane's ability to dodge is almost inhuman.

That's three shots. Three bullets.

How many does that gun hold?

I pick myself up and rush forward. Hugo is momentarily distracted with Crane, stepping back hurriedly as Crane approaches, knowing full well that if Crane's hands come into contact with him, he's as good as dead.

He fires again and this time, Crane is a tick too slow. The bullet grazes his thigh and he drops to one knee without even a cry of pain. Just a flesh wound, I think, but I haven't the time to check. I charge Hugo. He turns, just in time to lift the gun, but he has no time to fire before I've thrown all my weight behind a fist to his face. Beneath my knuckles I feel the satisfying crunch of his nose. His head whips to one side and he staggers. Before he has a chance to orient himself, I lurch forward to hit him again.

This time he has the forethought to block with his free arm. When he attempts to raise the revolver again, I grab for it, fingers wrapping around the barrel, shoving it up so when he fires, the bullet goes uselessly skyward.

Hugo growls and slams his head into mine. The collision sends stars across my vision. I nearly lose my grip. Nearly, but not quite. If I retreat now, he'll have a prime window of opportunity to put a bullet in me.

I twist the gun, bending his wrist at an odd angle. Just when I think he's about to relinquish his hold, he juts out a leg, uses it to hook the back of my ankle, and pulls my leg out from under me. It's all I can do to latch my hand into his hair and ensure that he goes down with me.

My back hits the muddy dirt road with enough force that it steals my breath a moment. Hugo's fist connects with my face. Once and then again and again, until all I can taste is blood and dirt and rain. I try to get a leg up to plant a foot against his stomach but cannot get enough purchase in the mud to do so. Finally he pulls back, and he still has that godforsaken gun in his hand. He shoves it against my chest, just above my heart.

If there was ever a God in the heavens above, I'm praying now that Hugo did not have a means of reloading this gun.

It clicks.

I let out a shaky laugh, coughing on the metallic taste of my own blood.

Not even because he isn't so smart after all, but because Crane has come up behind him, eyes alight with fury, and he locks an arm around Hugo's neck. Hugo's eyes fly open wide, mouth agape as though to cry out. He grabs at Crane's arm, claws at it, to no avail.

The trees rustle with shadows and thousands of whispers. The colour of Crane's eyes shift, black to corpse-white, and the dead grow restless.

I choke on a gasp, scrambling away, not wanting to be caught up in whatever is happening. Hugo convulses. Gasps. The colour drains from his face as swiftly as the life leaves his body. His massive arms twitch, slacken, and drop to his sides. Crane releases him; he slumps to the ground, a husk of a man.

"You killed him," I manage, voice scarcely above a whisper.

Crane straightens up, staggers back. He doesn't answer me. Instead he collapses to all fours, clutching at his chest, gasping.

I push to my feet, swallowing hard. "Crane?" He doesn't respond. Cautiously, I inch toward him. "Nathaniel?"

He shudders, claws at his shirt, his throat, wheezing. Before I can decide whether to reach for him or not, Crane's body goes rigid, tremoring with tension, and he begins to cough. A heavy, wet sound. Droplets of blood fall from his lips, all but disappearing into the mud.

Then he stills. Even his ragged breathing quiets. I can quite literally feel the wrongness of him, that what I am looking at is no longer Nathaniel Crane, but something else with his face.

He slowly sits back on his haunches, then rises to his feet, no longer hindered by the injury to his arm or leg. When he turns to face me, his eyes are still those of a corpse, yet deep set in his pupils sits a pinprick of red that takes me back to Mordaunt's ghost howling at us from his graveside.

I step back, a lump in my throat. No, no, no. This is not what was meant to happen. Crane tried to take Hugo's spirit the same way he took Philip's, the same way he almost took Carlton's, and something has gone horribly wrong.

"Crane. Nathaniel. Listen to me, if you're in there…"

His mouth pulls back into a snarl with a low, guttural growl that sounds more beast than human.

The moment I see him poised to lunge, I run.

I leap over Hugo's body, rushing down the road, back

the direction we rode on Rogue earlier. A furious howl fills the air, nearly paralysing me into losing my footing in the mud.

There is no way I can outrun him. I'm too exhausted, and he no doubt has plenty of energy to wear me down. But I need to buy myself time to think. I rifle through what James told me about Evenbury and Reverend Thomas, about the spirits possessing live people. This is the same, is it not? Which means if I can exorcise the ghost from Crane…

And yet, *how?*

Aunt Eleanor went over many things with me, but it wasn't as though anyone wrote down a rite of exorcism for me to keep in my back pocket.

Prayer, though. I can do that.

And the crucifix. Alice's necklace, still around my throat, the metal pendant pressed against my skin. I am not defenceless. I can do this.

I round the bend, ducking off the road into the trees. I press my back to the base of one of the tall red trunks, catching my breath. Crane's footsteps rapidly approach, and he stops in the middle of the trail, realising he's lost me. He throws his head back and howls again, nearly stopping my heart in my chest.

I squeeze my eyes shut.

Deep breaths.

Benji expelled those spirits at Carlton's home. I can send away a single spirit and save Nathaniel Crane. I must. Failure is not an option.

I remove the necklace from my neck, wrapping the chain about my fingers. Mustering my resolve, I inch back around the tree, watching him, waiting for him to approach close enough that I can make a grab for him. Damn it all; I wish I'd had the foresight to check Rogue's saddlebags for rope, or knives, or anything else that might have aided me in this fight I didn't know I was going to engage in.

When Crane passes as close to my hiding spot as I think he's going to get, I lurch around the tree, throwing my arms around his shoulders and shoving the cross against his chest.

"God the Father in heaven, have mercy on us. God the Son, Redeemer of the world, have mercy on us. God the Holy Spirit, have mercy on us..."

Crane tries to rip away from the cross, but only succeeds in backing into my arms, allowing me to tighten my hold on him. He shrieks in fury and pain, thrashing like a trapped animal. He claws at my arms. When that does not get me to release him, he ducks his head and sinks his teeth into my forearm, hard enough that the words catch in my throat and makes me gasp in pain. The thick wool of my overcoat is the only thing that prevents him from drawing blood.

I choke out the next lines of the prayer. Crane begins to sag in my arms, relinquishing his bite on me, howling and screaming.

It's working. Isn't it? I think that it must be.

It has to be.

In a burst of defiant energy, Crane reaches behind him and grabs hold of me—my hair, my shirt. He doubles forward, yanking me, hauling me off my feet and over his head, throwing me to the ground before him. The words are pushed from my lungs and I wince, the crucifix cutting into my palm.

Crane looms over me, teeth bared. He's going to rip my throat out. Could do it without a second thought, and that is how Benjamin will find my body.

I shove the cross up against his jaw, desperation flooding into my voice.

"You do not belong here!" I shout. "Nathaniel Crane, take back what is yours!"

When he tries to jerk away, my free hand shoots up and grabs a fistful of his hair, holding him in place. The sheer strength coiled in his limbs makes even that difficult, but it's working. He twists to try to free himself even as I begin to speak my prayer again.

The combination of blood on my hands, our positions, and the mud and rain and Crane's inhuman strength has him finally wrenching free, but he does not go far and I do not stop praying. Crane slams the heels of his hands into the dirt on all-fours, a howl catching in his throat, degenerating into a whimper and then heavy coughing. The wheezing returns, and he again clutches at his chest.

"Lamb of God, you take away the sin of the world, spare us, O Lord. Lamb of God, you take away the sin of the world, graciously hear us, O Lord..."

He's in pain. Or Hugo's spirit is, I am not sure which and it does not matter. What matters is that he's being rendered unable to attack, and if there is anything left of Nathaniel inside of there, he needs to fight to regain control.

He rasps out a single word—*"No!"*—and gasps, open-mouthed and retching, and I watch in horror as shadowy, bony fingers reach out from his mouth, followed by an entire hand and an arm and—

Some unearthly spirit crawls its way from Crane's lungs, smoke and shadow, a malformed, writhing creature that half slithers, half crawls a few feet away, steadily gaining more and more of a solid form.

It looks like no one, and yet I know precisely who I'm witnessing.

Hugo.

Crane has not moved. He's trying to get to his feet, ends up on his side in the dirt, panting. The thing that used to be Hugo is still recovering, but it turns, red pits where its eyes used to be shining bright, lips pulling back to reveal a set of blackened, sharp teeth. It growls, low, reverberating through every bone in my body, and it looks more beast than man.

The fear shakes me out of my shock. I grab Crane, hauling him to his feet, shouting at him that we need to go and we need to go *now*. He clutches at my shirt, his legs not cooperating as we stumble off into the woods.

I move as swiftly as I can with Crane's nearly dead weight hanging off me. I don't know what direction we're headed, how far from the main road we're traveling, but for now I just need distance. Distance, and a few moments for Crane to get himself together. He's got to know what to do about this, doesn't he?

Eventually, Crane's legs give out completely. I have little choice but to help him ease to the ground and prop his back against a tree. The shadows beneath his eyes are heavy, and blood from his coughing stains his lips.

He drops his head back against the tree, eyes closed. "Leave me. I won't be able to keep up."

"Benji and Sid would never forgive me if I did." I crouch before him, desperately trying not to let my fear get the best of me. "What in the hell just happened?"

"I couldn't hold him," he mumbles. "I already took Philip and Louisa… Too much."

That answers that about what happened to Louisa. "Then...what? His spirit is just a vengeful creature running rampant out there? Will it hurt anyone? Will it possess someone else?"

He sighs, tiredly swiping at his mouth, licking at his lips. "It can. I'm not strong enough to stop him right now."

"Then let's get you to town, get you rested. Then we'll come back..."

"He'll find us before that happens. Go on. Get back to the others."

"I *said* I'm not leaving you. There's got to be a way to figure this out."

"You can't fix everything," Nathaniel Crane says.

I go still. *You can't fix everything, Preston.* Benji had said those exact same words to me. They had stung at the time, left me feeling helpless and frustrated. Now, it only fuels my anger.

I grab the front of his shirt. "Look, you prick. We're in this mess because of you! You're not going to just give up on me because you're *tired*. Get off your arse, Nathaniel Crane, and help me deal with the mess you've made."

Crane opens his eyes. He chuckles, which was not the response I had anticipated. "You sound like Sid."

"Good. She seems to be one of the only people you listen to." I offer a hand. "Are you getting up or not?"

He sighs. But, finally, thankfully, he reaches with his good arm and takes my hand, letting me help him to his feet. "I make no promises except to do what I can."

I force a tight, humourless grin. "That's all any of us can do."

26
PRESTON

I STARE OUT OVER the trail and Hugo's corpse lying in the centre of it. There's no sign of the creature, but that doesn't mean anything. It's too dark. He could be in any shadow nearby, waiting for us.

"What's the plan?" Crane murmurs beside me. I notice his eyes darting to Rogue's body, flashing in pain and discomfort. I imagine seeing her just lying there like that is almost as upsetting as her death itself. Even when this is over, I haven't a clue how we'll deal with her.

I lick the salt and rain from my lips. "We aren't in any shape to out manoeuvre or fight him physically. So...we've got to outsmart him." I nod toward his body. "I've encountered a creature like him before. We destroyed him by destroying his remains. If we burn Hugo's body, the creature ought to be dealt with."

His eyebrows shoot up. "You want to start a fire in the middle of a forest? Are you daft?"

I glance skyward. It's damp out and it smells like it ought to rain any second now. "Clear a space around him, best as you can. Unless you've got a better idea, this is all we have."

Crane opens his mouth, closes it again, sighs. "There should be some flint in Rogue's saddlebags. What are you going to do?"

I straighten up from my crouch, rolling my stiff shoulders back. I hardly feel limber or rested enough to have a go at this, but it is what it is.

"I'm going to distract him," I announce. "I'll lure him away and keep him there as long as I can. Work fast."

Crane doesn't attempt to stop me as I make my way out into the middle of the road. I have this plotted out in my head...more or less. I know how to get back to the beach from here. If I lead Hugo there, I'll have him out in the open, away from Nathaniel and his own corpse. There will be no place for him to hide, no shadows for him in which to lurk.

I flex my numb hands and lift them around my mouth. "Only cowards hide in the dark, Hugo! Come on out!"

At first, nothing.

Then the trees rustle on either side of the road. A few paces ahead, the creature that was Hugo steps out into the moonlight.

It has fully taken shape. Even more massive than it was in life, Hugo towers over me a good foot now, beady red eyes scorching and its limbs too long for its body. There is something inherently animalistic about its facial features, cloaked in dark shadow and misshapen, yet something about the cut of its jaw and the ridge of its brows still looks very much like the man lying behind me.

I've got the crucifix clutched in my hand. How much good will it do me against Hugo now?

Suppose we're going to find out.

"Come on then! Let's dance!" I grin at the way my words seem to enrage it, whether it understands me or not. More beast than man, it drops to all fours, still almost as tall as me, and it charges.

I whip around, taking off down the road. Tired though I may be, I've had just enough time to gather myself, to get that rush of energy needed to continue for a bit longer.

Hugo tears after me around the bend, further and further up the trail. I could swear I feel its breath against the back of my neck, feel it swiping at me, claws grazing the back of my shirt.

Don't look back. Do not look back. Just run. Focus and run.

It's getting too close. Rather than head for the turn-off, I dart into the trees. Here, Hugo's size makes it harder for it to navigate, as it has to weave through the same towering red trees and branches that I do. I cut across to the beachhead trail and crash out onto it a fair bit ahead of Hugo.

Dirt changes to rocks, then sand. I hadn't thought to consider that sand is significantly harder to run across than dirt. I pick my feet up higher, straining every tired, worn muscle to *go, go, go*. If I can reach the wet sand and rocks near the water's edge, it will be easier to maintain my footing.

Only there do I skid to a halt and turn. Hugo is just now loping out onto the beach, moving effortlessly across the sand. When it spots me, it throws its head back and bays like a bloody hound that's caught a scent.

God, please tell me Nathaniel is doing his part.

I don't wait for the beast to get too close before I begin to pray, preparing to thrust the crucifix at it the second it nears. Hugo tosses his head, infuriated by the words, perhaps even slowed by them, but they are not stopping it completely. It approaches until I've got the ocean at my back, the ice-cold waves rushing in to lap at my shoes. But then it only circles me, doesn't attack, and I think the prayers must be doing some level of good. It paces around me like a caged lion, all teeth and claws and dead, dead eyes and rotting skin.

It's distracted. Good. That was all I needed. I can keep it here as long as I must.

Except my voice is cracking from exhaustion and overuse and the cold.

The creature lunges, not grabbing for me, but close enough that I think it might, and I stagger back until the rocks beneath my feet give out and I'm slipping. Falling.

The prayer is disrupted. Before I can continue, the waves rush in, washing over my face. Saltwater fills my mouth and lungs as I inhale out of reflex. The creature is on me, claws digging into my chest and shoulders, pinning me to the ground.

The waves recede and I cough up water, try to get out the next verse of the prayer before the next tide can come in. Above me, Hugo's mouth twists up, pleased. A sickly-sweet aroma fills my senses, rot and dirt and blood. It leans down, voice barely intelligible beyond the rumbling growl in its chest.

"Little sheep, eaten by the wolves."

I cough again, scarcely able to get a proper breath in with the weight atop me. "Fuck off."

The water rushes in once more, threatening to swallow me whole.

If I drown, I wonder if the tide will carry me out to sea.

The crucifix is still in my hand. I reach up, blindly searching, shoving the metal against one of the massive hands pinning me down. There's a snarl, far away, beyond the sound of rushing water in my ears, and that hand jerks back as though burned.

It's just enough. I thrust the crucifix up into its face. The water recedes. I see the cross burning into the side of Hugo's face, white-hot, smoking. He tears his head away, bellowing, and it's *just enough* for me to shove that second hand off me and roll away before the tide returns.

I get to my feet, circling around Hugo, putting it between the ocean and me. I shove my crucifix hand forward, forcing my voice to cooperate.

"Almighty God, through your only Son Jesus Christ you overcame death and opened to us the gate of eternal life…"

Hugo rears up onto two legs again, tossing its head, letting out a bloodcurdling scream.

It has nothing to do with my praying, I realise. Nathaniel must have the body burning. Hugo tries to step around me. I shove the cross in its face, and I pray louder. I need to keep it here, no matter the cost.

It swipes at me. I'm not fast enough to get away.

The burn of claws across my face is blinding. Blood fills my mouth. Red fills my vision in my right eye, making my other one blur, and the pain brings me to my knees. I refuse to let it stop me. I raise my voice, all but screaming the prayer up at Hugo just to be heard over the sound of its roaring.

Hugo lifts its arm, ready to attack again.

The waves rush in. A series of familiar, deafening howls fills my ears. A shape catches the moonlight behind Hugo, knee-deep in the water, dead eyes locked onto him and long, dark hair clinging to her face and body in wet tendrils.

Ellie rises from the foam and latches onto Hugo's back, fingers digging into the beast's chest. She sinks her teeth into its shoulder, fighting him back several steps into the sea. Hugo writhes in pain, its skin beginning to smoulder and crumble to ash, never a break in its blood-curdling scream.

Every step Ellie drags him, every piece of him that falls away, the more I wonder if I shall walk away from this with my hearing intact.

Hugo burns to pieces before my eyes, held prisoner by Ellie's gnarled, dead hands. Finally, a high wave crashes defiantly over them. The creature's smouldering body crumbles, sizzles, curls of steam and ash rising into the air.

Ellie is gone.

I collapse back into the sand.

Is it over? I'm afraid to think that it could be.

I watch the ocean, halfway expecting Hugo to rise from the tide again, angrier and more dangerous than before.

The beach remains quiet.

My head spins when I stand. Delicately, I touch my face, feeling the split flesh there, four angry wounds, one across my eye. I still cannot see anything through it. The pain, though, is dim, and I wonder if I'm simply in shock, if I'm too fucking exhausted to feel much of anything—even relief.

I dust the sand from my clothes. To the sea I say, softly, "Thank you, Ellie." And then I start up the beach, every step an effort.

Crane will be waiting for me.

Benji will be waiting for me.

God willing.

27
PRESTON

I FIND CRANE SEATED next to Rogue, a hand resting against her neck. It's begun to rain again. The disgusting scent of burning flesh fills my nose, makes my stomach turn. But I haven't the energy to be sick. Crane has cleared all the brush away from Hugo's body. The rain will no doubt put out the flames before long.

I sink down beside Crane, absently resting a hand upon Rogue's side.

"Thank you, girl," I murmur. "For looking after us so well."

Crane's lashes lower. His fingers curl into her mane. "I'll have to come back to bury her."

"Going to be a tough job for one man with the use of only one arm."

"Fuck off."

"That was an offer to help."

He glances at me and does a bit of a double take. "The hell happened to your face?"

"Hugo happened. Bastard couldn't die without leaving his mark on the world, I suppose." I wonder if it will scar. How annoying. I'm a little more concerned about the vision in my eye returning, though.

We sit in silence awhile. It's almost companionable. Almost.

But the sun has long since vanished. The fog is rolling back in. We need to be getting out of here unless we want to be stuck another full night out in the cold.

Crane favours his injured leg when he walks but refuses to let me help. I keep the pace slow for him as we make our way along the road, which is significantly slower going than when Benji and I came out this way on horseback. We walk for the better part of two hours before we hear hoofbeats on the trail up ahead and spot lanterns through the fog. My legs threaten to buckle.

When Sid's face appears before us on horseback, alongside a man I don't recognise, I could cry out in relief.

28
BENJAMIN

I AM WARM FOR the first time it what seems like years. Too warm, almost.

Beyond Sid helping me onto her horse, I remember little. Vaguely, I recall strong arms helping me out of the saddle, into a house. Someone removing my shirt. Prodding, pinching, stinging at my side.

Sleep claims me. Fitful, uneasy, plagued with nightmares, but sleep nonetheless.

The next time I open my eyes, everything swims in my vision. I'm covered in a layer of sweat, struggling to kick the blankets off.

"You've got a bit of a fever," a voice croons at me.

Mother?

I look up at her. Dark hair. Dark eyes. Gentle hands, cool against my forehead. A singsong voice.

"Here, take some of this. It will help."

She puts a spoon to my lips. I drink without question. It's bitter, thick going down. But if Mother says it will help, I believe her.

"There we are," she says. Gently, so gently. "Can you talk? How are you feeling?"

This time, my eyes blur with the onslaught of tears. I swallow thickly. "I've made a mess of all this," I whisper. "It's all my fault."

Every bit of it. I intervened with Carlton. I forced Preston into coming here to put Ellie to rest. Everyone who has died here is dead because of me.

And I still do not know if Preston is among them.

She strokes my damp hair back. "I don't think that's true for a second. Why don't you get some more sleep? Promise, things won't look so bleak after you get some rest."

I cannot get the words past my lips any longer. Whatever she gave me works fast to drag me under.

This time, my sleep is deep and dreamless.

The room is dark when I wake, save for the steady flickering of a candle on the bedside table. Silent as it is, I instantly know that I am not alone.

Upon turning my head, I see Preston slouched in a chair at my bedside. He has a hand over mine, our fingers laced together and, oh, God, he looks as though he's travelled to hell and back again.

He's shirtless, cuts and scrapes marring his torso and arms. There are thick bandages across part of his face, over one eye. The bruising on his body is so dark I can see it even in the poor lighting.

But he's alive. Good Lord above, he's *alive*.

I choke on a sob.

Groggy, I force myself onto my side, pushing up onto an elbow, whispering his name. My movement startles him awake, his eye fluttering open.

"Benji, oh, thank God."

I ought not to be moving, I think, and yet I cannot stop myself. I lack any sort of grace or coordination as I claw my way off the bed, desperate to get close to him, to get my arms around him.

"Hey now, you're supposed to be resting," Preston says, but he does not stop me. He puts his arms around me in turn, pulling me against his chest, onto his lap. And he holds me tight, so very tight, betraying the calmness he's so obviously trying to exude.

I sob against his throat, relief and guilt and happiness all rolled into every tear. Nothing I could say would come out at all sensical, so I don't bother trying. So long as I can hold him, so long as I can feel him, that is all that matters right now.

"It's all right," Preston whispers against my hair. "We're both all right. It's all over now."

I cry until I'm too drained to shed another tear. My head has begun to clear, the medicine from earlier losing its effect. When I touch a hand to my side, I feel no bandages, but a wide row of stitches. The flesh is warm to the touch, painful, but not unbearable. Certainly not as painful as being stabbed.

I draw back to get a better look at Preston, gingerly brushing my fingers against his jaw. "Your face…"

He grimaces. "Better it was my face than my throat, eh?" A distressed look must pass over me, because he swiftly cups my cheek against his palm. "Hey, hey… None of that. Just scratches. They'll heal."

"And if they scar?"

"Well, then I'll have quite a story to tell people, won't I?"

I sniff, swiping a hand across my eyes. "Where are we?"

"A farm not far from town." He shifts, slides his arms beneath me, and lifts. Just enough to relocate us to the bed, which is really too small for the both of us to lie side by side, but he sits and permits me to stay in his lap. When he reclines, he draws me to his chest, where I rest my cheek against his shoulder. "Owned by Jeb and Belinda Folger. Sid told them we were attacked by a group and scarcely managed to get away with our lives. I guess they bought it. They were able to tend to your injuries, and mine. Crane's too."

"He's all right?"

"A bit worse for wear, but he'll survive. Stubborn bastard."

That's a relief, although I'm not certain why. Crane likely does not consider us on friendly terms, no matter what has transpired. I wonder if Sid feels the same. Still, I think I have Nathaniel Crane to thank for Preston being here with me now...even if I also have him to blame for this entire mess.

I close my eyes, tired all over again. "Tell me what happened?"

Quietly, I listen as Preston recounts the events since I watched him fall from the edge of the cliffside. It takes great effort not to cry all over again by the time he's finished. I missed so very much. I should have been there to help, to keep him safe.

Preston cards his fingers into my messy hair. "If you're blaming yourself, don't."

Easier said than done. But I'm not about to wallow in self-pity—at least not in front of Preston. But, oh, I have so many questions for Crane now.

"The notebooks... Do we have them?" I ask.

"Sid grabbed them back at the cliffs. Imagine they're in Crane's hands by now, or they will be whenever he wakes." Preston yawns. He couldn't have slept well in that chair and hasn't had nearly the time I've had to rest.

So I fall silent. Sure enough, it isn't long before Preston's breathing evens out and his arms around me have gone limp and heavy. I remain with him for an hour, simply savouring the feel of his nearness, the steady and familiar beat of his heart. I'm loath to get up and leave his side.

I do eventually untangle myself from him and get out of bed. A dull, throbbing ache radiates with every movement. My rucksack, tattered and filthy, lays on the floor near the door. Everything inside is a mess, too, but I manage to find a shirt that is at least relatively clean to slip on.

The farmhouse is dark but warm. A faint aroma of spices hangs in the air. It's comfortable. Safe.

I follow the scent into a kitchen, where Sid stands alongside a woman with dark hair, plaited and pulled forward over one shoulder. The woman turns, smiles.

"Oh, you're awake."

Her voice strikes a chord in me. This is the voice I heard as I drifted in and out of sleep earlier—not Mother at all. "Yes, um, Miss…?"

"This is Cora," Sid says with a lopsided grin. "She's the Folgers' daughter. Been helpin' us look after you and Nate."

I dip my head into a polite nod. "It's a pleasure to meet you, Miss Folger. I cannot thank you enough for your kindness and hospitality."

"Please, just Cora is fine. Come in, come in. Would you like something warm to drink?"

"That sounds wonderful," I admit, stepping further into the room. Cora offers me a steaming mug of apple cider. It almost scalds going down, but it's such a pleasant sensation after being cold for so long. I fold my hands tightly around the cup, letting the curls of steam lick at my face.

"There's some leftover sausages and a few hardboiled eggs there from supper," Cora says. "Help yourself. I ought to leave you two to talk."

She exits the room. Sid watches her go intently and with a look of near disappointment. She sighs and swivels her attention to me. "First time I got her to myself since we've been here. Thanks a bunch."

My eyebrows lift. "Was I interrupting something?"

"Well, no. Not yet." She sniffs, reaches for her own cup. "How're you feelin'?"

"Sore, but alive. Thanks to you." I draw a chair over to have a seat. Sid props herself on the edge of the table.

"And your friend?"

"I spoke with him briefly and left him to sleep. He needs it. Is Mr. Crane all right?"

To that, her gaze diverts off to nothing in particular. "Yeah, he's... I mean, he's *alive*. A bit out of sorts. Think he pushed himself too hard."

I bite at the inside of my lower lip. How much will she tell me if I prod? If she's feeling congenial, then this might be my only chance to get any answers. "What he did to Philip..."

"Louisa, too," Sid adds, sipping from her mug. "He took them both out."

A pause. "What was it that he did? What is he?"

A faint scowl tugs at her features. "He's a goddamned person. What else would he be? He's just..." She sighs, runs a hand over her face. "It ain't my business to tell Nate's story. If he wanted you to know, he'd tell you."

Blast. So close. "What will you two do now?"

"We still got a job to do. I have the notebooks and they belong to our employer." She shrugs.

Suppose that answers the question of what happened to the books. What a shame. Miss Bennett would have been able to make some sense of them. I hope the notes we took are still in order and will be of some use.

Sid sips at her own cup. "Say, I wanted to ask you somethin'."

"What is it?"

"The ghost. The one you said was attached to me." She hesitates. "Is he still here?"

My gaze shifts. He is, of course. The vaguest shadow lurking at her side. "Always."

She looks down into her cup, tapping a finger against the rim. "Don't suppose he's said anything since you first brought it up?"

"I'm afraid not. Not that I've heard." I study the spirit, whose dead eyes have found mine and are locked on me. "Do you know him?"

There's a long pause where I think Sidney is debating how much she wishes to tell me, if anything. "My pa. He died a few years back. Accident, workin' the railroads. I was the only family he had left after the war."

She's alone.

I know that feeling, don't I? No real family to speak of. "Can you sense him?"

"Oh, hell, I don't know. Sometimes I think..." She stops, shakes her head. "Sometimes I feel him, like he's looking after me. I get these intuitions now and again, like...these strong feelings. About people, about places. It started after he died and

I kinda always thought it was him, helping me out."

A smile touches my face. "Has he ever steered you wrong?"

She snorts. "Nah, but I oughta get better at listening. Never did feel right about Hugo, and I ignored it."

"And what about me? What sense do you get from the two of us?"

"You really wanna know?" Sid pulls up a chair to sit across from me, slouching back.

"I don't see why not."

"Well, I get good feelings from your friend. Like he's dependable, I guess. From you…" At this, she eyes me, seeming to select her words with care. "It changes. Mostly, it's good. A quiet, soothing sorta feel. But now and again, like back at Carlton's…"

I frown when she trails off. "Yes?"

She sighs, rubbing the back of her neck with a shrug. "You scared the hell out of me."

That was not the answer I'd expected. It must show on my face, because Sid laughs.

"Don't look at me like that. It's the same sorta feel I get off Nate a lot of the time too. I think when you two are doing the ghost-thing, it just sets off warning bells."

No one has ever told me before that I frighten them. I'm not certain what to do with that information either. When it's clear I'm at a loss, Sid smiles and stands, placing her cup upon the counter.

I look down into my drink, debating. I still have questions, but they ought to be selected carefully. I suppose there is really only one that matters right now. One that I don't believe for a second she will answer, unless our conversation has left her feeling particularly agreeable.

"…What is The Order?"

Sid goes still, before slowly turning to face me again. "That's not a question you need an answer to."

"But it is. Our friends—the ones you mistook us for—if they're involved, if they're targets somehow… I want to keep them safe." I frown. "You know what that's like."

She braces her hands against the countertop, silent. Tapping her fingers against the worn wood. "If you wanna keep them safe, then you tell them to keep their noses out of things. Stick to hunting local spirits and get out of the big stuff."

"The big stuff… Do you mean like the possessions that happened in Buckinghamshire?" I'm getting somewhere. I don't yet know where, but *somewhere*. "Sid, please…"

She whips around, pinning me with a cold stare. "Look, I like you, kid. I'm glad we didn't have to kill you, but make no mistake that we would've if it had come down to it. Because of this chase you took us on, we gotta explain to our boss why we're down three people. If you think I'm gonna add onto our troubles by telling you shit I ain't supposed to, you got another think comin'."

She stalks out of the kitchen, leaving me alone with my thoughts and a rapidly cooling mug of cider.

29
PRESTON

TWO DAYS PASS before Mrs. Folger lets me look at my face in a mirror. The stitches are neatly done, but no less gruesome. While I can't say that I've ever worried much about my appearance, even I have to admit the scars these are going to leave behind are going to prompt an absolute fit from my family back home.

What does bother me is my right eye. It's still healing, they say, but no one could give me a proper answer as to whether I'll ever be able to see out of it again. A nuisance, more than anything, and certainly one I could do without.

I'm given leave to have the bandages off now, at least, so long as I'm careful and keep the wounds clean. Now and again, I catch Benji watching me with an indefinable look etched into his features. He's feeling better himself, but he tires easily and naps throughout the day. I try to lay with him and no one seems to question it—at least not to our faces. Small blessings. He touches my face at night and I know he's blaming himself for this, which only makes me all the more determined to assure him I'm unbothered by this new addition to my physical appearance.

"They're just scars," I murmur against his hair. "They're proof I survived."

Does such a response make him feel any better? I'm not sure. But he doesn't press me on it and I'll admit, having him reach out to touch me just to reassure himself that I'm all right is not a bad feeling.

Sid, being the only one not horribly injured from our last several days, has taken to helping around the farm. In part, I think, trying to thank the Folgers for their hospitality. Not only in housing us, but in feeding us, too—and they've refused any payment for their assistance. Also in part because she seems quite fond of Cora Folger, puppying around after her and making eyes at the girl not unlike James makes at Esher. Maybe I'm overthinking it. It's hardly any of my business.

I have not seen hide nor hair of Crane. At one point, I'd been certain he would emerge from the room he is sharing with Sid—namely, when Sid, Mr. Folger, and some of the other nearby farmers, set out to deal with both the bodies of Hugo and Rogue. I offer to go along to help, but Mrs. Folger insists I stay put. Crane doesn't make an appearance. I take that as a testament to how poorly he's feeling.

Or maybe going back there hurts too much. I don't pretend to know.

Any time I try to ask Sid about him, she shrugs and says, "He'll be fine. Give him some time."

We seem to be made of time right now, with none of us in any hurry to be anywhere else. Although I would be lying if I said I wasn't eager to take Benji and get as far away from here as we can.

On the fifth day, I wake to find myself alone. It's almost disorienting to reach for Benji and not find him there. I slide out of bed, wash, dress, and apply some more salve to my various wounds before emerging from my room.

The Folgers are out and about, busy with the farm. Sid waves me over when I step outside.

"Mornin'," she calls.

"Good morning." I squint. It's a clear day out for a change, though still chilly, still damp. "Have you seen Benji?"

"He and Nate went out for a ride a bit ago."

My stomach about bottoms out. I swallow hard. It's fine. It's all fine. "Where?"

She shrugs. "One of the nearby beaches. Why? Worried?"

"The pair of you did chase us down and hold guns to our heads," I say dryly. "Is there a horse I can borrow?"

Sid laughs and waves me off. "C'mon. I'll go with you."

We saddle one of the horses Sid managed to find running loose in the woods. It's apparent she's growing more familiar with the area surrounding the farm, because she takes several winding trails to one of the beaches without hesitating to wonder if she's going the right way. The trail drops us right out onto the beach where we can see another horse tied to a tree and grazing on dewy grass. We leave ours there with it and venture out onto the sand.

I see Crane first, seated atop a boulder with his back arched and head bowed. Reading, it seems. Sid wastes no time in scaling the rocks to join him. I continue, however, walking between the climbing limestone cliffs and the water.

Benji stands up ahead. His shoes are off, trousers rolled up to his knees, shin-deep in the water. His head is tipped back and his eyes are closed. The wind slides through his hair, caresses it from his face. He does not move, does not speak. He's simply existing in the moment.

He looks at peace.

And he's beautiful.

I could watch him all day like this. I do, for a while.

When I finally approach, he hears me, opens his eyes and tips his head to look my way. His mouth curves up into a smile. "Good morning."

"Morning," I greet, coming up beside him. "Woke up without you and got a bit worried."

"I'm sorry. I did try to wake you, but you were sleeping like the dead." Benji takes my hand. His skin is cool to the touch, and there's sand on his skin as though he's been playing in it. Sure enough, I spot a small castle-like mound constructed not far away, although it's going to be destroyed by the rising tide before long.

To his apology, I shake my head. "I see you got Crane out of his room. How'd you manage that?"

He shrugs. "I didn't. I believe Mrs. Folger prodded him out, said he needed some fresh air and sunlight."

"How is he?"

"Hmm. Quiet. Distant. Aloof?"

"So, back to how he was when we met him."

"About, yes." Benji slides his gaze back to the ocean. "I tried to ask him about The Order. He ignored me."

That's no surprise, is it? We'd have better luck getting information out of Hugo's dead body. "So much for that."

Benji draws in a deep breath. The air is cold enough that it puffs in front of his face on the exhale. "He's reading the notebooks."

I peer back toward the boulder a fair distance away. Crane and Sid are still seated atop it. "And...?"

"And... I don't know. Clearly, he understands at least some of it. Do you suppose he'll share what he learns?"

"Unlikely," I mutter. When Benji squeezes my hand, I

turn my attention back to him. He smiles.

"Our notes appear to be intact. We still have something for Miss Bennett and Spencer and Esher."

Something is better than nothing. I draw him closer to my side and begin to stroll farther down the beach. "Speaking of… Now that this is all over, we have an important question to figure out the answer to."

He *hmm*'s. "Where we go from here?"

"That would be it."

"I think we've proven that wherever you choose to go, I will follow." Benji says this easily, as though there's not a question about it at all. Except there is, because—

"We came all this way for me, Benji. Where we go next is up to you." I halt, pull him to me, and brush a stray curl from his cheek. "Compromise, isn't it?"

His long lashes lower in reflection. "Can I think about it? Just a bit longer, until we have to leave here?"

I chuckle. "You're lucky I'm not the sort who needs everything planned out ahead of time, eh? Take all the time you need."

He smiles widely, and it might be the first time he's smiled at me like *that* since—ahh, since before his mother died, isn't it? So mired in his grief and trying to figure himself out that nothing has brought such happiness to his face until now. I'm glad for it. Benji rises on his tiptoes, presses a cool kiss to my lips that tastes like an ocean breeze, and murmurs against my mouth, "Thank you."

30
BENJAMIN

TWO DAYS LATER, we wake to Sid and Crane preparing to leave. They're taking a single horse, which I suppose means they're leaving the other one for us—a surprising show of kindness, really—and their meagre belongings are already packed by the time Cora sends us outside to say our farewells to them.

Crane has scarcely spoken a word to us since he began to come out of his room. Oh, he's been a perfect gentleman to our hosts. Even with his arm in a sling and a bit of a limp to his gait, he's insisted on helping around the farm as much as he can. We all have, as our strength has begun to return. Although my chores have consisted mostly of tidying up about the house and helping with the cooking. I've learned a few things from Mrs. Folger and Cora, and also taught a few things, too. As it turns out, the Folgers immensely liked some of my Chinese recipes.

Now, Crane glances over, seems disinterested by our presence, and resumes readying his horse. I wonder if he's named this one. I wonder if he'll grow as attached to him as he was to Rogue.

Sid dusts her hands on her trousers and flashes us a grin. "Come to see us off?"

"We didn't even know you were already planning to leave," Preston says.

She shrugs. "Can't stay here forever. We got things to

do, places to be. Shame, though; wouldn't have minded stickin' around a bit longer."

I try to hide a smile. "Will you write to Cora when you're gone?"

"Don't get sassy with me, boy." She sniffs, steps over to us, and plucks the Stetson from her head. Rather than lean up, however, she grabs Preston by the front of his shirt and yanks him down so that she can place the hat on him. He blinks once, startled, and touches it absently.

"What?"

"You've been eyein' it. I can get another." She draws back, studying us. "Will you be going back across the pond after this?"

I smile a little. "We haven't figured that out yet. I suppose we ought to make up our minds soon."

She nods, expression sobering. "You remember what I said, right?"

Stay out of the big things, right? "I remember."

"Good. I'll see you around, maybe." She ruffles my hair in a way that feels oddly sisterly and makes me wonder if she has a little brother or sister somewhere. Then again, with the way she fusses over Crane, one would almost think the pair of them are siblings too.

Sid returns to the horse where Crane is waiting. She says something to him and he shakes his head, hands her the reins. He pauses a moment, scowl…and then turns to march over to us with a purpose.

I expect him to give an awkward goodbye, perhaps prodded by Sid telling him to mind his manners. Instead he comes to a halt before us with a severe twist to his features.

"You two should go home," he says. "Go home and tell James Spencer and William Esher to keep their heads down and watch their backs. They've already got in the way once and I can't promise they'll make it out if they do it again. Same goes for the pair of you."

That was not at all what I expected. Preston tenses, shoulders squaring. "That sounds like a threat."

Crane frowns. "It's not a threat. It's a warning. The Order is bigger and stronger than all of you combined. This isn't a game."

"So you'll leave us with that vague and mysterious explanation and no answers to any of our other questions," I say softly. "If that's all we have to go off of, you know perfectly well we cannot be satisfied with that."

He shoves his good hand back through his hair. Sighs. "Christ. Tell them… They know me. We've met."

A frown tugs at my brow. "So you've said. When? Where?"

"Buckinghamshire." Crane pauses, mouth pulled thin. "I was working undercover in the household of Lord Claude Wakefield, keeping an eye on someone."

Preston's eyes widen. "The Reverend?"

"The Reverend."

"Then you're the one who assaulted the bobbies and set him free, weren't you?" Preston bristles, taking a half step forward.

Nathaniel doesn't so much as flinch, doesn't skip a beat. "I did. I broke him out, and then I killed him."

That takes the wind right out of Preston's sails. "What—why?"

"Because he knew more than he should have," comes the easy reply. "Which is precisely why I'm not telling you more than that."

Crane turns away, returning to Sid and their horse. He accepts her help getting into the saddle, letting her handle the reins.

Before they leave, he looks back at us one last time with a curt nod. "Take care of yourselves. And each other."

31
PRESTON

I T'S TOO QUIET without them here. Less tense, less worry about waking with a gun in my face, and yet...

Still too quiet.

We linger for another week. The physician visits to clear Benji for travel, though he's instructed to take it easy. I'm given a bottle of salve and some pain medication as well for the trip.

Even the night leading up to our scheduled departure, we still haven't a clue where we're going. Or, at least, I don't. I've patiently waited for Benji to think it over.

We visit Drake's beach one last time to watch the sun set. Benji chases the tide in and out, collecting shells and stones and odd circular husks that Cora calls sand dollars. He admires each and every one, but never keeps them. Instead he places them in patterns and shapes or words upon the sand, where they will no doubt be swept away by the next high tide. Leave it to Benji to find such joy in fleeting beauty.

I watch him in fascination as he takes extra care with the shells tonight. He seems at home in this place, with the ever-present breeze ruffling his hair, the way the sun has left the crests of his cheekbones pink. This weather, the ocean, the beach and sand...it suits him.

After he's compiled the shells—in the shape of horse

today—he joins me higher up on the beach where I've sat upon a massive felled tree trunk. He plops down into the sand at my feet, dusting off his hands.

For a few minutes, we merely watch the sun sinking beyond the horizon, before he says, "I think we ought to return home."

Honestly, I expected as much. After everything we've been through, he's got to be exhausted. Homesick. Even I am, a bit. I miss my family.

But it was the principle of the thing; I wanted him to *say* it. I wanted him to tell me what *he* wanted, and of course I will oblige without complaint.

"Back to Boston, then," I say, reaching down and sliding my hand through his hair. "Maybe we can find more of that pie you liked."

Benji tips his head back to peer up at me. "I only mean, we ought to return home to tell Spencer and Esher and Miss Bennett what's happened. They might need our help. We could write a letter, but what if it doesn't make it?"

My eyebrows arch. "Help them... Even after all Crane said, you want to get further involved in all this?"

The look he gives me is patient. "Do you for a moment think Spencer and Esher will refrain from investigating just because they were told to?"

Esher would. In a heartbeat, I think. But— "James wouldn't, I have to agree."

"And are *you* satisfied with not seeing this through?"

"Not in the least," I reluctantly admit.

"Then they'll need help. As much as I would rather not get involved in such dangerous activities, I'll not leave our friends to deal with such things alone, either. Nor Miss Bennett."

I slide my fingers along the soft slope of his jaw. He leans into it, presses his cheek into my palm.

"Right then. We go back to Whitechapel; we deliver the notes and information to Aunt Eleanor. We help to do…whatever it is they need us to do. And then what?"

"And then…" Benji pauses, turns his head, presses a kiss against my palm. "And then I thought we might see Italy. Or China. Australia?"

My mouth threatens to curve into a grin and I fight it back. "You want to keep travelling? What happened to settling down, laying roots somewhere?"

I can feel his smile against my skin. "I did not say we have to travel forever. We're young. We have our whole lives ahead of us. Who's to say our roots need to be laid down where we were born?"

"You're certain? This is what you want and not what you think I want?"

Benji takes a deep breath, straightening back up to return his gaze to the horizon. "You know… I was so scared to leave home. I've been scared to do a lot of things. I was afraid to deal with ghosts. I was afraid of telling you how I felt. I was absolutely terrified at the idea of living life without Mother there to always ensure things were good and safe.

"But I'm not a child anymore. I want to be someone Mother would have been proud of and I think I can do that best by being with you, by seeing the world. By not being ashamed of who I am and what I'm capable of."

Never have I been prouder of Benjamin Prichard than I am at that moment. Not that how he was ever bothered me, but he's right. I can't fix everything. I can't always protect him. Hell, I've proven that I can't always protect myself, either. I feel I've watched him grow from the quiet, shy boy I met at Whisperwood into the sweet, brave man sitting before me now. Gentle and soft, yes. But not helpless. Not meek.

Funny. I never thought it possible to love him more than I did the first time I realised my feelings. And yet here we are.

I must be silent for too long, because Benji glances back at me. "All right?"

"Quite." I slide off the tree trunk to join him in the sand, where I can properly slip an arm about his shoulders and press a kiss to his temple. "Home. And then…the world."

Benji laughs, soft, quiet. Presses his face against the curve of my throat. "You *are* my world, Preston."

EPILOGUE
JAMES

"OPHELIA, YOU REALLY must come here before dear William sees you and has a fit."

From the rooftop, Ophelia licks her lips and peers over at me, disinterested. With a flick of her tail, she stretches her long legs out before her and...lies down.

Of course William would have a cat that is as difficult to deal with as him and I combined.

With a sigh, I heave the window further open and begin the careful process of crawling out of it and onto the roof. The slope of it makes this tricky, as does the fact that it's rained all bloody day, so the damned thing is slippery. Not that Ophelia seems to care. Really, I think she's quite fine crawling all over the way she does, but it stresses William immensely and a stressed-out-William is not something I care to have. The lower his stress overall, the better. Especially while he's doing his best to remain off his medication.

I inch away from the window, grimacing when I must release my hold on the frame to lean forward and grab the cat. Thank God Ophelia doesn't dart away as she sometimes does, as though this is some kind of game to see how close she can get me to falling and breaking my neck. I scoop her up one-handed and drag her to my chest, where she promptly begins to purr.

"Bloody cats," I mutter, carefully crawling my way back inside. "Why couldn't we have found a dog? I wouldn't have to rescue a dog from rooftops and trees."

"No, instead you'd be explaining to me why everything in the house was chewed up," William says.

I nearly tumble the rest of the way into our bedroom. He's seated at the edge of the bed, watching me in quiet amusement. Ophelia squirms free from my grasp and all but throws herself into William's lap, acting the perfect angel.

"How long have you been there?" I ask.

"Since I watched you wriggling yourself through the window out there."

"You could have said something."

"I was enjoying the view." He scratches behind the cat's ears fondly. I must say, for however much of a headache she can be, she brightens dear William's day. Even when his mood is poor and melancholy has its hold, he still gets up to ensure she's fed every morning, and she seems to sense when he needs her there at his side. Every night, she sleeps at the foot of our bed. Usually, we wake with her on the pillows between us.

I refuse to admit that perhaps I am, just marginally, a tiny bit fond of her.

With a sniff, I shut the window and fold my arms across my chest. "Your feline is a demonic entity."

"So are you, and yet I keep you both around." He lifts his free hand. In it is a piece of paper. "Two telegrams just arrived."

"Oh, I do enjoy mail." I start to reach for it and note the peculiar look upon his face. Almost immediately, I step back. "...Who are they from?"

"One from Miss Bennett about a job." He holds it out, but with the other, he hesitates. "And your mother."

That…is not mail that I much enjoy. At all. Ever. Mother's letters come infrequently and when they do, they're normally stunted and aloof, or else lecturing me about not coming home for a holiday or birthday or special occasion. I haven't been able to bring myself to return. I've no interest in seeing their new home with my uncle still there.

And I cannot—I *will* not—get past the fact that *he* still gets to be a part of this family while I have been all but ostracised and pushed away. I've not even seen my parents since graduation.

It would be easier if they'd just let me be. Let me enjoy my new home and life with William. I don't need any of them.

I incline my chin, debating, then take the gram from Miss Bennett and turn to head for the door.

William sighs a bit, shoos the cat from his lap and rises to follow me. "You ignored the last two, sweetheart. What if it's important?"

"There is little my mother could want from me that I would care about right now. If it's that important to you, *you* read it."

I do not mean to sound so cold to him, but this is still a subject I prefer to avoid. William chooses to keep in at least some contact with his own family, even when their letters upset him. I have no interest in hurting myself in such a fashion.

He dogs my heels all the way downstairs to the kitchen, where I fully intend on stealing a biscuit or two that he baked yesterday. William lingers in the doorway, watching me as I lean against the table and consume my treat while opening the letter from Miss Bennett.

It is, of course, regarding work. Two more clients interested in our services. Both local, which is good. Although the money from our Buckinghamshire case was much appreciated and needed, I *am* doing my best to go easy on poor William's nerves.

"Someone in Limehouse says the ghost of their dearly departed grandmother is puttering about and causing problems," I muse. A little old lady ghost. That ought to be entertaining. "Oh, this one looks interesting… A coroner near Hyde Park is having some odd occurrences. Bodies moving about or going missing, shadows, voices. That sounds right up our alley, doesn't it? Miss Bennett says he's been by twice this week asking after us."

Silence.

I glance up, cramming the remainder of the biscuit into my mouth. William's got the other telegram in his hands, open now, but his eyes are on me, wide and uncertain.

My stomach sinks and suddenly the food in my belly feels uncomfortably heavy. I know that look and I do not like it. It means nothing good. I want to march right out of the house to avoid hearing whatever it is that is about to come out of William's mouth.

I swallow hard and brace myself.

"Sweetheart," he begins in a tone so achingly gentle it's enough to break my heart. "Your mother requests you home immediately. Your father has passed away."

FROM THE AUTHORS

ANOTHER BOOK DONE, and what a journey this one was. 2019 threw a lot of obstacles our way and made finishing book three difficult. We're sorry it took so long. This next step in the *Dark is the Night* world is a big one and introduces some major players for what's to come.

We always make sure to thank our betas in this, but this time, we have to give them *major* props. Not only did they do an incredible job, but they did it around the holidays and on a super tight deadline. Karen, Kristin, Kaye, Shannon, Pidge, Jada, Beedoo… You all are *amazing*. It doesn't matter how much work goes into a first draft by the authors. If it weren't for amazing betas and editors, books would seriously suck.

Another special shoutout to our editor, Natalie. Again, working on a tight deadline over the holidays and snagging every little thing that got missed through all the other various rounds of edits. She helped to put the final shine on this story that it needed.

And, always, thank you to our readers. You allow us to continue on this journey with James, William, and their friends. Happy New Year. Let's make 2020 a good one.

Printed in Great Britain
by Amazon

20279929R00180